BETWEEN

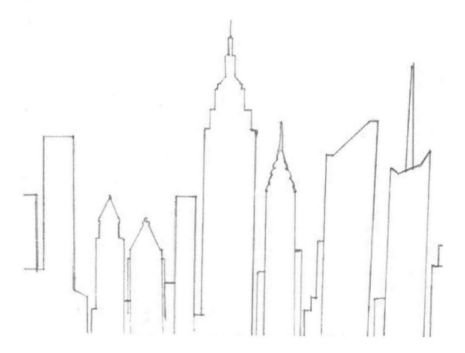

a novel by Sarah Lynn

ALL THAT GLITTERS PUBLISHING

All That Glitters Publishing,
an independent imprint
Canton, OH, USA

First Edition: October 2021

The publisher is not responsible for websites (or their content)
that are not owned by the publisher.

ISBN: 978-0-578-30394-9 (Paperback)

This book is dedicated to young women everywhere who have nurtured an unrelenting dream with fierce protection. For the ones who have dreamed of a better life and took a chance.
And to the ones who have lived, loved, lost their dreams, and found the courage to rebuild.

You are the dreamers, the starry-eyed hopefuls, and the lifeblood of this world. Don't ever lost your hope. Hope keeps us going and keeps this world turning when the future seems so unclear.
Storms don't last forever.

Good things are coming.

"For surely, I know the plans I have for you, says the Lord, plans for your welfare and not for harm, to give you a future with hope."
Jeremiah 29:11 (NRSV)

CONTENTS

ACKNOWLEDGMENTS

To Havilah, Ben, and the Truth to Table Community:
Without you, this book would not have seen its completion…
at least not any time soon!

Thank you for your content, teaching, and fierce
encouragement.

PREFACE

Eva's tiny frame shook as she looked down at her champagne-colored phone to see his number ring across the screen for the very first time. This ownerless, untraceable number had assaulted her for years, but only through text - never an actual call. She accepted the call with no greeting and waited for the thing that would tell her everything that had been kept in secret for so many years.

Only he didn't speak. Instead, heavy breathing took the place of an answer.

Eva's heart began to pound loudly enough for her to feel as if it would shake her insides loose. Like the first time. But this wasn't the first time, and the pounding wasn't accompanied by the familiar race of butterflies. This time a new feeling began to rise from deep inside of her.

She waited. Five excruciatingly slow minutes went by.

Nothing.

Five more minutes went by.

Still, nothing. Nothing, but the thick sound of his shallow breath, mocking her with his delay. Eva looked around her apartment now darkened by midnight shadows; a sense of dread crept over her. Something was very out of place.

10 minutes...more breathing.

Her stomach began a sickening descent as she began to understand that this was not the hopeful anticipation of a love reunited that she was feeling. No. It had been traded for something else. Something far different.

...five more minutes...still nothing.

1

Eva began to feel acutely aware that she was alone in her apartment with a possible stranger on the other end of her phone, and it terrified her. He knew where she lived. He knew she was alone. He knew every move she made from the time she woke up in the morning to the time she laid her head down at night. And now, she felt something she had never associated with him before.

Danger.

She quickly moved her finger to press the touch-screen button that would end the call.

"Hi...."

It was him, but in a text message. Not a recognizable voice that she could finally put a name to.

"Hi...Why aren't you saying anything?" she replied, scared, but frustrated that although he'd finally gathered the courage to call, he was continuing with this charade of text.

"I can't...please say something."

"No... I can't...it has to be you. You have to speak. You called me. You speak first. Please."

"I'm afraid."

Eva sighed and smacked the door frame as the only outlet for her frustration. *"Please...we're so close. Please, say something."*

More breathing.

"How is it that you're even able to text me while we're on the phone?"

"Same way you are. Eva, please believe me...I love you. I love you so much. Nothing will keep us apart once we're together. I won't ever let you go. You and I are one, we always have been. I love you. I love you so much!"

Eva trembled as she paced her shadowed apartment. *"I know...I know you love me. Please say something...you're scaring me."*

No response. Eva grew more and more uneasy. *"Okay...I'm hanging up now. You're really scaring me."*

"No! Eva, please don't!"

"Then say something! I'm not going to stay on the phone with you and text you at the same time! This is freaking ridiculous!"

"I'm sorry, Eva." A low and dark whisper came across the phone that chilled Eva to the core. Now, even more confused than ever, she quickly ended the call.

As the anxiety began to rise, she ran to the front door to lock it, then to the windows, and then drew the sheers. She climbed into bed and pulled the covers up as high as she could; her wide forest-green eyes searching the blackness of her room. Everything inside of her screamed that something was seriously not right.

Then it came again.

"You hung up on me!"

Another text.

"You scared me!"

"Eva, please, I love you! I was just afraid!"

"No. You are really frightening me now. Please stop texting me. Please leave me alone!"

Eva sank into her covers as she tried to slow her own breathing. Try as she might, she could not shake the innate doom that was seeping throughout her entire body, mind, and soul. Would he come for her in the middle of the night? He might be angry if he realized he was losing what he deemed as "his" property. Would he lose control of himself and try to overtake her? She had seen how violently he could attack with his words, the rage buried deep inside of him. Was it only a matter of time before his attack became physical? The elusive one who had held her heart prisoner for so long. Would he now come to claim her as his own and make the prison real? Which she could never escape from, for only he held the key. And that cage was invisible to everyone around her.

She never imagined she would feel unsafe at his hands, but his breath, his dark whisper. Adoration was fast turning cold as Eva's heart of hearts alerted her to the danger that loomed so close by. She had become his prey. He'd set a trap long ago for not just her, but her mind...her heart...her soul. And he'd bound them up so tightly until it was too late for her to realize she had entered his inescapable lair willingly.

Eva opened the drawer of her nightstand and felt for the cold, hard steel of her gun. As much as she hated having one in the house and had protested learning how to shoot, she was glad to have the protection should the need arise for her to defend herself. Eva said a small prayer as she closed her eyes and tried not to think about the implications of what she had just opened the door to. Worn out and mentally exhausted, she finally fell asleep.

***

Location: NYC - 5 Years Earlier

"Be there soon!"

Eva waited for the check next to her text to confirm that her message had been received.

Nothing.

Hmm, she thought to herself. *That's odd. He always gets my texts. Oh, come on, Evie. It's probably nothing but your own insecurity. He's probably just busy getting ready and not by his phone.*

Eva rushed around her New York apartment in her final attempts to beautify herself for her date with Mr. Man, the guy that she adored, but who made her stupidly nervous at the same time. And after their recent time apart, she'd been waiting for what seemed like an eternity for this date.

Jetsetter that he was, Mr. Man's travels had taken him out of the city just a week after their first date, leaving a very impatient Eva waiting almost six weeks for his return. They had gotten together a few times after he returned to the city of glass and steel, but something about their recent encounters just didn't feel right.

It's just not the same, she thought as she grabbed her lightweight, cream-colored jacket and swept out the door. Thoughts of what could have happened while he was away plagued her mind and she intended to confront him this evening to put her ever-growing what-ifs to rest.

Her street on the Upper East Side was a buzz of spring-thaw activity that evening. Eva stepped off the gum-spotted sidewalk, hailed a taxi, and mentally ticked off possibilities of what she could have done to contribute to Mr. Man's recent coldness. She hadn't spoken to him much while he was away; hardly at all., actually. Not that she hadn't wanted to. She kept her distance partly to avoid bothering him and partly because she didn't want to seem like one more desperate, needy girl. After all, Mr. Man was a hot commodity in this concrete jungle and for some reason that she could not figure out, he had chosen to pursue her. And she was going to be different. None of her old insecurities were going to sabotage this budding relationship and she was going to make sure of that. After all, they were already off to such a good start. Friends first, it had taken him a good year before he could work up the nerve to approach her in taking the friendship one step further… their first date… and on Valentine's Day, no less. That alone told Eva this had to mean something.

The city whirled by in a hectic, shiny blur as the taxi took her from Upper Manhattan down to Lower Manhattan. Eva stared out of the window from the backseat of the yellow cab and watched as the setting sun raced across the glass of each rapidly passing building. The nauseous feeling in her stomach only increased as she neared his street. The cab came to a stop on the corner by his apartment building. She looked down at her phone...still no response. Her stomach sank deeper. This was very much unlike him.

Nope. Something is definitely not right, she thought to herself as she paid the driver, slid out of the cab, and stepped onto the curb. Eva's long, wavy, deep reddish-brown hair blowing in the breeze as the cab sped away. Looking up at his apartment, her large dark-green eyes sparkled in the early evening sun; or the "Magic Hour" as they called it in her line of work. She slowly took one step and then walked closer to his front stoop.

"I'm here. Waiting downstairs." Eva sent a quick text to let him know she'd arrived and was waiting for him.

No response.

It had been 20 minutes since she had sent her last text. There was no way that he hadn't seen it by now, even if he had been delayed, or was having some sort of a fashion crisis. The sinking feeling deep in her chest refused to be denied now as she stared at her message screen and waited for him to reply. *He's probably just on his way down.*

She waited. Still nothing.

Eva dialed his number and tried to control her voice. His phone went straight to voicemail. *It's turned off...*

Her heart sank into her churning stomach. *No...this isn't happening*. It was slowly starting to sink in. *He's not coming...he doesn't care.*

Eva allowed herself a full 20 minutes from the time she got to the sidewalk in front of his apartment until her self-respect gently nudged her to turn around and go back home.

Don't cry, she told herself, climbing into the cab that had stopped for her raised hand. *No, don't be that girl, Eva. Be strong. Be...*

But Eva couldn't hold back the pain of rejection any longer. Tears flowed from her mascara fringed eyes like a deluge, blurring the harsh edges of the city through the taxi window...blurring her truth.

1 BIG APPLE

"Good morning, New York!"

The alarm clock blared, jolting Eva out of a quiet sleep. Well, as quiet as you can get in the big city, anyway. But no matter. She had grown quite accustomed to the honking taxis, incessant jackhammers, unrelenting sirens and fire trucks, as well as the random people yelling outside of her window, far below on the sidewalk for no reason. You name it, she could hear it. Yes, even in Upper Manhattan and even 10 floors up.

Noise was no respecter of heights in the big city, but Eva didn't care. To her, that beautiful noise was just another reminder of the life she had dreamt about and built for herself all on her own. Yes, sir. Eva had done it, small town girl in a big city world, all by herself, and all on her own terms. Or at least so she thought.

Eva reached over to turn the alarm off, opened the sheer gossamer aqua curtains, and slid back under her covers to snuggle with her pillow just a few minutes more. Eva squinted towards the window through sleepy eyes and swept her soft burnt-colored waves out of her porcelain face.

"Oh, that sparkling landscape!" she thought to herself as she gazed out at that concrete jungle. From her viewpoint, it almost looked as if you could leap from one roof of a building to the next. Eva smiled a sleepy smile and breathed a sigh of contentment.

Eva was every bit as in love with that city now as she was when she first moved there from her small hometown in Virginia two years before. It had been a struggle to break free from the confines of her hometown just outside of Virginia Beach.

Many of those around her did not approve of her decision, which made it all the more difficult to leave, but the friction also fueled her wanderlust fire even more. Eva's almost every decision had been made for her from the time she was a child; school and social activities, college, what she would major in, what she would grow up to be. It all boiled down to one thing - control - and the free spirit that was embedded into her from birth could not stand to be kept in a cage any longer. She had a purpose, she had a destiny, and she knew she had to go, she had to at least try…or she would regret it for the rest of her life.

So, she ignored the naysayers, packed up her bags, bought a one-way ticket, and left that small town without looking back. And as her plane ride took her further from her prison and closer to her dreams, Eva thought to herself, "I will never let anyone, or anything control me ever again." And although she would jokingly tell her friends back home that she and New York shared a love/hate relationship, that city represented one thing to her…freedom. And she wouldn't trade it, or the stress that came with it, for anything in the world. She was finally free. Free to dress how she wanted, say what she wanted, think what she wanted, go where she wanted and be what she wanted. Eva was a new woman, an independent woman and no one was going to take that away from her ever again.

Eva stretched one last time and gracefully stepped out of bed and into her fuzzy bunny slippers; the one part of her old self that she had kept from home. She walked over to her closet to decide on her fabulous attire for the day: ink blue, dressy jeans with a white three-quarter sleeve blazer, a champagne silk camisole blouse with matching champagne stilettos. The shoes, of course, went straight into her purse. Eva had done the "running frantically through the city in your high heels while trying to look like Carrie from 'Sex and the City'" thing for about a minute before she tossed that unrealistic notion to the birds and opted for a comfy commute in her sneakers or flip-flops; weather depending, of course.

She left her long, naturally wavy hair down and swept her bangs to the side as she brushed her teeth. A little blush, mascara, and quick swipe of lip gloss and she was out the door of her peaceful apartment and onto the streets of chaos along with the millions of other New Yorkers making their routine morning rush hour mad dash to work.

***

"Hey there, Tony!"

Eva greeted her favorite street vendor with a smile as she purchased her morning coffee and bagel.

"Hey there! Light and sweet?" Tony replied, grinning back from behind the cart counter. Tony was like a big brother to her; always joking, always teasing.

"Hey! Who you callin' light and sweet?" Eva furrowed her brow, leaned her head back and teased Tony in her best pretend New York accent.

"Hey, fo'get about it!" Tony played back with a wink and a smile. He knew very well she liked her coffee the old-fashioned way with cream, but still teased her every morning for not jumping on the "milk and sugar" bandwagon as was the city coffee staple for just about every other New Yorker.

"Shootin' anything big today, Eva?" Tony asked as he handed her her morning fuel and change.

Tony was referring to her job in the magazine industry and although she could have easily been a model, Eva's work found her on the other side of the camera; shooting the shoot, directing the models, the product, or wherever her job led her to that day and having a blast all while doing it. This had been her childhood dream and she was actually living it.

"Just your typical fashion shoot today, Tones," which was Eva's nickname for him.

"Hey, what do you think?" Tony put his hand on his hips and flashed the goofiest male-model grin he could muster. "I'll get a couple of the other guys together and we could all post our crafts-o-grub. They could call it 'Street Vendor Chic', apron and all, huh?" Tony suggested, nodding and pointing to the coffee-stained canvas tied around his neck. He was clearly very proud of his idea.

Eva placed her finger on her chin and furrowed her perfectly manicured brow, pretending to give it some thought. "Hmm...I like. Have your people talk to my people. I'm sure they'd go nuts over it."

Tony changed his character, now pursing his lips. "Zoolander. We could all pose like Zoolander."

Eva glanced up from her coffee long enough to give him one of her infamous "you must be joking" smirks. "Listen, I gotta run," she said glancing at her watch and turning to head towards the subway.

"No-go, huh? Shucks." Tony snapped his fingers and shook his head at the ground to tease her. "Okay, well, have fun today, Beautiful!"

"You know it!" Eva winked back at him and went on her way.

***

About 15 minutes and one very packed subway ride later, Eva rushed through the giant steel doors of *Highline Magazine's* corporate headquarters and (bagel in mouth) traded her sneakers for her stilettos. *Highline* was the go-to magazine for just about anything; fashion, décor, city living, travel...a little bit of everything. And Eva had been blessed to be taken on staff as one of the magazine's most prized young photographers; second only to Ramona Stevenson, the industry's most seasoned best.

"It's all in the eye, Cupcake," Ramona's trademark saying. Although she could be tough at times, Jewish-born and bred New Yorker that she was, Ramona had taken Eva under her wing as her protégé when Eva first came to *Highline*. Ramona noticed her talent right away which evoked an instant respect for her young apprentice.

"Honey, you stick with me," Ramona had told her in a thick New York accent. "By the time we get done with you, you're gonna be the cat's meow around this town. Everyone will wanna hire you, Honey. You got that natural eye...that whaddya call it? ... Vision! You's got vision! And that sass ain't bad, neither. I ain't nev-uh seen a country girl with so much sass as you!" Eva could be reserved at times, but she definitely had some feistiness in her and Ramona got a kick out of that, especially knowing that Eva was from Virginia...or 'The Sticks' as Ramona loved called it.

"Hey, I'm not from the country!" Eva had first retorted, "You have to drive at least 30 minutes to see a cow!" An endearingly innocent comment that always brought a chuckle to her city-slicker colleagues.

But she didn't really mind the teasing. A city of concrete and steel can be cold and with her friends so far away, it felt good to know people cared about her enough to look out for her. Ramona reminded her of the classic stereotypical 'bad aunt' with no filter and she loved it.

Just as Eva was getting into her office, in sauntered Peter, the magazine's young, snooty office assistant. "How's that marathon training going?" Peter asked sarcastically as he handed her the shoot schedule for the day. "I saw you hobbling pathetically out of your sneakers and into your...," Peter looked down his nose at her feet and gave a disapproving sniff, "...heels."

Eva ignored the jab, turned back to her desk, and picked up her camera to adjust the settings for the first shoot of the day. From the moment she'd met Peter, she didn't trust him. Something deep inside told her that he was as sly as a fox. Her intuition was only solidified over time, as he proved himself to be a gossip and troublemaker, even causing another photographer, Paul, to lose his job. Eva found out later that Peter had switched a major shoot schedule without telling Paul, so that it would look like he had purposely missed the shoot. Peter's ulterior motive was to replace Paul. It was an act of jealousy as Peter had always drooled over Paul's photography position.

Peter made no qualms about tearing down the character of other people and twisting truths to gain attention and make himself appear important to get what he wanted; something that never sat right with Eva. She hated gossip and hated to be around it even more. Eva was promoted into Paul's position before she had learned the truth about what happened, which fueled Peter's contention towards her even more. The only thing that kept him from messing with her, too, was that Ramona was his aunt and the owner's sister and she would have had his literal hide if he ever tried to sabotage Eva. Eva had always had a hand of protection on her life, something that she never had been able to figure out.

Eva didn't like the fact that she had to work so closely with Peter and entrust him with some of the most important details of her job. But he was the owner's nephew, employee by default, and he was not about to go anywhere anytime soon. So, Eva did her best to be kind to him hoping it would turn things around.

"Well, the shoot will be starting soon. Looks like we better get down there." She stated matter-of-factly, gathering her shoot papers, and coffee.

"Don't worry, sweetie. My aunt wouldn't dream of starting without you," Peter snarked.

Eva looked him in the eye. "Peter, it's obvious that you aren't happy with your position here, but you can keep the sarcasm and blatant disrespect to yourself." Eva grabbed her camera, walked past him, and headed down to the set, where Ramona was already there waiting for her and directing the set designers.

"Well, would ya just look at that?" Ramona called in her thick Yiddish-New York accent and waved her over. Eva jaunted over to Ramona, trying not to fall down in her heels, and gave her cotton candy-haired mentor a hug. Ramona was a wild card when it came to fashion. You never knew what she was going to pull out of her closet next, classic Chanel, or, ripped jeans, blazer, and funky scarf. Today it was the latter.

"Hiya, Gorgeous. Are you a sight for sore eyes or what? I've had Peter up my behind all morning. Askin' all kinds of questions, 'Auntie, when can I shoot? Auntie, when can I edit?'...I told him he can start when he actually gets some talent without making me look like an asshole. I tell ya the Peter Circus never ends around here."

10

Eva shrugged her shoulders, shook her head, and smiled. She didn't know what to say without insulting Ramona based on the sheer fact that like him or not, Peter was still her mentor's family.

"You got your clicker ready, Baby doll? Big shoot this mornin'. We've got the big wigs over here from L.A. And they are dying - dying to see your work."

"Got it right here, Mon's." Eva set her camera bag down and started unpacking it.

"Oh good, Honey. By the way...did you happen to see who's editing today?"

Eva looked over the schedule. "Oh...Alex? Yeah, he'll do a good job," she said without looking up, not wanting to give herself away.

She was glad it was Alex and not one of the others and not just because they had formed a friendship. Alex cared about his work and always put in his best, even on the days he felt less than motivated.

Although he was tremendously talented and reliable, editing was not his passion. Dealing with the models, and all of the drama that could go with it, tried his patience to the absolute extreme. Alex's deepest desire was to go into any kind of work that would bring him closer to helping less fortunate people, but family issues and lack of time left his dreams wanting. He would have to switch gears completely to go back to school for the degree, but the timing was off. Instead, his plan was to endure the industry until the time was right to redirect his life. And he still gave 100% in the meantime. That's just who he was. He wasn't the type of guy to half-ass anything.

They had met back when Eva was hired at the magazine, a little over two years prior. Alex was one of the magazine's most coveted freelance editors. Freelance meant he would pop in and out on occasion as needed, which ended up being quite often.

He and Eva had become fast friends and would talk for hours while they worked. Work, family, life -- no subject was left unturned. They worked well together, and Eva felt safe with him, one of the few men who hadn't come on to her since she moved to the city and Eva had been relieved that she wasn't going to have to keep this one at bay. Nothing was more frustrating than having to maintain a professional relationship with a completely idiotic pervert, which in her experience, was just about every man on earth. Although now that they had established a rapport, she was beginning to wonder what it would be like to be in a relationship with him. A guy so refreshingly different from the other guys that she knew.

"He was askin' about you the other day, you know." Ramona chimed in, as if she could read Eva's thoughts.

"Oh?" Eva's eyebrows raised slightly in curiosity.

"Well, it was more like telling on himself! Honey, it was the cutest thing, 'Do you think she likes me? I think about this girl all the time. I can't get her out of my mind. Do you think she would go out with me?' Yadda, yadda, yadda." Ramona crossed her arms and rested her chin on her thumb and pointer finger and stared off as if she was deep in thought. "I nev-uh seen a grown man trip over his words like that." She straightened up sharply and shook her head as if to jolt herself out of her thoughts. "Anyways...he asked for your personal number which, of *course*, I gave to him! And he's gonna call you tonight," Ramona stated nonchalantly.

Eva's jaw dropped in surprise. "Ra*mona!*" Eva couldn't decipher if she was angry with Ramona or relieved that she stepped in where she herself would not have had the courage.

"Oh, Honey, who you kiddin'?" Ramona tapped her on the backside. "Lighten up, would ya? I smell love in the air and it ain't just cupid. Besides you know what day is coming up." Ramona ended her sentence in a sing songy tone and gave Eva a nudge and a few raises of her eyebrows.

Eva looked down and smiled shyly. "Valentine's Day," she whispered. *Me? Does he really want to spend a day that represents something so special with me?* Eva on purpose did not date much. Although she had grown up in a church, she was not religious, but she also didn't believe in randomly going out with men she could not see herself marrying. And that meant no superfluous dating. It was kind of a self-discipline thing she held to keep herself from unnecessary relationships...and unnecessary pain.

"Yep, that's right, Valentine's Day. And you've got the hair for it," pointing to Eva's dark red locks. "Now don't you be an idiot and turn him down when he calls. Good girl like you needs a good man to take care of her."

Eva gave a little smile, trying to hide what she was feeling. Inside, she was full of excitement and anticipation.

Just then, the bell to start the photo shoot rang out and the dance-pop music could be heard on the speakers to mark the beginning of the session.

"Okay Honey, shoot's on," Ramona put her bejeweled hands on her hips and leaned in towards Eva. "Go get it, Boo."

Eva brought her camera up to her face and moved it around, pretending to photograph her mentor. "Smile for me, Dahhhling," she purred.

Ramona pinched Eva's cheek, took her chin gently like a mother, and tilted her head back to look at Eva tenderly. "Go, Doll."

12

2 ALL THAT GLITTERS

The gym was busy that evening. Eva had rushed to her neighborhood's state-of-the-art gym just as fast as she could after the last shoot of the evening to work out some of the day's stress. Yoga was usually her anti-stress weapon of choice, but today she needed a good run where she could zone out, organize her thoughts from the day, and reset her mind.

Eva finished her run and was just walking out to grab a dinner-to-go on the way home to her apartment when her phone rang.

Oh, no, she thought. *What in the world do they want now?*

It was not unusual for an entire shoot to be scrapped last minute, which by default meant an emergency for everyone involved. Eva was looking forward to a relaxing evening at home and the last thing she wanted to do was go back into work. She looked down at her phone and breathed a sigh of relief. *Kate.*

Kate was a close friend from back home who called at least once a week to check in and make sure Eva was okay. She had always supported Eva's dreams but was still concerned for her friend living in the big city. Kate knew Eva's tender heart and wanted to make sure she wasn't taken advantage of in any way. Although Eva had expressed her lack of faith years before, Kate never gave up the hope that one day Eva would have an experience that she could not deny. Kate also knew that Eva lived her life on her own terms, which would leave her at the mercy of her own decisions, or other people, without a covering. They did not always agree or see eye to eye, but Kate knew she was the only spiritual influence in Eva's life and wanted to be there for her to help guide and direct her, and to be a support and perhaps one day that would speak to her on a higher level.

Eva answered her phone. "Well, hello, stranger," she teased. "What's the good word?"

"Hey there, Big City Girl!" Kate's pet name for her. "Just calling to check in. What's new? Anything good?"

"Well, funny you should ask...but you'll never guess what Ramona told me today."

"Oh, My-lanta," Kate chimed in her quirky wit. "What the heck is that crazy woman up to now?"

"What isn't she up, too? You know Ramona. Anyway, you know the guy I work with, Alex?"

"Yeah?"

"Apparently, he's been asking Ramona about me. And she gave him my number."

"She did not."

"Oh, yes. Yes, she most certainly did."

"Geez, what a stinker. That woman is something else, I tell ya."

Eva laughed, "Oh, believe me, I know it! I work with it every day. So, I guess he's going to call and ask me out, or so speaks Ramona. I guess we'll see about that."

Kate could hear the hesitation in Eva's voice. "Well, I guess that's exciting. How do you feel about that?" she asked gently.

Eva paused, then answered slowly, taking one thought at a time, mulling it over in her mind. "Fine...I guess. I mean I've known him since I started at the magazine. We work well together. He's super nice and polite. He's always treated me with respect. We seem to get along very well. I don't know. I guess I'm hopeful. I don't know...We'll see." Eva was trying desperately to hide a vulnerability that she would not dare let seep through her new-found city armor.

"Aw...okay." Kate could read her friend like a book. "I know you don't want to get hurt. And I definitely don't want you to get hurt. Just take it one step at a time, okay?"

"Yeah, no worries. Thanks, Kate." Eva was relieved that Kate was one friend she didn't have to explain herself to.

"Anytime, Eves. Keep me posted!"

***

"Home sweet home!"

Eva sighed as she unlocked her door and walked into her reprieve. Her

14

cozy apartment was her oasis from the crazy, brash world outside and she loved the evenings where she could just relax. Eva had finished her dinner and was just drawing a deliciously scented bubble bath when her phone rang again.

"Seriously?" she sighed impatiently, turned off the running water, and grabbed her phone. It was *Highline*. "Can't I get two freaking minutes to myself in this city?" she said out loud as she answered her phone.

"Eva's not home, please leave a message after the beep. 'Beep'," she answered sarcastically.

"E-Eva?" questioned the very confused-sounding voice on the other end of the line.

Eva put her hand over her mouth in surprise and stiffened up straight…It was Alex.

"Oh…H-hi, Alex. I'm sorry. I thought you were someone I didn't want to talk to," she answered sheepishly. Although there was no way he could have known the precursor to his phone call, Eva felt ashamed. Even though the city had made her strong and edgy, the old ghosts from her past still haunted her. And shame was one haunt she just couldn't shake although she wanted to. She just didn't know how.

"Hey, Eva…uhh, you okay? I can call you back later if this is a bad time."

"Oh, no! Not at all! I was just, just…no, it's fine." Eva smacked herself in the forehead. *Stupid. Stupid. Eva, you are such a goof.* Self-deprecation was her familiar friend and mantra.

"Well, listen, I just wanted to call and let you know how great the shoot turned out today. You did a fantastic job. The angles, the frames, the filters…you really know how to make an editor's job easier. I hardly had to retouch a thing."

Eva was glad Alex couldn't see her blushing cheeks over the phone. "Oh…gosh, thanks. I mean, it was nothing really, an easy shoot. All I did was point and click." Accepting compliments was not Eva's strong suit and she was usually quick to laugh one off.

Alex chuckled gently. "Well, you did fantastic. I always look forward to working with you."

"Well, I'm not all that special, but thank you. I like working with you, too."

"Well, I should let you go. I know you've had a long day and probably just want to relax."

"Oh. Sure, okay." Eva's heart dropped slightly. She'd thought this was going to be the much-anticipated call that had been the hot topic of the day.

I knew it, she thought to herself. *He's not interested. Probably thinks I'm a nut, just like everybody else. I probably scared him off with my oh-so-charming greeting.* "Well, I'll see you later, I guess. Thanks for the call, Alex. Have a great night!"

Alex broke in before she had a chance to hang up. "Well, um…actually there is one more thing I wanted to talk to you about. I was wondering if…uh…you would be interested in spending some time together tomorrow evening?" He squinted his eyes on the other end of the line and waited for her response.

Eva caught her breath. "Oh…yeah, did you want to go over the proofs or something?"

"Um, I mean, we can do that if you want. But actually, I really just wanted to see if we could spend some time together. Truth is…Eva, I really enjoy talking with you. But I know tomorrow is Valentine's Day, so you might already have plans?"

"No, that sounds great. I would love to.*" 'Cause I'm the only loser with no plans on Valentine's Day.* It didn't even occur to her that Alex had no plans on such a special day either.

"Awesome! Alright, well, would you like to come over? I can make dinner…lasagna…my specialty."

Eva's nerves halted her. She wasn't ready to be alone-alone with him. She was terribly insecure when it came to dating and being alone with him under the circumstances would be too much for a starter.

"Oh, you don't have to go to all of that trouble just for me!" Eva exclaimed apologetically. *I'm not worth the effort.* "Why don't we just meet at Union Square and go from there?"

Alex's mood sank a little on the other line. He'd been wanting to do something special for her to let her know how he felt about her. He tried not to let his disappointment show. "Um, sure, yeah, okay. That sounds good. Seven okay?"

"Seven is great. See you then. Thanks, Alex."

"See you then."

Eva was a ball of nerves. By now, the bathroom was a sauna as she stepped into the perfumed tub, tea in hand, and let the bubbles soothe her stress away.

***

Alex hung up the phone riddled with doubt. *Maybe she doesn't feel the same way I do.* It had been a challenge for him just to pick up the phone and call her. Since his talk with Ramona, he'd felt confident in his decision to pursue Eva. But her reaction felt detached and uninterested, leaving him to question himself.

Alex sat down on his couch and took a sip to help ease his nerves.

Well, he thought to himself, *I'm sure she gets approached by typical yahoos every day. I don't blame her for being guarded. But how can I prove to her my feelings are real?*

***

Eva stood on the corner of Broadway and 14th as people rushed past her. It had turned out to be a very frigid Valentine's evening and Eva had herself bundled up as much as she could while still looking somewhat presentable for her date with Alex. Puffy, black coat and cream-colored knit hat with a pompom on top and matching fuzzy gloves. *Yep, nothing says romance like the abominable snow girl*, Eva had told her reflection with a frown back at the apartment.

"Eva!" a voice shouted out behind her.

She turned around to find a very freezing looking Alex standing there with a single, white rose in his hand. She couldn't help but smile shyly. Terribly nervous, she had to force herself to look him in the eyes. "Hey, Alex," she said quietly.

Alex gave her a very debonair smile and leaned forward to give her the rose, as if he were presenting her with a very rare and special gift. Eva reached out very slowly and gingerly took the rose, almost as if she ws afraid it would bite her.

"Thank you, Alex," she said almost in a whisper. It had been years since anyone had given her flowers. It was one more thing that she truly believed she did not deserve.

With his hands in his pockets, and a bounce on his feet he asked, "So, do you like hot chocolate? I know a place where they have the best hot chocolate in the city!"

"Ooh, that sounds great!" Eva replied, "I love hot chocolate!"

"I was thinking we could grab a cup to keep us warm while we walk around."

"It's a plan, sir." Eva took his arm and let him lead her across the street to the shop just around the corner from Union Square.

Eva followed him into the chocolate shop and stood beside him while he ordered from the chocolate bar. Alex paid the cashier and took the cups of the steaming, velvety liquid.

"Your cocoa, Madame," he said in his best French accent as he handed Eva her cup.

Eva looked up into his dark eyes and took the cup. "Merci beaucoup, mon ami."

"Oh, la la!" He replied, lifting his eyebrows a couple times to compliment his character. "Try it. You'll love it."

Eva pursed her lips, blew softly across the surface of the sweet drink to help cool it down, and took a sip as Alex watched her wide-eyed with all the hopeful anticipation of a puppy dog.

"Holy crap! This is heaven."

"Interesting dichotomy, but yes. You like it?"

"Oh, my gosh. It's so good, I love it!"

"Whew! So, you're not one of those weird one-offs that hates chocolate. That's good."

Eva punched him playfully in the arm.

Alex furrowed his brow and pretended to rub his arm. "Got to look out for the knock-outs from a knock-out."

Eva giggled.

"So, what would you like to do?" Alex asked with a bounce in his voice.

"I don't know, really. Want to walk until we find something?"

"Sure!"

They walked out of the chocolate shop and turned down a very crowded Broadway towards St. Mark's Place. Eva walked just a step behind him. Alex took note of it without saying anything. "I can't believe how cold it is!" he exclaimed as they walked, trying to break the ice.

"I know," replied Eva. Although it was awkward given there was no longer an unspoken barrier between the friendship, Eva still felt comfortable with him. She listened to him go on about his day while they walked. Finally, they reach the sushi place he wanted to take her to. They stepped inside and walked to the back wall.

"Okay, now watch this." Alex stepped forward and turned towards Eva as if he was about to teach her something new and extraordinary. "See, you can pick your sushi from one of these little cubbies," he explained pointing to the plexi-glass compartmentalized wall. "And then you press this little button next to it and the chosen raw delicacy goes all the way down this conveyor belt to the counter where our friend in the red cap there rings us out," he ended with a flourish of his hand grandly gesturing to the short, black-haired man behind the counter. After Alex made a selection for the both of them, they walked to a counter in the front and sat down together. The brightly lit sushi cafe was empty aside from the two of them.

"Guess the cold weather's keeping them away, huh?" Eva joked with a smile.

"Yeah, well if that's the case, they don't know what they're missing," Alex gave her a wink. "So, tell me more about your family. What was it like growing up? You mentioned before that your parents are not in the best of health, right? What is that like being so far from home?" Alex had been wanting to know Eva better for a while now and now that he finally had the chance, it seemed his questions sprang forth like a gushing fountain.

"Hmm." Eva pondered his questions for a bit and tried not to let him see her frown. Although her childhood had not been bad according to most standards, it was not her favorite memory and she always felt awkward explaining it to other people, as if the truth about her dysfunctional upbringing might send them screaming in the other direction.

"Well, I mean, it was just your typical middle-class family, really. My dad owned a small business. We went to church on Sundays. Florida vacations during Spring Break. You know, the usual," Eva smiled at him softly.

"Were you lonely?" Alex's knowing eyes met hers with a sweet mixture of compassion and curiosity.

Eva was surprised at his intuition. "Oh...well...yeah...yeah, I was. I mean I had everything I could have needed." She didn't want him to think she was complaining. "They didn't spoil us with unnecessary wants. But there were times where I felt that I was...disappointing...that I couldn't quite measure up." Eva stopped talking, lingering on her last thought.

Alex read her face, which now held a distant gaze as if she were a million miles away. He hadn't wanted to make her feel uncomfortable and ruin the first evening that they were spending time together with a mental cross-section. "Hey," he lightly nudged her arm with his elbow. "You wanna get out of here? Go someplace quieter, cozier? I'm sure a pop culture-ridden sushi cafe is not the most comfortable place to talk about this kind of stuff. You know what I mean?"

Eva looked up at him and watched his face. *Wow...he's sensitive*, she thought to herself. "Sure. Where would you like to go?"

"There's a place by where I live. It's quiet and cozy. A neighborhood spot more conducive to talking. Lola Lounge...have you ever been there?"

"No, but it sounds perfect."

Alex held out his hand to help her down off the stool and gave her a soft smile. "Your chariot awaits, my dear." Eva blushed and smiled shyly at the ground while she gently took his waiting hand and hopped off her seat.

Alex took her slender arm in his and gently drew her to his side to keep her warm as they stepped out once more into the cold night air and Eva continued her conversation about her family as they walked to the cafe.

"...I understand," came Alex's soft words as they reached their destination. "Performance-driven."

"Very much so," she said with an undertone of sadness.

"I get that. Ever since my brother became such a huge success, my family has been waiting on me to grow up and get a 'real' job."

"Umm, do they not know that you are an editor for the most successful magazine in the city?"

"It doesn't matter to them. Throw the word 'freelance' in there and all bets are off."

Eva looked at him with empathy. "I'm sorry. I can soo relate to that. I don't know if there is anything that I could do that would be seen as right in my family's eyes unless it earned them a trophy or a compliment. As if my accomplishments have any bearing on their own lives."

Alex stopped her in front of the door, took her shoulders gently in his hands and spoke very softly, "Well, I'm a firm believer that the people who are exceptionally critically interested in what others are doing are not as willing to turn that mirror around on their own lives. In short...people want to work on other people's lives more than they want to work on their own. You get my drift?"

"Yeah, I do. That's so true."

"And anyway...you are more than alright in my eyes."

Eva caught his dark eyes, but quickly looked away. She wanted to make herself believe him. Again, came those self-deprecating thoughts. *You wouldn't feel that way if you really knew me.* She really liked him but feared if he got too close to know the real her, he wouldn't want anything to do with her.

His eyes wanted to follow her face, but he knew it would make her self-conscious. "Well. Let's go inside before you freeze to death!" Alex joked trying to lighten the mood. He held the door as Eva walked in ahead of him. The lounge was dark and softly lit with candles. Sheers of purple silk and velvet were draped gracefully around the room. There was hardly a person in the room aside from the young woman behind the bar. It felt peaceful, warm, inviting.

They found a table in the corner by the front. Alex sat down first and took off his coat. Eva sat down, slowly took off her pom-pom hat and looked at him. She'd seen him so many times before, but this time something was different. It was as if she was discovering him for the first time.

Could it be? No. Eva tried to chase the thought away, but it lingered. All of the sudden, looking at his strong-jawed face in the candlelight, it was as if she'd had an epiphany. *He's...is he really...? No.* The strange look on her face betrayed her silence as his own became inquisitive.

"What?"

"Nothing," Eva shook her head quickly, causing her waves to dance slightly around her shoulders, golden shimmers of candlelight catching highlights in her hair.

He stared at her for long enough to make a don't-look-at-me girl self-conscious. "You're beautiful," he whispered softly.

"What...me? No." Eva furrowed her brow and shook her head again as if the very notion of her beauty was ridiculous.

"Yes...you are. And the inside surpasses. Why else do you think I'm here with you?" His words were soft, but firm.

"I honestly have no idea!" she laughed. "Well, actually...there is something I do want to know. What on earth did you say to Ramona?"

Alex burst out into a loud laugh. "Ramona! You got to love her! So, she told you about our 'top-secret' conversation, huh?" he joked, making air quotes.

Eva threw him a teasing wink. "I might have had a clue...for real though, I'm curious. Will you tell me?"

"Well...I told her what anyone who feels a certain way would say."

Uh-oh.

Alex took a big breath and leaned a bit closer. *Here goes nothing*, he thought to himself.

Eva tried to avert her eyes, but he wouldn't let her. He held her gaze. "Okay. So, I know this is the first time we're actually hanging out and I know this might sound intense, but I don't think I can hold it in anymore. So, I'm just going to bite the bullet and say it anyway. Eva...you are special. I've never met anyone like you before. You're kind, compassionate, and sweet...even when you think no one is looking. Even with Peter...the way you handle him knowing he is out for your blood is awe-inspiring. Not many people could hold their composure in the face of adversity on a daily basis like you do. And your presence is just...it's indescribable. It's like being in another realm. Seriously every time I'm around you, I just get this sense that...," he took her hand, "...you are light and everything else is dark."

Eva stared back at him, half in wonder, half in disbelief. No one had ever spoken to her in this way before. "Wow...I'm...flattered. I guess?" Eva didn't know what else to say. She still found it incredibly hard to believe that anyone could feel this way about her.

Alex's voice became intense, "Eva, I know we work together and that might be tricky, but I don't believe this is just a coincidence. The way we are so compatible, like we're cut from the same cloth. I trust you completely for some reason...and I have a hard time trusting anybody. But with you, it's easy...like breathing. I know I'm gushing, but I really like you...a lot...you're special...and I want to see where this will lead. The crazy thing is, I've never met anyone I've wanted to take that journey with until I met you. So, let me stop rambling now and ask you. Can we?" Alex ran out of words and looked down for a second, then back at her in hopeful expectation.

Eva hesitated; her words caught in her throat. She was afraid. Afraid of getting hurt. Afraid that her flaws would prove to be too much. Afraid, afraid, afraid. But she also knew that she didn't want to pass up a chance for happiness. Maybe this was finally her time to learn what true love felt like.

"Okay," she finally answered. "I mean, I think I want to see where this will go, too." Her eyes slowly met his to see his reaction; still so afraid to look at him.

An easy smile formed across his face. He breathed a quiet sigh of relief, not knowing he'd been holding his breath. "Awesome."

Eva smiled back for a minute. "...and on that note...I must depart." Eva looked down at her watch. It was 10:30 p.m. "It's getting late...I wish I could stay longer, but I really better go. I've got to be at the office early tomorrow."

"It's okay," Alex said reluctantly, but still smiling. He didn't want the night to end, but knew he had to let her go for now. Eva's 'yes' was enough to carry him through the rest of the night even if he had to spend it without her. They both stood up and made their way through the door and out into the icy winter night.

Snow had begun to fall and whiten the city afresh, making the moment even more picturesque; the two of them standing there on the city street, with the cottony snow falling gently all around them. Alex broke the silence, "Let me hail you a cab."

"Nah, I actually thought I'd just walk home," Eva teased.

"Ye-ah...totally not okay with that!" Alex countered with a protective tone in his voice. And Eva let him. It had been a long time since anyone had made her feel special enough to be guardable. She giggled softly to herself, enjoying the attention. Just then a cab pulled up, ready to whisk her away into the winter night.

"And now...I'm going to kiss you," Alex announced as if to proclaim something grand. Eva wasn't sure if it was a question or a statement, but she did know that she wasn't ready.

Alex began to lean in, ready to make good on his statement. Eva felt the anxiety begin to rise within her. *Oh, my gosh! He's going to kiss me! Wait! No! I'm not ready!* It was all happening so fast. He came closer until his lips were almost to hers.

"No!" Eva exclaimed...almost shouted into his mouth, turning her head away just as he was about to make contact. "I'm sorry," she whispered, "I can't. I mean, I'm not ready for that."

A really surprised Alex backed away, dropping his head in disappointment. "It's okay," he said quietly, too embarrassed to look at her.

Eva could hear the disappointment in his voice but didn't know what to say or do to soothe it. It had taken a great deal of bravery for her to even agree to meet him for a date, but a kiss was too soon. "I'm sorry," she said, shaking her head apologetically as she climbed into the cab. "Look, I have to go...I'll call you when I get home, okay?"

"Okay," he replied softly and closed the door behind her. Eva waved from inside the cab as it pulled away. She didn't see that Alex's smile was gone as he watched the cab take her away into the frigid winter night.

***

Eva made sure to adequately beat herself up the whole taxi ride home and then up all eight flights of stairs to her apartment. *I need to call him...so he doesn't think I was blowing him off.* She plopped down onto her couch and mustered up all the strength she could to pick up the phone and call Alex. She was so terribly shy when it came to guys in general, let alone a guy who had just spilled his guts about how he felt towards her. She truly did not believe she was worth any of his effort or that she even had a right to call him and explain herself. After all, she was always screwing up.

"Hello?" came a cold half-whisper from the other end of the line. It didn't even sound like him.

23

"Oh…hi…Alex?"

"Yeah." Coldness.

"Hey, it's me…listen, I just wanted to let you know I got home okay. And actually, I just wanted to let you know that…. I didn't kiss you because I wasn't ready. And I've been sick and didn't want you to catch it…It's not that I didn't want to…I just wasn't ready." *And I didn't want you to think I'm a horrible kisser, or have bad breath, are too inexperienced, etc….*Eva mentally abused herself as she checked off her own irrational shortcomings in her head.

"Don't worry…I'll get you eventually."

Eva paused and then let out a nervous laugh of relief. She could hear the teasing in his voice but was still unsure of how to take that. "Yeah…maybe…if you're lucky!"

She could feel Alex loosen on the line as he laughed softly in his normal warm tone. She always had a way of getting him with her quick and feisty responses. "Goodnight, Eva."

"Goodnight, Alex. I'm sorry."

"Hey, it's okay. I mean, I got to admit, I was super confused after the conversation we'd just had before I leaned in for the kill, but I think I understand now. You just need to take it slow."

Eva nodded her chin into the phone. "Uh huh, definitely."

"Okay. Well, goodnight then."

"Goodnight."

Eva hung up the phone. Whew! Damage control, check.

***

Alex hung up the phone, took another sip, and let his glass comfort him to numbness until he fell asleep. *This girl has the power to hurt me…whether she means to or not.*

3 SIGNALS CROSS

"There she is! Live and direct from uptown Manhattan!" shouted Tony, spotting Eva walking down the street towards his cart.

Eva, sporting her black oversized "Jackie O" sunglasses, knee-length silver, faux fur coat and black leather boots, stopped in her tracks. With one hand on her hip and one hand behind her head and the best duck face she could muster, pretended to pose for her friend. "How-f dat?" she muffled through her pursed lips, not breaking her pose. Tony was one person she felt she could be silly with that wouldn't judge her and his big brother vibe only validated her comfort.

"Ha, ha! It's super! And hey, since you've already got those luscious lips puckered, how's about a kiss?" Tony leaned over to hand Eva her coffee, closed his eyes, raised his eyebrows wide, and puckered his own lips in expectation.

"Yeah, nice try, Tones. Knock it off," Eva playfully smacked his arm as she took her coffee and stepped aside to make room for the other customers. Tony snapped his finger as if to say darn and crossed his arms pretending to pout.

"Always the jokester," she said, taking a sip of what she considered the best brew in town.

"Hey, somebody's got to liven things up around here," Tony replied nodding towards his growing line of customers scowling down at their smartphones.

Expert at his job, he also knew their orders by heart and worked fast to whittle down the line as he chatted with Eva who was not only his friend, but favorite customer. "So, yesterday was a big day. You do anything special?"

Eva blushed and looked down at her cup. "Well...yeah...actually. A friend I've known for a while took me out on a date."

"Really? Oh, wow. How did that go?"

"Not bad...pretty good...yeah, pretty good." Eva smiled at her friend.

Tony could sense the tension in her voice. "Listen, doll, this guy gives you any trouble? You let him know, yo. This guy ain't afraid to kick some ass and take some names, capiche? Especially a sweet sugar pie like you."

Eva turned to the side and gave him a defiant smile over her shoulder, "Don't you worry, Tones. I can take care of myself." And with that, she turned around and twinkled a 'goodbye' with her fingers over her shoulder as she headed down the street.

***

Highline was a buzz of activity that morning, as Eva stepped in through the glass doors and looked around for Alex through the crowd.

Hmm, no Alex.

With his freelance schedule, it wasn't out of the ordinary for him not to be in the office. Eva was almost half-relieved to see he wasn't there. After her mishap the night before, she knew she would be embarrassed to face him. With not only starting a new relationship, but also working together, she knew she'd have to overcome her insecurity if they were going to make it work.

Eva stepped into her office, took off her coat and started sorting through the scattered mail that Peter had thrown on her desk.

"Well, honey...you know, I'm just dying to hear how it went," came a sing songy voice at the door.

Eva turned around to find Ramona leaning in the doorway with arms crossed over one of her vintage Chanel suits and a proud smile as if she were watching one of her babies go off to college.

"So, tell me everything," she said emphatically and waved her hands in the air at Eva as she brisked through the door. "How did it go? Where'd you eat? Did you's guys do the hokey pokey? Huh? Huh?" Ramona asked, raising her eyebrows, nudging her elbow into Eva's side.

"Ra-mon-a!" Eva's jaw dropped to the floor as she gave her boss a shocked look that her virtue should dare be questioned.

"Oh, honey, I'm just teasing. Relax. Good girl like you, I know nothin's gettin' near those knickers unless he puts a ring on it."

"Nice." Eva rolled her eyes and shook her head.

Ramona held her belly and laughed hard falling into a chair, "Oh, honey, you should see yourself. You're about eight shades of red right now! Alright, alright, so spill already."

"Well, he took me for hot chocolate and then-"

"No, no, no," her mentor shook her head with each no. "None of that boring stuff. Did you smooch the guy?? I know he's been dying to the way he looks at you. In fact, I was hoping NOT to find you here this morning you know what I mean.... wink, wink."

Eva gave her mentor 'the look' and shook her head at her pressing questions. She knew better at this point not to expect Ramona to listen to rebuke on her teasing. "Ramona, you are hopeless, you know that?" she said with a soft smile.

"No, sweetie. I'm a hopeless romantic," she corrected reaching for the proofs from yesterday's shoot that Peter had also tossed carelessly on Eva's desk. "That Peter...," Ramona muttered, shaking her head at his messiness. "Remind me to kick his ass later, will ya? Aaaand, I'm still waitin' to hear you tell me the good stuff. So, did you guys lock lips or no?"

"Well...no," Eva posed her response almost in the fashion of a question. She bit her lip and watched for her mentor's response tentatively, anticipating disappointment.

Ramona looked up over her glasses at Eva without lifting her head. "No...? You mean to tell me the guy finally gets the you-know-what's to ask you out and you don't even kiss the guy? Oh, sweetie," Ramona shook her head. "What the hell." She put one hand on her head and closed her eyes like she had a headache.

"I couldn't. I mean, I just wasn't ready. It was only our first date, you know?" Eva flustered. She didn't want to admit how self-conscious she was when it came to that.

"'Ready?' Honey, I mean what in the hell are you waitin' for, a grand parade?" Ramona waved her hands through the empty air in front of her.

Eva shook her head, "No... I just. I was afraid. I haven't been out with anyone in so long and I was afraid of...messing things up. I called him right after to explain, but I'm afraid I already discouraged him."

"Oh, honey, believe me. A hot little thing like you don't need to be afraid of nothin'. He should be the one to be afraid of screwin' things up. Anyways, I unda-stand. You take your time and when it's right, you'll know."

"I don't even know if he's still even interested anymore. I mean, he hasn't even texted me since we spoke last night. I thought for sure he would have at least said some small thing by now. Guys usually don't wait that long to reach out when they really like someone, right?"

"Why don't you text him now? And let him know what a great time you had. Soften the blow of kissin' rejection, if that's the case," Ramona nodded in approval taking her glasses off and resting them under her chin.

"I didn't reject him, and you really think so?"

"Oh, yeah," Ramona waved her glasses in a flourish. "Men love that. It helps them get out of their own heads, when they know for sure that a gal is interested enough to do the talkin'."

"Okay...yeah...maybe I'll do that."

"Good!" Ramona tapped the arms of her chair in affirmation and stood up. "Now, that we got that outta the way, we can get down to business. These pics are killa, by the way...killa. The boys from L.A. are def gonna love'em. And they loved you even more."

"They did?" Eva looked up, a pleasant look of surprise on her face.

"Yeah, honey. As if that was even gonna be a question." She took Eva's chin tenderly. "I'm proud of you. Hiring you was the best decision I ev-uh made around here."

Eva smiled her thanks at her mentor. She'd learned to live her life in the stale coldness of negativity; first from others, which then taught her to be her own worst enemy. Now starved for encouragement, she could always count on Ramona to believe in her, even when she didn't believe in herself.

"And you know what will make me even more proud?"

"What?" Eva inquired softly.

"Text the guy."

Ramona gave Eva a wink and sauntered out the door and down the hall.
***

"I just wanted to let you know, I had a great time last night. Thank you for everything. I hope to see you again soon."

Eva pressed send and exhaled, realizing she'd been holding her breath. *Let's hope he doesn't think I'm absolutely bat-poo crazy.*

"Ping!" chimed the phone.

Wow! That was fast. Eva looked down to read the message.

"Me, too!" it read. "We'll get together again soon."

Eva smiled. Still, part of her wished there was more. She wanted the ask that would solidify their next plans and not keep her waiting to really find out if he wanted to see her again.

The next couple of days were a blur with work, and with no word from Alex. She thought for sure he would have called her by now. *I knew it. I scared him off. He's not that interested in me.* Suddenly her phone rang. She looked down. It was him. She let it ring a few times before she answered. "Hello?"

"Hi, Eva."

"Oh, hi, Alex," Eva responded easily, not wanting him to think she was over-eager. "What's up?"

"I just wanted to let you know, I'll be out of town for a couple of weeks.

Eva's balloon of hope deflated. "Oh...you will?"

"Yeah, I've got a big editing job out in L.A., and I want to visit my brother while I'm out there."

"Oh. Okay, I understand."

"Yeah, I'm packing now. I just wanted to call you before I got too busy."

"It's okay," Eva said softly. "I mean, I was hoping we'd be able to get together again, but I understand if you need to go."

"Yeah, I'm so sorry, Eva. It was kind of a last-minute thing. We'll get together again when I get back in a couple of weeks." His answers were short and lacked the tenderness they held of just a couple of nights before. "Sorry, I'm super busy right now. I'm leaving in an hour. I'll talk to you soon, okay?"

"Yeah, okay. Sure," Eva tried to sound enthusiastic. "Hey, have a good trip, okay?"

"Thanks, Eva. We'll talk soon."

Soon. Eva hung up the phone. Not two seconds later, did it ring again. "Hello?"

"Well, I'm glad I wasn't waiting for that phone call!"

"Oh, hi, Kate."

"So, were you ever going to tell me about your date? I've been sitting on pins and pine needles here!"

"I'm so sorry," Eva soothed her best friend. "I've been just a little distracted here." She gave her friend the details and waited for her response.

"Hmm?"

"Yeah, I mean he sounds like he really likes you from everything you've told me he said to you that night. And the white rose and all...maybe he's just distracted with work. Give it time. And wait and see how he is when he gets back from his trip. I mean, you've only had one date. I know he basically poured his heart out to you, but don't get ahead of yourself. Oh, Collin says 'hi', by the way."

Eva could hear the protective tone in her friend's voice. "Yeah, you're probably right. Hi, Collin."

Collin was Kate's husband. She'd been through the world's most horrible divorce before she met him. Collin was the perfect man for her. A strong man of faith who respected and valued her in a way her first husband hadn't. They were deeply in love and Eva, having watched her friend's first marriage fall apart first-hand and then witnessing the courtship from the budding of the new relationship through to the wedding, she admired their union.

Kate and Collin were unified, bonded in every way. There was nothing he wouldn't do for her. Kind, considerate, compassionate, patient...a godly man who knew how to lead. And always very polite to Eva. Eva remembered the first time she had met him. He had taken the time to get to know his then future wife's best friend, knowing she would be a staple in their lives. A gentleman. Eva used her friend's marriage to set the standard for her own future. I want a marriage like that, she'd muse.

"Evie, you know I've had my share of heartache. No need to rush things. Just take it slow. God will show you if it's right."

"Yeah...God," Eva replied almost in a scoff. She didn't know the same God Kate knew. Eva's god was an authoritarian, ready to punish her at every slip. Making her reach for things just out of grasp, never bringing them close enough to materialize; awarded on merit and Eva always fell short. Eva was bad in her god's eyes; undeserving of his hand; having to search high and low for her life, while her god sat up in heaven shaking his head at her in disapproval. No, Eva's god did not deem her worthy of anything...especially happiness and love.

"Just give him a chance."

Kate was talking about Alex, but for the first time in two days Eva wasn't thinking about Alex. She felt a slight stirring in her gut that told her Kate's words may mean more... a plea for something deeper.

4 MILES APART

"Ping!"

"Mmf."

Eva slowly turned over underneath her silk cream-colored comforter and soft Egyptian cotton, pale blue sheets and opened her eyes. 4:30 a.m. *Who on earth could be texting me at this hour?*

She picked up her phone and opened her message. Alex.

"Hey, sweetheart. Just wanted to let you know I landed safe in L.A. Talk to you soon!"

Eva smiled half-asleep and rolled back over hugging her pillow drifting now into a deep sleep. He may have been distant earlier, but he'd cared enough to let her know he had arrived at his destination intact and that was enough to give her the peace she needed to rest easy.

***

Eva rushed around her home back in Virginia making the final preparations. She was late and everyone was waiting for her. Her mother was waiting for her at the bottom of the steps. "Eva, let's go! The limos have already left. You're just going to have to go like that."

Eva ran down the steps in her pajamas, hair and makeup undone. She'd hoped to have time to prepare herself, but she would have to make do with what she had on. "Coming, Mom!"

They climbed into Eva's old Mercury and raced to the church. When they arrived, Eva found Alex waiting for her at the altar in a tuxedo, his face a mix of worry and relief.

"Thank GOD!" he exclaimed as if his very life were hanging in the balance. "I thought you'd never get here." He reached towards Eva to take her hands and pull her towards him.

Eva startled awake with a gasp. *A dream. It was just a dream.*

***

2 weeks later...

"Nothing??" exclaimed Charlie, Eva's closest guy friend in the city. "Not even a 'Hey, how ya doing? Wish you were here?' Geez, what is wrong with this guy," Charlie pondered shaking his head into his straw of pop as if the very notion was ridiculous.

Eva had met Charlie, a struggling actor, through one of her freelance gigs, when she had first moved to the city. The two had become fast friends. Charlie had not hidden from Eva the fact that he was not only interested in her, but very much ready to date her at the drop of a hat.

Although they shared much of the same artistic interests, Eva was not attracted to him in any sort of romantic way and strictly saw him as a friend.

Still, they were able to make the friendship work. Although he could be immature and annoying at times like a little brother, Eva enjoyed his company. Charlie kept her grounded and could make her laugh with his simple humor. Charlie was from a small town, too, and Eva felt as though she could relate to him. They would often spend time hanging out near Union Square or in the village checking out comedy shows, new cafes, or just walking through the streets, seeing what they could discover. The friends' go-to option, of course, was Eva's favorite ice cream shop downtown, Frankie and Johnny's.

"Seriously, Eva, this guy is lucky enough to actually have the chance to go out with you...like out-out...like more than what you and me are doing here just having some ice cream...like it's a known-thing you both are interested and working towards a common goal and he doesn't even have the decency to keep in touch with you while he's away? What's up with that?"

Eva sighed and pushed her chocolate peanut butter chunk ice cream around with her spoon.

"I don't know Eves...if that was me, I'd leave absolutely no room for doubt," he spoke gently, wanting to be tender toward Eva's sensitive spirit.

"Well, Charlie, you're a guy. What do you think I should do?" Eva inquired purposefully.

Lose this guy. Charlie's thoughts were selfish. His feelings for Eva were much deeper than he ever let on, but he was willing to suppress them for the sake of their friendship. Just being near her gave him life. She added color to his world. And he wanted her to find happiness, even if it couldn't be with him.

"Well, Eves...guys love it when the girl takes the initiative, you could just call him." Charlie hated to give advice that would win another guy his own case, but also knowing the depth of her feelings for Alex, her happiness was at stake.

"You don't think he'll think I'm too forward?"

"Eva, he's a guy. And guys are stupid. Trust me, I know. I am one. We don't think about things nearly the same way as you females do. If you want to talk to him, call him. Maybe that's what he's waiting for. I mean, you all but ran in the other direction when he tried to kiss you. Maybe his confidence is down."

"For Pete's sake, I wasn't ready. How many times do I have to explain that? What was I supposed to do just throw all of my virtue out the window in lieu of attraction?" Eva lowered her head, feeling the familiarity of shame creep over her. "I mean...he did reach out to let me know when he landed in L.A. Doesn't that mean something? You don't just tell anybody that you got somewhere safe."

"Yeah, Eves, and then L.A. happened. He's probably just busy."

"Yeah...maybe...Ugh, I can't think about this anymore," Eva shook her head in frustration which made her angel hair to float around her face. Charlie wanted to reach out and touch her soft locks, but he restrained himself.

"Okay, so, I'm just going to call him." Eva stood up, grabbed her coat, and leaned down to give Charlie a big kiss on the cheek. "Mwah! Thanks, Charlie!" she beamed giving him a big bear hug. "You're the best!" she exclaimed as she headed out the door.

"Yeah...So are you." Charlie returned softly, almost in a murmur. Only Eva didn't hear him. She had already merged with the hurried traffic of the sidewalk rushing off towards home to make her call.

Charlie watched her through the window as she made her way down the sidewalk until she was out of sight...a single tear skimming down his face.

***

Eva poured the steaming-hot water from her grandmother's hand-me-down silver kettle into her etched glass teacup and watched the tea stain the water in ruddy-brown rivulets from top to bottom. She sat down on her vintage lavender velvet chaise and looked around her apartment that had become an oasis of warmth that she loved to come home to. The soothing cream and gold tones of color, elegant and shimmering gauze-like fabrics and soft, warm lighting had a calming effect that could soothe her no matter what was going on inside of her or outside of her apartment on those clamoring city streets.

Sigh. Eva took a sip of tea and leaned back, resting her head in her hand and gazing out the window. Over the past two weeks, snow had turned to rain. A beautiful thing happened in the city when it rained at nighttime. Clouds descended just above the tops of the buildings and cast a beautiful luminescent pale-yellow glow from the city lights; one of Eva's favorite things about her not-so-new-now home. Peace.

"Ring!" Eva sat up with a start and looked at her phone. *Alex.* She reached over to put her tea down on the glass coffee table and answered the phone. "Hello?"

"Hey, Gorgeous."

"Oh...Alex? Hey. How are you?" He sounded different than normal...cockier, almost arrogant. "How is your trip going?"

"Good so far. You wouldn't believe all of the celebrities I've gotten to hang out with since I've been here. And the parties? Ah-mazing."

Parties? Celebrities? That's not like him. Alex was normally very down to earth, unmoved by the things of pop culture. Eva began to wonder if the two weeks he had spent in LA had begun to infiltrate his mind. The parties, the beautiful women, the recognition. Alex's brother was a well-known producer in Hollywood and one of America's most-noted playboys. Eva had never followed pop culture as it never impressed her, but she knew enough about Alex's brother to know that the life he lived was reminiscent of a modern-day Babylon; an excitement that Eva knew she could never compete with for his attention.

"Oh...that's nice." Eva was disappointed. It had been so long since they had spoken, and she was hoping their first conversation in two weeks would have proven him eager for her. Missing her. And here he was sounding so different, so...L.A. A far cry from his gentle-toned conversation over candlelight just two weeks prior.

"Yeah, listen, I've decided to stay another two weeks. It was kind of a last-minute decision."

Eva didn't respond.

"But don't worry, I haven't forgotten you. We'll hang out when I get back to the city, cool?"

With that cocky attitude? No... not cool...this is most definitely not cool. Eva decided to hold her frustration. After all, he was on vacation and perhaps he wanted to spend some more time with his brother. Perhaps the work was much more than he had anticipated. *I mean, we're not even truly official yet.* Still, despite her best efforts to think positively about the delay, something told her there was more to it than what he let on.

Don't let him know you're upset. You'll just push him away even more. "Yeah, okay, that sounds good. See you in two weeks."

"Bye, hon."

"Bye."

"Oh, and Eva?"

"Yeah?"

"...I miss you."

***

Eva sat at her desk looking over the proofs on her laptop from her most recent shoot.

Fix that. Adjust this. Correct that coloring.

Eva kept a running list in her head of things she would want to go back and edit later.

Knowing *Highline* would be short an editor with Alex out of town for so long, she decided to adjust the photos herself to save the magazine time, a skill she had learned working alongside him for so many hours.

"So, you and Alex seem to be quite the hot topic around here," interrupted Peter as he sauntered into her office unannounced. "I heard the two of you seem to be getting along quite famously," he continued sarcastically.

"I'm sure you have," Eva responded unamused, not looking up from her work.

"Personally, I think work relationships are a bit messy."

Eva gave Peter a serious look. "Did you have anything important you needed to discuss?"

Peter continued, ignoring the fact that she had asked him a question. "Kind of unprofessional, but that's just my opinion," he responded smugly with a shrug of his shoulders and a flare of his wrists.

"Well, good. I'm glad it's just your opinion because I don't remember asking you for it." Eva looked up at him with a look of intent. "In fact," she took her glasses off, "I don't remember asking you to barge in here without knocking first. I don't remember asking you to throw my mail or my work across my desk like you're scattering corn to mice like a freaking Cinderella. And I most certainly don't remember asking you to pry into my personal life like it's any of your damn business."

She stood up and walked towards him, backing him out of her office. "So, the next time you want to waltz in here like you own the place and start digging into my private business and how that supposedly relates to work, I suggest you first show me a card that says you're the damn CEO of this company. Because that's the only way you might even come close to getting away with it."

Peter was flustered silent for the first time in the whole time Eva had known him.

"Until then, we're done here. When you have something to discuss that is work-related and pertains to your job or mine AND you can be respectful, you can knock first. Okay? Buh-bye." Eva closed the door in front of him, leaving him standing there with his mouth open in shock.

Eva slowly walked back to her desk, fighting guilt the whole way. She knew she couldn't continue to allow him to walk all over her, but still a part of her felt cruel. *Who are you kidding? Who are you to stick up for yourself? Who do you think you are, anyway, the Queen of Sheba? It wasn't really a big deal, you shouldn't have said that.*

Outside of Eva's office door, Peter was fuming. He turned slowly on his Gucci heels and started down the long hall, cursing Eva with each prowling step. *Oh, honey, you absolutely do not know who you're dealing with, do you? But...I think I can find a way to make you learn.*

5 SECRET ADMIRER

"Oh, my-lanta, what kind of people are they growing over there in that crazy city, Evie?"

"I know, right?" Eva had just finished telling Kate about Peter's latest shenanigans. "Do you think I was too mean?"

"What? Mean? Heck, no. Are you kidding? Way too easy on him. If it was me, I would have given him the what-for...without losing my Jesus, of course."

Eva laughed. It wasn't often she saw calm Kate fired up, but when she did, look out. Kate was a force to be reckoned with and she took no prisoners.

"You're so sweet, Eva, even when you're angry. You could yell at someone, and they would think you were giving them your holy blessing or something."

"Oh, yeah, 'cause we all know how religious I am," Eva replied sarcastically.

"Gosh, I hope not," teased her friend.

"Wait...what?" Eva was surprised at her friend's counter.

"Eve, there is a difference between being 'religious' and having a faith relationship. And I hope someday you'll know the difference. I think you will."

"Don't hold your breath."

"Eh, you talk a good game now, Eve, but just wait...pretty soon you'll be shouting it from the rooftops!" Kate knew how to speak to her friend with just enough pressure to make her think and just enough humor to keep it light and keep her laughing.

"We'll see." Eva, suspicious by nature, wasn't as sure.

"No, Eve, you'll see...in a way you never have before...and then everything will change."

***

Eva snuggled into her pale-pink silk jammies with black pipe-trimming, climbed into bed, and grabbed her laptop. With the week she had, she just wanted to zone out and forget about life for a while. She logged onto Profile, her social media homepage. The icon at the top of Profile told her that she had a new message.

That's odd, she thought, not recognizing the name or profile picture of her messenger. The guy looked about her age, had no shirt on and had a shaved head. Eva didn't like that look. Just the picture alone was enough to turn her off. *Who the heck is Cyrano?* She opened the message.

"Hi, Eva! Long time, no see! How are you?"

Eva racked her brain...*who in the world is that? Guess there's only one way to find out...*

"Hi, who the hell is this?" Eva replied. She didn't believe in beating around the bush, especially when it came to strangers. If this guy needed to go, she was going to find out quickly so she could get rid of him in a hurry and get back to her night.

"Just an old friend from high school! Who happens to be a huge fan of yours! By the way, I think it's awesome what you're doing in NYC! I bet you everyone back home thought you'd never make it!"

Eva furrowed her brow at the screen in confusion. She didn't remember this person from high school. Maybe it was someone else messing with her, which she did not appreciate one bit. If that was the case, she was going to get to the bottom of it.

"Okay, so are you going to actually tell me who you are, or do I need to edit my resume to add Mystery Solver? I don't recognize your name or picture. And editing my resume is such a pain in the butt."

"Haha! Well, we were in marching band together."

"Oh, yeah? How do I know you're really someone I went to high school with? You don't look like any of my friends...or anyone else I knew for that matter. Prove it."

"Well, you were in the kick-line, and you always wore your hair in French-braided pigtails with ribbons. I had such a huge crush on you! My name and profile picture is not who I really am!"

No crap. Eva was irritated. She couldn't figure out why this person would choose to hide behind a false name and picture. *If this mystery person thinks they're gonna mess with me at my expense, they've got another thing coming.*

Eva wasn't in the mood for games, and she was leery of people from her hometown digging for info on her, trying to find out what she was up to in her life to numb the boredom of their own lives. Eva's big move had been a hot topic of gossip when she left, and it had been a fight for her to push through her own doubt without adding the unsolicited opinions of others. She wasn't about to feed into that again and decided to put this creeper in his place.

"Look, I'm flattered, but if you aren't going to tell me who you are, I'm not going to continue a conversation with you. I really don't have time for this."

"Okay, okay. You got me. I didn't know you from high school. I just knew you wouldn't talk to me unless I made it sound like I knew you."

Eva was more confused than ever now. She racked her brain trying to think of who else it could be. It wasn't uncommon for someone outside of her fellow high school alumni to know this superfluous detail about her. As her life experience had expanded, and she had begun to meet new people, she could think of several people she'd compared high school stories with at one point or another in the friendship or relationship...and Alex had been one of them. Could he be testing her now?

No, she thought to herself. *He can't be THAT paranoid...could he?* Eva remembered a conversation between the two of them where he had described to her how much of a struggle it was for him to trust anybody...even those he felt closest to, mostly because of his brother's fame. Most girls Alex had dated had only wanted one thing, the chance to get close to his brother in the hopes of selfishly acquiring fame and fortune for themselves. Once they realized Alex was not a man to be fooled, they would drop him like a hot potato; leaving him heartbroken, insecure, and sometimes even discovering these women would have another guy on the side as back up. Alex had admitted to fabricating tests if he felt his love interest could not be trusted.

Eva wondered if this anonymous admirer was Alex doing that very thing now.

If he is testing me, I'll just have to show him that he can trust me. Eva didn't like it, but she could understand the situation from his perspective. *I didn't even kiss him...after a beautiful date. He's probably wondering if I'm truly even interested in him. And he is so far away right now...on the other side of the country! He's been burned so badly before...maybe this is his way of testing the waters...to see if I truly am who I say I am... if I'll be faithful while he's away. But why the anonymous emails?*

Eva decided to stop responding. If this mystery person was Alex, she wasn't going to add to his history of doubt by making herself suspect in his eyes. She was going to show him that she was a woman of integrity. And if it wasn't him...well, that was just creepy.

Eva closed her laptop, set it aside and drifted off to sleep.

***

"Holy crap, Eves! Slow down!"

Charlie mounted his horse and tried to catch up to Eva as fast as he could.

Eva's laugh carried high through the wind along with her hair as she rode Epiphany, Central Park's most prized horse, as fast as she could hoping her friend would catch up.

"Aww, what's the matter, Charlie? Can't-cha keep up?" Eva teased back over her shoulder and smiled as she dug her riding boots in again for another sprint. The lazy Sunday afternoon had found the two horseback riding at The Stables in Central Park and Eva was loving it. The trees of Central Park framed the clear, blue sky, which held only a bright sun, no clouds. Eva felt as free as the wind around them.

"Raised horses!" Charlie yelled after her, goofily pointing his finger at his friend. "RAISED! HORSES!"

Eva threw her head back and laughed at her friend's silly way of telling her that he couldn't quite cut it on an equine like she could; a fact not many knew about her.

"Oh, al-right, Mr. Slow Poke!" Eva laughed breathlessly and halted Epiphany who promptly whinnied and slowed her pace. "Steady, girl," Eva patted the Epiphany's mane and spoke softly to her equine as she jumped down to wait for Charlie. Holding onto the reins, she stepped in front of the well-groomed horse and gently took her long horsey face in her hands.

As she looked into the horse's eyes memories came flooding back...

Eva's grandparents had raised horses in the country just outside of her hometown in Virginia. On weekends, she would go to her grandparents' farm to help them with the horses and to visit her own horse Arabia. Arabia was an Arabian horse who had a will as strong as its own beauty. Eva had been the only one that could tame her.

The horse had been a rescue, and no one had been able to connect with her except for Eva. Her grandfather had tried and was promptly thrown, miraculously unharmed. Her grandmother had not had much more success with Arabia. But from the moment Eva looked into that horse's eyes, something had clicked. The connection the two had was like a dance. Eva could simply take Arabia's long face in her small hands or run her hand down

40

the length of her smooth coat to calm her. Eva would call her name from the hill next to her grandparents' house and watch her come galloping across the open green pasture anticipating the promise of carrots, oats, or simply time with her owner.

Then, one unexpected day, Eva had come to the stable to find that Arabia had been sold by her parents. "She's too much of a distraction," her parents had told her. "You'll be headed off to college soon and that horse is way too time-consuming. We don't want her getting in the way of your studies."

"That horse?" Eva had retorted rebelliously. "That horse is way more than just a horse. That horse is more of a friend to me than you'll ever be!" And with that she ran to her room, slammed the door shut, and sobbed for a week.

That memory was one loss that still stung enough to matter. Coming to The Stables was Eva's way of getting her equine fix and making amends with her past. Epiphany reminded her so much of Arabia and Eva would visit whenever she could to ride and be carefree for the afternoon.

Charlie, wheezing, finally caught up to her. He put one hand on his hip and the other elbow on his horse pretending to lean out of exhaustion. "You and that horse look like you're in the middle of a serious conversation. I can come back?"

"Oh stop," Eva slapped her friend's arm, giggling. "Race you to the Reservoir?"

"Yeah...yeah...you go on ahead, you crazy thing.... I'll catch up".

The ring of Eva's phone startled them both.

"Oh...it's Alex! Hold on a sec, okay?"

Charlie grumbled and rolled his eyes at her as if to say, 'are you serious?'

"Hi, Gorgeous."

Eva blushed, "Hi, Alex. When did you get back?"

"Oh, no, that's actually what I'm calling to tell you."

"Oh...was your flight delayed?"

"No, hon, it's going to be another two weeks."

The brightness left her eyes.

"Two weeks?" Eva looked out of the corner of her eye at Charlie and turned away from him.

She didn't want him to see that she was getting upset.

"Yeah, I just. I'm just having such a good time here that I'm not quite ready to leave...is that alright?"

Eva kept her feelings to herself. "I mean why? Did someone else approach you for a job?" Charlie jumped down and walked over to her sensing

41

something was wrong and gently took her elbows, forcing her to look at him.

"What?" he mouthed. Eva shook her head, but Charlie persisted. Eva shook her head again and held up her finger telling him to wait.

"No, nothing like that. I just feel like I need more time here, that's all."

"Look, Alex, if this is your way of blowing me off-"

"No! Eva!" he interrupted her before she could finish her sentence. "I'm not blowing you off, I swear. We'll get together as soon as I get back, I promise."

Eva hesitated. "Okay," she responded quietly.

"Look, I got to run. My brother's having a party tonight and I need to help him get ready for it. Talk to you later, okay?"

"Yeah...okay." Eva knew what that meant, further opportunity for him to forget about her. A simple girl from Virginia, there was no way she could compete with the big lavish parties that L.A. boasted.

"Bye, Sweetheart. Don't you go getting another boyfriend while I'm gone. Okay?"

She knew he was teasing, but she wasn't in the mood to laugh. She didn't want him to think it would be okay to continue to keep her waiting like this with no communication in between. "Bye, Alex."

Eva hung up and gave Charlie a puppy dog look.

"Ah, geeez!" Charlie put his hands up to his head. "What is wrong with this guy?? He's got the greatest woman on earth waiting for him back home and he don't know. If that was me, I'd have been back before I left. I mean I'm standing here with you right now and I already miss you!

Eva shot her head up and looked at him in surprise.

"I... mean...," Charlie stuttered and gestured to the air as if searching for his words. "I-I just mean that if I said all of those things that he said to you that night and was away from you for that long, it would be very hard not to communicate to you that I missed you...that's all."

Eva chose to ignore the deeper meaning behind Charlie's words and avoid conflict, but also to save his dignity. She knew it had to hurt on some level for him to see her with someone else and she didn't want to add salt to his wound.

"So... I guess it's a good thing I have friends like you, huh?" Eva said softly trying to save his confidence.

Charlie gave her a sideways smile and bumped into her with his elbow playfully. "Yeah."

"Come on let's get out of here. It's getting late and I need to get home before Monday gets here."

"What are you going to turn into a pumpkin?"

Eva frowned and gave him a scrunchy face as she hopped back up onto Epiphany to head back to The Stables.

"Seriously, Eva...how interested in this guy are you? He just doesn't seem to be very...attentive. Or considerate for that matter."

"No, he is very sweet and caring when he's in person," Eva defended her Mr. Man. "It's just the environment he's in right now. Once he gets back to the city and sees me, I know it will be different. I know his heart...he would never hurt me on purpose."

Charlie looked over at his friend, whose horse was now trotting just slightly up ahead of him. He was concerned.

"So, if this relationship continues...and you know how he operates while he is away.... are you going to be able to handle that?"

Eva held her response.

"Eva?"

"Yeah," Eva responded definitively, now concentrating on Epiphany, petting her, making kissy noises at her; enjoying her last moments on the horse before she would have to hand her back over to the stable hands.

"You know I'm always here for you, right? Anytime you need me."

"Yeah, Charlie." Eva smiled sweetly at her friend. "I know that."

6 SWEET RETURN

Eva stood on the street corner near Alex's house and took a deep breath. It was the two's first date since Alex had left for L.A. six weeks prior. Eva had spent what seemed like an eternity in front of her closet trying to decide on the perfect 'homecoming' outfit for their get-together. Now that spring was coming, and with the break in the weather, she had a few more options aside from bundling herself up into an unrecognizable oblivion. She'd finally decided upon dark jeans, a gauzy, flowing white shirt and pale gold wedges; her hair in easy waves pulled loosely half-up at the crown of her head, with just a few pieces surrounding her face.

She looked up from her daze and saw a tall, dark figure walking towards her on the opposite street corner. It was just before sunset and the sun was illuminating Alex from behind in such a way that almost made him look mysterious, like a hatless urban cowboy sauntering up the street.

The minute she saw him, all the doubts of his absence fled, and she forgave him for being so neglectful while he was away. It had always been difficult for her to stay angry at anyone she cared for deeply. And now that he was back home and ready to spend time with her, she didn't care what had happened in the past couple of months. She was ready to move forward with a clear mind and an open heart.

Eva smiled and waved, trying to contain the butterflies in her stomach, before prancing across the street to greet him. "Hi," she said softly with a doe-eyed smile, gazing up at him.

Alex didn't say anything but stared at her for a minute. Then, without any warning, he swooped down to draw her in for the longest hug. When Eva went to pull away, he held her just a few seconds longer. And she let him.

Having her so near again helped him remember how important she was to him...a comfort...like home.

"Eva...I didn't realize how much I missed you until just now," he whispered into her perfumed hair, finally pulling away.

"Well, I should hope so...what took you so long?" she teased him.

Alex looked at her as if he was studying her for the first time. He took her hand as they started down the street.

"I honestly don't know."

***

The cafe was crowded that night as they sat down at a comfy table in the corner and waited for their order. Eva wanted so badly to ask him if he had met someone else while he was away and if that was the reason for his absence, but she decided to hold her tongue. Again, her insecurities plagued her. *I don't have any right to ask him that. It's not like we're engaged or anything.*

She decided to try another way. "So, how was your trip? I didn't really hear much from you while you were away. I was kind of...surprised." Eva waited for his answer tentatively, as if she were afraid that he would be annoyed with the question and snap at her.

"Yee-ah, about that. There's something I need to tell you."

Eva's pre-conditioned response caused her heart to sink. *Here it comes.*

"I'm...not really...."

Eva closed her eyes into a wince and braced herself for the rejection.

"...a phone person."

Eva opened her eyes. *Whew. That was close.* She thought for sure he was getting ready to tell her he wasn't interested in her anymore, or that he had met someone else more appealing. Or, or, or.

"Yeah, I really just wanted to give my full attention to...everything that was there in front of me while I was out there. It's not often I get to see my brother. He's so busy with movies and... partying. Seems like he goes right from one movie to the next. I really try to spend as much time with him as I can, when I can. I just wasn't ready to come home."

"I guess I can understand that." She wanted to tell him how hurtful it was or that she felt neglected when he chose not to keep in contact while he was away after pouring his heart out to her and that she didn't understand why he didn't want to talk to her more, but she was afraid it was too soon to tell him so many things. That bearing her heart would only make her appear

45

desperate and needy; some of the very things that Alex was against.

He had told her many times before that she was different, and she'd planned to prove him right. So, she let it go. There would be plenty of other times for discussions of that nature and she didn't want to ruin their first night back together with a potential argument.

"So," he started, "I've been thinking."

Eva looked up at him inquisitively over her straw. "About what?"

"Yeah. I've been thinking about school, actually. Eva, I am getting so tired of this editing gig."

"You are?"

"Heck, yeah! I want to do something more with my life, make a better contribution." Eva could feel his passion behind his words as his eyes became more focused. "I've always wanted to go into social work, but I'm thinking counseling specifically. I know it will be a long haul, but I feel like if I'm not doing anything, I'm just wasting time. And the longer the clock ticks by, the further I feel it slipping away. I want more out of life than this. I want an actual future that's going to matter." He looked at her intently, watching for a reaction. "What do you think?"

Eva was excited to see him motivated for a purpose that would make a difference. "Well, I think it's wonderful. Yeah, you should definitely do it!" she encouraged.

"You do?"

"Yeah! I mean, I know this is something you've been thinking about for a long time. I remember you talking about it way back when we first met."

"But I mean, how do you think it will affect this?"

"This. This. What 'this'?"

"This...us." Alex gestured back and forth between the two of them.

"Oh." Eva was surprised by his question and tried not to look confused. Alex was most definitely a mystery to her. He'd just spent six weeks practically ignoring her and now here he was talking about the future; referring to her and himself as an 'us.

Eva had spent time talking to him on a deeper level before, but now that things had moved from professional to personal, she was getting to see a bit more of his personality than she had before. And his 'come and go' approach to the relationship just confused her even more.

"Well...," Eva hesitated, she wasn't sure how to respond, again fearful of saying too much, but at the same time wanting to express herself in the hopes that they'd settle into some kind of normalcy by default. After all, how could she expect him to give his all when the relationship had no clear definition? She still blamed herself for the epic kiss-fail. *Maybe if he sees that I am serious, he'll trust me enough to become serious.* "Well...I don't know. I mean...what do you see happening here? Because if you see what I see-"

"What? What do you see?" Alex interrupted her with a grin. "Eva...do you want to have my babies?"

She knew he was joking, but the serious nature of the question startled her. She slowly let out a laugh. It was the first joke he had made since that night on Valentine's Day that seemed so long ago.

Eva gave him a wink. "Well...maybe we could just start with a walk."

***

"Now how in heaven's name did you manage to get a horse and buggy to come all the way down here to the East Village?"

Alex had surprised Eva when they stepped out of the cafe with an evening carriage ride.

"Oh, I have my ways."

More mystery.

Alex held out his hand to help Eva into the carriage and pretended to tip his non-existent hat to her. "Your chariot, Mademoiselle."

Eva smiled, took his hand, and climbed into the carriage. "Merci, monsieur!" Alex followed in behind her and whispered something to the driver, who then turned around and flashed Eva a toothy grin. "Hiya, Light and Sweet."

"Tony?! And in a tailcoat, no less!" she turned to Alex. "Wait a minute, how in the heck did you...?" She turned to Tony, "And you?" And back again to Alex, "How did you...?"

Alex laughed heartily, finding her sheer confusion adorable in that moment. He grinned at her and gave her a flirtatious look out of the corner of his eye. "I told you...I have my ways."

Eva met his eyes in confused wonder, her own eyes betraying her. *Mr. Man knows a lot more about me than I realized. I wonder what other secrets he's keeping.*

She wondered if he had been watching her or had someone else watching her while he was on his NYC hiatus, but then immediately chased the notion out of her head. *No...he can't be that paranoid.* In the very moment those words crossed her mind, she remembered the email from her anonymous admirer. She tucked the thought away into her mental "save for later" file, not wanting to kill the mood or the sweet effort he had put into preparing the evening. There will be plenty of time for questions, she thought to herself and decided instead to be fully present in the moment.

"So, where are we going?"

"You'll see. I wanted to take us somewhere where we could talk. Just the two of us."

Now, he's talkin'. Eva had been waiting for time alone with him where they could actually have a serious conversation and not be interrupted or listened in on.

The carriage took them through the city streets to Washington Square Park and stopped right underneath the arch all aglow in its nighttime glory. Alex jumped down first then put his hands around Eva's tiny waist to help her down. But Eva tripped on her way out and ended up not so much hopping down but falling...right into him. "Oh, crap!" she gasped.

"Woah!" Alex wrapped his arms around her tighter to keep her, and himself, from falling.

"I'm such a klutz!"

Alex could have let go, but he held onto her just a bit longer. He looked into her face, now flush with embarrassment, then into her green eyes, bright with the shock of her faux pas. "No worries," he whispered softly, gazing down at her. It was the first time in a long time that she had heard tenderness in his recently blunt voice. Eva gazed back up at him as if in a daze, she wasn't afraid to be in his arms this time. Was this her chance to make up for her hesitation on their first date?

Just then he slowly released all but her hand and led her out from underneath the park's arc. "I have a little surprise for you."

"Seriously, there's more? I didn't think you could top that one, but hey, I'm game."

Alex squeezed her hand slightly. "Look around," he directed her gently. "What do you see?"

Eva slowly surveyed the small park. Then she saw it, her mouth dropping open in awe. Alex had strung a tree with lantern lights and laid a red and black checkered blanket on the grass beneath it. Tony had also left the carriage and was now setting a basket on the corner edge of the blanket. Alex slipped him some money. "Thanks, man. I'll take it from here."

"Yo, no problem," Tony replied. Then he tipped his hat at Eva, "M'lady."

Eva giggled. "Thanks, Tones...you are such a goof!"

"For you? Ehh, fo'get about it! You deserve it. Enjoy your evening,

Beautiful."

And with that, he left the two alone and he headed back to the carriage. Eva noticed that Tony's endearing farewell had won him a slight 'look' from Alex.

"Eh, it's nothing," she assured him. "Tony is a really nice guy. I see him practically every morning."

"You're a beautiful woman, Eva. And with a heart of gold to boot. I'm not surprised he would speak so comfortably with you...or find you attractive."

Eva wondered if there was deeper meaning to his words than what he let on, but in the magic of the setting, she didn't want to talk about Tony.

"Please...come sit down," Alex coaxed, gesturing to the blanket. His smile was soft and warm.

Eva walked over to where he was and sat down on the fluffy, red blanket. "So, what else have you got up your sleeve? Is there an orchestra in that basket or something?"

Alex laughed. "Um, no."

"A puppy?"

"No."

"Elvis?"

"E-va!" Alex was laughing. He found her innocent humor incredibly adorable. "Well, now it's really going to be a letdown. All I have is tea."

"Tea? Heck, yeah. I'll settle for that. I love tea! What kind?"

"A little birdie told me. You're favorite. Mint Chocolate Yerba Mate."

"Okay, you are really pulling out the big guns here."

Alex winked at her, poured a cup, and handed it to her, then poured himself a cup and sat down beside her. He looked at her. One of her deeper copper tendrils had found itself in front of her eyes, put there by the breeze. Alex tenderly brushed it aside, the black of her lashes framed memorizing pools of green. "This is nice," he said softly.

Eva held his gaze, "Yes, it is." She wondered if being in his presence was all it took for him to remember his feelings for her. *But I can't always be with him. What if I do something that causes him to back away again? And at what point will my absence mean more than my presence?* Eva couldn't help but turn the thoughts over in her mind. She wanted this time with him, but she didn't want to continue to experience the painful neglect of the past six weeks again.

"Eva, can I ask you something?"

"Sure."

"What do you think about family?"

"Do you really feel like talking about that again? Tonight?"

"Not like your home family, but family...as in... raising one?" His question was so confident and unmoved.

"Oh....Uhh..." *Holy crap, that was fast. This guy goes from zero to 60 in no time flat.* "I don't know. I mean, I know that I want one eventually, but I wouldn't want to raise one here in New York. You can't give a child a normal life here. Kids need a yard to play in and space to run around. Just watching mothers drag their strollers up and down the subway steps is enough for me to say 'nope'. I've watched the kids here and they aren't...kids! No normal four-year-old should know what udon noodles are. Seriously, they're exposed to way too much at such an early age and they act so serious! Not that it's bad to culture your kids, but kids should be kids for a while before they get into all that crap."

"I couldn't agree more. Man wasn't meant to live stacked one on top of the other. If I had a family, I would move out of the city, so I could raise them in a proper setting."

"Yeah." Eva sipped her tea, swirls of steam curling up from its surface into the air. "My thoughts exactly."

"I think you would make an amazing mother, Eva."

Eva almost choked on her tea. "You do?"

"Oh, yeah. You're very patient. And sweet...not like these city girls."

Eva raised her eyebrows. "Well, that's debatable. Clearly you have not seen me on my ugly days."

"Eva, your so-called ugly days are a walk in the park compared to these crazy New York chicks. I've seen you angry and it's more like a disgruntled bunny."

Eva laughed, "disgruntled bunny," she repeated out loud to herself. "Nice."

"And the way your nose crinkles up...," Alex shook his head. "Man."

Eva raised her eyebrows and decided to test the waters. "Yeah, I know what you mean about crazy."

"Yeah?"

"Yeah...someone sent me a message on Profile the other night. Only I don't know who the heck they are. They were saying they knew me from high school and all this, but I don't even know the person. He knew some pretty specific details about me, though. That's odd, don't you think?" Eva watched him, waiting for a response, but Alex didn't say anything. He stood up and started to pack up.

"We should get going."

Eva's heart sank. *I knew it. I ruined it. Eva, you're so stupid. Why can't you ever learn to keep your mouth shut?*

"Yeah..." Then he turned to her out of the corner of his eye and with his handsome smile said, "There's actually one more spot I'd like to take you to."

Eva looked up at him; confused again but intrigued. He rarely responded to her how she expected, but she was trying to keep up. Eva had assumed the worst as usual and his response once again proved her wrong. She stood up, picked up the blanket, and started folding it.

"And we'll have to take a cab," he continued. "I couldn't get Tony to take the carriage off the island of Manhattan. I think it's a law or something."

They finished packing up and Alex took the blanket from her. Switching the basket to his other hand, he hailed an unmarked cab. "We'll just leave that there," he said, gesturing to the trunk of the tree. "Tony's coming back to pick this stuff up." Alex put their tea picnic at the base of the trunk and then the two climbed into the backseat of the cab.

Eva looked out the window trying to hide her excitement. She wasn't used to being pampered but was absolutely loving it. She broke her gaze from the storefronts that zoomed by. "So, mister, where are you taking me to now?"

Alex paused for a moment then took her hand.

"You won't believe this...but I actually found something in the city that shines almost as brightly as you..."

***

"Brooklyn? I remind you of Brooklyn?"

"Okay, well, technically it's not in the city proper, but it's still one of the five boroughs, so it counts."

Eva stepped out of the cab and waited for Alex, wondering what he had up his sleeve. He finished paying the driver and stepped out after her.

"Aw, what's the matter, Ethel? Ain't you never been off the big island before?" He teased in a southern drawl.

Eva didn't skip a beat. "Of course, but only for cheesecake," she quipped with a grin.

The more time she spent with him, the more comfortable she became. Maybe the six weeks away was what he needed to get himself thinking...to see if he was really ready to commit to a deeper level of relationship after living single for such a long time. And if that was the case, Eva was glad he had gotten out of his system whatever it was that he needed to get out of his system while he was away, so that their reunion could be that much sweeter.

"Where are we going?" Eva asked as they walked.

"You'll see."

Alex took her hand and led her down a sidewalk away from the main streets.

"Uh-oh...You're not going to try and kidnap me, are you?" Eva teased.

Alex gave her one of his mysterious sideways glances and squeezed her hand. "Only if you're lucky." He stopped walking abruptly at the point that the alley widened, letting out into a big open area. "There...look." He leaned down towards her and pointed out to the side of where they were standing.

Eva looked up. "Oh...wow!" Her face glowed with delight. "I've never seen anything like this before!"

Alex had taken her to the rocky bay in downtown Brooklyn right in between the Manhattan Bridge and the Brooklyn Bridge overlooking downtown Manhattan. The alabaster city was lit up tall against the black of the night sky and the water in front of them sparkled with a million crystals; reflected the city's towering glory of glass and steel. Alex took her closer, down to the rocky shoreline. The rocks were large half boulders, sharp and bumpy.

"Do you like it?"

"It's beautiful," Eva whispered.

Just when they had walked as far as they could to the shoreline without running into the almost boulder-sized rocks, Alex smiled slightly, stepped in front of her and held out his hand.

"Come on."

"What?"

"Let's go!"

"What...you mean out there?" she asked, pointing to the rocks. Eva looked around. The other people in the park were sitting in the concrete amphitheater-style seating. She realized that he was inviting her to step out further with him, where none of the other shore-dwellers had dared to venture, uncharted territory.

Rocky ground, she thought to herself. She could hear the water rippling against the jagged rocks.

"Do you trust me?" Alex still had his hand out; waiting with a look of hopeful expectation mixed with fear that she might decline his proposition.

Eva bit her lip and delayed, glancing up at him almost apologetically for her hesitation. "I'm frightened," she whispered.

Alex whispered softly to her, "I won't let anything happen to you, I promise...Please?"

Eva took a deep breath, closed her eyes, and took his hands.

Alex leaned in and whispered softly to her. "Sweetheart, you're going to have to open your eyes to see where you are going."

"Oh, duh. Of course," she responded, smacking herself in the head.

"Yeah, that's another thing...I hate it when you put yourself down like that. Will you please stop doing that? You shouldn't be hurting yourself that way."

Eva frowned but nodded. *That's gonna be a tough one.*

"Good." He smiled and cupped the side of her head gently in his hand. "Are you ready?"

Am I ready, Eva thought sarcastically to herself. It was rare that she ever felt ready for anything.

"No fear."

Eva nodded her head in agreement and repeated the sentiment with slightly less confidence than his. "No fear."

He brought her close. "Hold onto me tight, okay?"

Eva nodded and he started to lead her out onto the large, ragged rocks. His steps were quick and deliberate. Eva's steps were slow and unsure, as if one false move on the uneven terrain would scatter both of their bodies onto the broken rocky shoreline. Alex climbed out further and further away from the shore, one step after the other. Eva held tightly to his hand, afraid to go too far from land, afraid that they would get arrested. Afraid, afraid, afraid.

Just then Alex stopped when he found a rock big enough for the both of them to stand on. He turned to face her and then put his hands on her shoulders and turned her to face him. "Come over here." Alex motioned for her to step onto the rock he was standing on. The rock was slightly higher than the one she was standing on and Eva had to step up to meet him. Alex wrapped his arms around her firmly so she would feel more secure. "Now...look."

Eva held onto him and looked around in complete awe, her face aglow from the mass of electricity generating all around them. From this viewpoint, they were so far from shore, it seemed as if they were right in the middle of the bay between the two islands Manhattan and Brooklyn, with the two illuminated bridges on either side of them: hemming them in. The black water rippled softly against the rocks around them, sparkling like diamonds all around them from the electric building illumination across the bay. It was the brightest, most gorgeous place she had ever been at night.

"So... what do you think now?"

Eva was so taken in by the stunning atmosphere that she could hardly breathe, let alone speak. She hugged him tightly and leaned her head against his chest, staring at her beloved city in childlike wonder. "It's beautiful," she breathed.

"True...but...nothing compares to you." Eva almost didn't hear him; she was so lost in the scenery. Alex took his finger and lifted her chin slowly up to look at her, their faces just inches apart, and stared into her eyes. "I could get lost in that green," he whispered and kissed the very tip of her nose lightly.

Eva couldn't help but notice the symbolism in the evening. Here they were, standing on a space hardly big enough for both of their feet, in the middle of a body of water, far out from what was safe and level ground...and he was asking her to trust him...an obvious metaphor to the relationship. Eva knew it wouldn't be easy, but her heart told her that this was genuine, and his promise of safety only made it less difficult to give in to him.

A single tear slid down Eva's cheek; she was deeply moved.

Alex cupped her porcelain face and wiped away her tear with his thumb. "I don't want to see you cry, Eva...ever."

Eva smiled through her tears at his tender caresses. With every passing moment of the evening, she was becoming more and more sure that everything was going to be okay, and that this was the man for her. An idea jumped into her mind and broke Eva from the trance. "You know what this would be perfect for?"

Alex laughed softly. "I can only guess."

"Our next photoshoot!"

"Wait...what?"

"Yeah. We could get the set crew and the-"

"Eva-"

Eva continued, "-makeup crew and the-"

"Eva-"

"I mean I know it would kind of be a pain in the butt to get everyone out here, but-"

"Eva!"

She finally stopped talking and looked at him. "What?"

Eva opened her mouth to speak again, but Alex leaned down suddenly and pressed his lips against hers, not giving her the option to continue. Eva was shocked at first, but her heart soon quickly overcame her fear and she melted into him. Eva wasn't afraid this time. His kiss was slow, passionate, and deliberate. And she could feel all of the emotion he had been holding back.

He finally broke the kiss and gazed down at her; his dark eyes full of love. "Do you always talk this much during special moments?" he teased softly with a squeeze.

Eva blushed and pressed her forehead to his chest.

"Only when it matters."

***

Back in Manhattan, the yellow cab was waiting to take Eva home from Lower Manhattan.

Alex held Eva tight in his arms, not wanting to let her go. "Do you want to come up for a little while? We can talk a little more."

Eva wanted to spend more time with him, but she knew that if she made that decision it might lead to something she was not ready for that she might regret later. She was not the kind of girl to give herself so freely to a man without a solid commitment, and they had only just made up from the distance.

"No... not tonight."

Alex pretended to pout, but Eva went up on her tippy toes to give him one final parting farewell on the lips as the taxi started to pull away without her.

"Wait!" they both yelled, laughing together, and tapping the car for the driver to stop.

"I'll call you soon," he whispered.

Soon. There was that word again, but she chose to hide her insecurities and smiled softly instead.

"Okay." Alex, sensing her doubt, gave her one last squeeze, breathing her into him and then let her go. "I won't hurt you, Eva."

Eva said nothing but gave him a delicate smile as she climbed into the cab. *I hope not...*

7 LOSING GROUND

"There's my sight for sore eyes!"

Ramona, wearing her trademark red lipstick, was sitting at her desk filing her nails when Eva stepped in the doorway of her massive oak office.

"Honey, you look like cupid slapped you on the behind. Wait! Don't tell me...Mr. Man finally got his act together, didn't he? Ooooh, I just knew it!" Ramona clapped her hands in excitement and bounced up and down in her leather studded chair. "Now get ya behind in here and gimme all the juicy details!" she commanded patting her desk. "And by the way, I already know the juicy details. Alex came in here this morning and told me all about it."

"Oh, he did, did he?" Eva walked in to sit down on Ramona's elegant velvet, cream-colored pintuck couch with wooden cherry-stained legs.

"Hi, Beauty." Alex had already beat her into Ramona's office and was sitting on one of the arms of the couch. It was all Eva could do to restrain herself and not run over to him. Although she knew Ramona approved of the union, she didn't want to appear unprofessional in front of her boss.

But Alex's heart led up him off the couch and over to her. He leaned down and wrapped his arms loosely around her waist and gazed into her eyes. "Hi, Sweetheart...I missed you."

Eva giggled and put her hands on his strong forearms. "Hi."

The two got lost in each other for what seemed like an eternity, almost forgetting Ramona was even there.

"Well, would ya just look at that?" Ramona had taken her glasses off and was resting her chin on her hand, watching the greeting. "I knew you two would finally manage to pull ya heads out of your own butts and get it togeth-uh! Listen, while I've got you two in here, let me talk to you for a minute."

Alex broke the embrace and led Eva over to the couch to sit down.

Ramona continued in her heavy accent, "Listen, you know I'm ya number one fan around here. I love you both and couldn't be happier for you...but, let me caution ya. Relationships is messy. Especially when there's work involved. And, Honey," she directed to Eva, "you know my a-hole of a nephew is looking for any reason he can to take you down. So please be careful. I'm trusting you both, so don't screw nuthin' up and give me a reason to regret giving you my precious holy seal of approval. Got it?"

Eva had known her as 'mentor', 'adoptive aunt', and friend, but now she was seeing her as 'protective mama bear'. The last thing in the world she wanted was to let down the one she looked up to so highly. She nodded encouragingly. "I understand."

Ramona turned to Alex. "And you," she said, pointedly narrowing her eyes.

Alex sat up straighter.

"You know I think of you as a son...but if you do anything to hurt this sweet angel from heaven, I will hunt you down and take you to get neutered, you unda-stand me?"

Alex held up his hands in defense. "Don't worry, Ramona." He looked back to Eva. "She's safe with me."

"She bet-tuh be. Alright now you kids get outta here. Big shoot in a few. Eva honey, grab your clicker and meet me downstairs in 30, will ya?"

"Okay, Ramona."

The two made their way back to Eva's office and closed the door.

"That Ramona...such a character!" Eva giggled walking over to her desk to get her camera.

Alex grabbed her hand and whirled her around, pulling her back to him. "I've been waiting all morning for this."

Eva sighed and closed her eyes as his lips met hers. *Heaven*. When he finally went to pull away, Eva held onto him, not wanting to halt the affection.

He ran his fingers through her hair. "Listen, I need to run. I have a meeting in a few and you need to go meet Miss Mona. Meet me tonight at Central Park southside, okay? Around 7?"

Eva smiled and nodded.

Finally, she thought as she gazed into his face, *my dreams of true love are finally coming true.*

***

The weather was warm that evening as Spring had begun to fill Gotham with its parade of colorful splendor. Central Park's trademark pink cherry blossoms were in full bloom against the bright orange dusk sky.

Eva hurried down the street to the corner where they had promised to meet on the Upper East Side close to the Metropolitan Museum. When she arrived, Alex was waiting for her.

Eva lighted on her feet and ran up to greet her muse. "Hi," she whispered, giving him a big hug. Only his look was distant again as his voice had been only a week before...almost cold and his embrace lacking, barely holding her. Eva was taken aback by his somewhat icy greeting; a far cry from the recent warm affections the two had shared just that morning. *He's had a full day*, she thought, *he must be tired.*

Eva went to pull away, then she noticed it. Eva looked up at him in confusion. *Has he been drinking?* Before she could say something, he took her hand almost roughly.

"Come on," he directed, stepping quickly.

Eva looked down at the ground, her brow puckered deep in thought as she followed him. She didn't understand what could have taken him from tender and loving this morning to short and abrupt this evening. *What have I done to upset him?* She couldn't imagine what the "something" could have been as they had not seen each other since their warm, tender kisses this morning. *Maybe it has something to do with work. Maybe Peter has gotten to him.* Still, she had not been prepared to find the smell of alcohol on him, a mark that seemed so contradictory to who he was.

Eva could feel her confidence slipping further and further away as she mulled the possibilities over in her mind. She chose to stay silent, hoping that he would confide in her. *He's been distant like this before*, she thought to herself. Still, even in his distance, the more time he spent with her, the more he seemed to warm up. *Maybe this is just how he is; a personality quirk. And the alcohol? He probably just had a drink to relax. Eva, you are turning this into something way bigger than it needs to be. It's probably nothing!*

Alex stopped on the sidewalk in front of the steps that led up to the museum. "Actually, I changed my mind. You want to walk instead?"

"Yeah, we can do that." Eva sensed an importance to be supportive, to put his wants above her own. That was her role. To Eva, engaging in a relationship meant losing herself to make the other person happy. The insecurities that haunted her told her that she did not deserve to be heard or to make her own needs known.

The two turned to walk into the park. He led her past the museum and into the trees where the paths wound like a serpentine next to the open field. Eva looked over at him as they walked. *Who is this man?*

He slowed his pace and turned to her, "You want a hot pretzel?"

Gosh, he is so random. "Yeah, that sounds good."

"Wait here."

Alex walked over to the pretzel cart, scenting the steamy air with its delicious doughy aroma. Eva noticed he had pulled his phone out of his pocket and was typing something.

Shortly after, her own phone vibrated in her jacket pocket. A notification telling her that she had a new message on her Profile account lit up her home screen. It was from Cyrano, her mystery admirer.

What in the world...is Alex testing me? When I am on an actual date with him?

Eva looked up to see Alex standing there holding a pretzel out to her. "Who was that?" he asked her.

Like you don't know. Eva didn't understand him, but she internalized it; believing she must have done something to make him question her. Living a life with fault ingrained in her, her filter told her to accept it and do the best she could to earn his trust back.

"I don't know," she dissimulated. "I don't recognize the name." Alex pursed his lips but didn't say anything.

Eva took the pretzel from him, and tore off a piece, and took a bite. The outside a shiny, dark golden-brown; contrasting flavors of sweet from the smooth crust with just the right amount of salt. The inside was warm and chewy soft.

"This is one of the things I love the most about New York," Eva stated, as if she were talking to the pretzel itself.

"So, do you get anonymous messages from men a lot?" Alex asked, almost challenging her.

Eva looked at him in surprise. "No," she replied softly. "I mean my friends communicate with me for sure, but nothing like this...," Eva decided now was her chance to turn the tables on him and see if he would fess up. "Don't you think it's strange? I mean, just some random guy messages me out of the blue, knows personal things about me, won't tell me who he is, hides his identity...it's almost as if someone is...testing me...you know?"

Alex's face hardened. "No...no, I don't know."

"Well, don't you think it's strange? I mean I can count my guy friends on less than one hand and none of them would-"

He interrupted her. "Eva! No. I don't know anything about this! Now, can we please stop talking about it? I didn't plan on spending the evening with you so we could talk about other guys."

No, she thought. *I've got to confront him.* "What is wrong with you?... have you been drinking?"

"Yeah. So, what if I have? Is that a problem?" His reply reeked of defense.

Eva wanted to say 'yes', but her old friend Fear was standing at the gates. "No. I-I mean, I guess not. It's just you don't...seem like yourself."

"Eva, how would you know? You hardly know me."

Eva's heart brimmed with anxiety. Her face flushed and she looked down at her shoes. She didn't know what to say. "I'm sorry," she whispered looking up at him apologetically. "I have no right to-...I didn't mean to upset you."

"It's okay, it's just..." He let out a heavy sigh and remembered himself as his voice softened. "Nothing, it's nothing. Let's just forget about it, okay?"

Eva searched his face, not understanding his sudden outburst. She wanted to explore his feelings, to help him work through them, but she thought better of it. *It will just upset him more.* She gave him a small smile, hoping it would break the tension and bring him back down to earth. "Hey, stop. It's me, remember?"

"Look, I'm sorry," he said softly, running his hand down her hair. "Let's just get out of here, okay?"

"Okay," Eva nodded. She took his hand and gave it a squeeze, smiling again to show him compassion. Eva was used to being the recipient of another person's anger. She was an expert at smoothing things over, even if it meant she had to die to herself.

"So," she said, changing the subject, "where would you like to go?" Eva hadn't realized they had walked so far. Their conversation had taken them all the way to Central Park South and 59th Street.

"Top of the Rock."

"Didn't we just do that?" she teased, referring to the romantic evening that they had just shared the night before on Brooklyn's rocky shoreline.

"Yeah...but maybe we can get a different perspective from up there."

***

Their walk from Central Park had taken them just ten blocks down 5th Avenue to Rockefeller Center and up the elevator to the observation deck.

Night had fallen by the time they set foot on the roof, the skyscrapers glistening brightly all around them lighting up the night sky like daytime.

"Wow!" Eva gasped taking it in. "Well, how do you like that for date material? Rocky ground and harrowing heights!" She leaned close to the glass and peered over the edge.

"Eva."

She turned back to look at him. "What? You don't like my cheesy play on words? Alright, I'll give it a rest."

"I'm constantly being compared to others."

Eva paused, and then slowly began to walk towards him realizing he needed to get something out and he needed to do it now. "I know that" she replied softly.

"People don't see me when they look at me. They see my brother's fame. I don't have an identity that belongs to me."

Eva took his hands, "Alex...It's okay...I understand."

"No, I don't think you do." Alex turned away from her. Eva walked up behind him and put her hand on his back. "I can see myself with you, Eva."

"Well, of course, you can. I'm standing right here," she joked, trying to break the tension.

Alex spun around and took her firmly by the forearms. "No, Eva. No jokes. I'm serious. And it scares the hell out of me."

Eva's smile faded to concern as she searched his eyes. Her voice became very gentle. "But...Why? Don't you trust me?"

"Of course, I trust you...because it's real."

"But you knew that before...didn't you?"

"Yes...but not like this. You listen to me. You actually care about me."

"Of course, I care about you. I wouldn't be here if I didn't. I wouldn't have climbed out onto the rocks with you if I didn't. Which, by the way, was terrifying."

"I know, but...this is a first for me."

"Hey...It's okay. I'm not exactly used to this kind of connection either."

Now it was Alex's turn to be bashful. He shook his head and looked at the floor.

Eva bent her head down to see his face. "Alex?"

He looked up at her from where he was sitting. "You wanna go?"

"Yeah," she nodded. "We can go."

***

After they left Rockefeller, the evening took them to a small cafe in the village. Alex stared at Eva across from the table, her face aglow with candlelight. The two had been silent up to this point, both contemplating the intensity of the conversation that had taken place just moments before. Alex was the first to break the silence between them.

"Eva, I'm sorry. I don't know why I freaked out like that."

"It's okay."

"No, it's not. I can't imagine what you must be thinking."

"I understand. And I'm thinking, you must be really scared." *I'm scared, too.*

Alex looked at her with all the softness of the night before. "Why do you have to be so damn sweet?"

"Well...that's debatable."

Alex stared at her deep reddish-brown hair glowing in the candlelight. "You are so beautiful, Eva. Warm. Safe. I feel safe with you. You feel like home, you know? You're so understanding. Even when I don't deserve it. I'm just tired, you know? I'm tired of fighting. Tired of fighting myself."

"I know."

"Eva, you don't know how many times, I've just wanted to fall asleep with you. To relax and just let go next to something that feels like home."

Eva blushed at the intimate connotation and the first she heard something like that directed at her.

"And it's after moments like these...I just want to hold you even more. You make my pain go away."

Eva leaned closer to him.

"To just hold you and fall asleep...yes...that would be good." Alex closed his eyes and leaned his head back, finally calmed down from the tension earlier in the evening.

Eva stared at him, her heart beating faster. No one had also ever made her feel this wanted before.

"Look...I'm sorry about earlier."

"It's okay," she said.

"No, I just...I didn't mean to snap at you."

"It's okay...I know it wasn't like you. Maybe just the influence of the alcohol and once you sobered up-"

"Okay, why do you have to bring that back up? I just apologized to you." He was clearly offended by her suggestion.

Eva squeezed her eyes shut, kicking herself for the rehash. "Agh, I don't know. Forget I said that. I'm sorry."

"And why do you always say, 'I don't know'? You do know...you just don't want to answer truthfully." Alex felt his anger begin to rise again within him as his voice intensified with every word he spoke.

Eva shook her head from his emotional whiplash. "What?" *Why is he doing this?*

"My ex-girlfriend used to say that when she was lying to me."

Ohh...Okay. Now this is starting to make some sense. Eva was hurt by his lack of trust, but she knew she couldn't let him compare her to someone who wasn't in his life anymore. She needed to make him see her for who she was. "Okay, well, I'm not your ex-girlfriend. Are you seriously accusing me of lying to you?"

"She never wanted me to know what she was doing, and I would find out later from other sources."

"Okay, stop. How did we even get on this subject? Remember when you said earlier that you didn't want to talk about the other men in my life? That's how I feel now with you talking about her. Please. Let's not ruin this evening."

"I loved her, Eva. She was my first everything and she completely broke my heart."

Eva closed her eyes in frustration and searched for the words that would diffuse the situation and defend her character at the same time. She sympathized with him, but she knew they couldn't continue to go back and forth like this. "Alex."

But his head was turned down and away from her, refusing to look at her.

"Alex, please look at me. I'm sorry...but I am not her and it's not fair for you to accuse me of something I haven't done. I waited faithfully for six weeks for you to come back. I wanted so badly for you to reach out to me while you were gone, but you didn't."

"Look, Eva, maybe we just aren't right for each other."

"Wait, what? How can you say that now after everything you said before? You're just scared. It's okay. I'm scared, too." Eva was beyond confused. Alex's words had wounded, but now that he was fired up, he couldn't stop. Eva sat there silent while he berated her; more like, complained to her. And with every impassioned word he spoke, Eva felt like it was more and more her fault. Finally, after nearly 15 minutes of arrows flying from his mouth, she broke her silence.

"Okay...So do you think we can get passed this? I don't know how we got here, but can we be done with this, please? It's one thing to discuss a matter, but we're getting nowhere here."

"Yeah, we can get past it. When were we ever not past it?"

"Alex, what's really bothering you?"

Just then his phone rang. Alex held it up to show her. "And look, there she is!"

"There who is? Your ex-girlfriend?... Wait a minute. You mean you're still talking to her? Regularly?"

"Yeah."

"As in, every night?"

"Is that a problem?" he snapped back in defense.

No, except the fact that I barely heard from you the whole time you were gone, but you have time to talk to her. Eva shook her head in disbelief at how the night had turned. Then it dawned on her.

"You're still in love with her, aren't you?" It was a statement more than a question.

"Yes. I love her...but I'm not in love with her. We aren't together. I meant everything I said to you. You're the one I want, Eva. She's just a friend."

Eva took a deep breath and looked down at the table. Her mind was whirling from confusion. "I think I should go." Eva stood up and turned to walk out the door.

"No, please wait," Alex jumped up to follow her. "Listen, you don't have to leave. I'm sorry."

Eva started down the sidewalk. "Look, I don't know what happened, but this night has gone terribly wrong. I think we should just go home and breathe for a minute. We can talk later, when I've had time to think, and you've had time to sober up."

"Sober up? So, what am I, a drunk now? Is that it? Are you going to judge me now just like everyone else in my life?"

Eva let him go on as they continued down the street to the main avenue where she could hail a cab. *Maybe he needs to vent so he can heal.* She had seen the deeper, compassionate, gentle side of him and that was enough to give her the desire to be patient with him. There would be other evenings, but she knew she had to end this one quickly before any further damage was done to either one of them.

When they got to the corner, Alex was still going. Eva turned to him and placed her hand over his mouth to calm him down, mouthing a "shhh."

No sooner did he stop his rant; did he immediately lean down to kiss her. Eva instinctively backed away, like anyone would who'd just been approached for intimacy after being yelled at for an hour, which fueled his fire even more. "So what? Now you won't even kiss me. Again? Oh, it's too late now. It's waaay too late now!"

Eva shook her head at the obvious. "Alex. You've just spent the past hour yelling at me and now your ex is calling you. What did you expect? I'm not exactly feeling romantic right now."

Just then a cab pulled up. Eva opened the door to get in and turned back to him. "Look. We've known each other a long time. I know you. I want to be here for you, but I can't do it like this. Please understand. I am willing to be patient, but you've got to meet me halfway. You can't bully me like this. I'll call you later." Alex shut the door after her.

Eva set her purse on the seat next to her and turned back to the window to say goodbye...but he was gone.

***

Eva sat at her glass kitchen table, staring at her laptop; bunny slippers in tow and hair pulled loosely up into a dark brownish-red pile on top of her head.

"Well, what in the world does it say this time?" Kate exclaimed through the phone.

"'So, I heard you're seeing someone. Are you enjoying your evening?'" Eva responded.

"Oh...girlfriend."

Eva had called her friend back home to discuss the most recent turn of events in the city, namely Alex's tantrum and her new message from Cyrano, Alex's presumed ghost-writer.

"I don't know, Kate, do you think he's testing me?"

"Well, I don't know why he would. You are the most trustworthy person I know, and I don't even live in that crazy city! I'm sure a born and bred New Yorker would think you were an angel, for Heaven's sake. If he is, Evie, you don't need that. Especially after the way he treated you the other night. Holy cow!"

Eva was quick to defend him. "Well, I've known the man for two years and he's never been like that before. He was just tired. Of course, my pushing didn't help either, I'm sure."

"Eva, a good man would let you talk about what is concerning you. Not everything is your fault. God isn't up there in some intergalactic space docking you for every time a person gets ticked off at you. Gosh, if He was, I'd be way in the red by now! The whole world isn't going to spin off kilter if you don't kiss a guy right when they expect you to or say just the right thing at the right time. It's not about what you do or don't do, Evie. You've got to stop blaming yourself for every little thing that happens. Let him prove himself to you! A man who loves God and who is truly worth your time will do that, Evie. He will pursue you the right way. And it's nothing you can make happen on your own. It will just happen. Because he will know what God is asking him to do when it comes to you. And God doesn't create this kind of mess of confusion."

"Kate, how can I look for that quality in a man, when I'm not even sure that I know God?"

"Well...," Kate paused. She didn't want to hurt her friend, but at the same time she knew she had to say what needed to be said. "Maybe that's something you need to think about. Because Evie...if you love God, you will love yourself...and if you are grounded in Him, you will know who you are and where you stand...regardless of what others expect from you. Because it's not about what others think...it's about what God thinks, and He loves you just the way you are. No action required on your part to earn that love. So, if that's true, which I believe it is, wouldn't you think He would mirror our human relationships after His?"

Eva sighed. *Here she goes with that God talk, again.* How could she trust a God she was so unsure of? A God she'd never met?

"Evie, you know I love you, but are you sure this is the right guy for you? I know you really like him, but, geez. You're only a couple months in and already he's causing you so much grief. He doesn't respect you."

"You don't know him, Kate. He's really very kind and compassionate. He's been through a lot."

"Um, hello? Have you forgotten? So have you, my friend. So have you. And I don't want to see you get your heart broken."

"I know what I'm doing."

"Alright, well, just do me a favor, okay? Promise me you won't marry the guy tomorrow if he asks you to, alright?"

The absurdity of that statement after the volatility of the evening made Eva laugh. "I said I was patient, not crazy!"

Kate chuckled, but inside she was worried for her friend. "Alright. Listen, I'm here if you need me."

"Thanks, friend." Eva hung up the phone and made some tea. She turned on the radio, but try as she might, she couldn't drown out that still, small voice inside trying desperately to tell her that something was very wrong.

***

Eva rushed through the street traffic of St. Mark's Place to meet Alex at Thompson Square Park. After almost three days of no contact, he had finally called her and asked her to meet him. Eva's heart went back and forth between feeling neglected and missing him. She knew he came from pain, and she wanted to be as understanding as she could, so she allowed the roller coaster in the hopes that her faithfulness would break through.

Alex was sitting on a bench when she arrived. She watched him for a minute, not letting him know she was there just twenty feet away, wondering what could have traded his tenderness for anger and hopelessness. He had been so open and loving with her and they had shared a special friendship before he approached her romantically. But now, he looked as though he was far away, turning something serious over in his mind.

Eva finally walked over to him slowly, feeling the weight of every step. "Hey, Stranger, mind if I join you?" she asked standing in front of him, a faint smile, her hands in her coat pockets.

Alex looked up at Eva, surprised to see her standing there. "Hi," he replied softly. "...sit down." He motioned for her to sit beside him.

Eva sat down beside him slowly, not breaking her gaze. *I must have done something terribly wrong.* She could sense this was serious. She wanted to offer comforting words, but she found herself lacking due to her own insecurities. "What is it, Alex?" she finally asked. "What's wrong?"

"Eva, I...I just don't think we are compatible for each other."

Eva looked down at her hands. She didn't say anything for a minute, taking it in before she spoke. "Why? Is it because of the other night? We both have fears and insecurities. We can get past this."

"We're just two different people."

"That hasn't seemed to be a problem until now."

"I know," he replied softly, "but we weren't working towards something until now."

Eva stayed quiet.

"Look, I'm torn. I think you are amazing, but I just don't know if it's going to work."

"Because you're angry with me." Eva started gently, afraid that the very sound of her voice would shut him down.

"No, sweetie, it's more than that."

"We won't know until we actually try...right? You're just going to give up because we had a fight?"

"I know... but there's too much at stake now."

Eva looked at him wondering what he meant by that.

"I really like you, Eva."

"I really like you, too. I'm not afraid of what happened the other night. "

"But I feel like it's going to be difficult, and I just don't know if I can give you what you need. It's like, I want to see where it might go, but I can't date you. But I still want to try to find a way to keep you in my life."

Eva kept her eyes on the ground. She had a million questions but lacked the confidence to voice them. She truly believed she had no right to ask him anything or to fight for what had begun to blossom. *This makes absolutely no sense. I know he's lying.* "Well...if that's how you truly feel, then...I guess there's nothing I can say." She couldn't look at him. Her avoiding eyes let him off the hook saved them both the embarrassment of owning up to what was happening between them.

"Alex!" a girl's voice shouted towards them from a distance.

Eva looked up to see where the greeting was coming from. A tall, skinny, young woman with straight dark hair was heading towards them briskly.

"Amber! Hey!" Alex stood up to give her a hug. Eva watched to see how the two interacted with each other. Alex's whole countenance had lifted when he saw her. The two seemed to know each other very well and seemed very happy talking to one another. Eva's heart sank as she began to realize the reason for his distance.

"Oh, Amber, this is my friend Eva!"

His 'friend'? Eva watched as the two seemed almost giddy together. *She doesn't seem like just a friend to me.*

"Oh," Amber replied as if this was not a new name to her. She greeted Eva with enthusiasm and bent down to give her a hug.

Eva felt awkward hugging the very person who was coming between them. *Obviously, she knows who I am. But who the hell is she?*

"Well, I'll let you two get back to your conversation!" Amber chimed. "So, I'll see you later, right?"

That did it. Eva knew she had already been replaced in that very moment. Alex glanced nervously at Eva and then back to Amber. "Yeah, that sounds good."

"Awesome! See you later!" She turned towards Eva. "Bye, Eva, it was such an honor to meet you!" Before Eva could answer her, she was on her way.

Eva didn't need to say anything; her face dripping with questions as the two started down an apartment-lined street, heading back towards Union Square. Alex led her over to a stoop and the two sat down once more. Alex walked up to a step higher than hers.

"She's...a friend of mine. I've known her for a long time." Alex said quietly, his face stayed down, but his eyes went back and forth between the ground and Eva.

"Oh," Eva said quietly. Eva put her balled-up hand lightly on his knee and looked at him helplessly, wanting so badly to fix the situation, but she knew deep inside that she couldn't. *I knew it...I don't fit into his world. I was such a fool to think I would. It's pointless to try to change his mind.*

Alex's phone buzzed in his pocket, and he reached down to silence it without taking it out of his pocket. "Listen...I better go. I promised my family I would meet them at the movies and that's probably them now wondering where I am. You wanna walk?"

"Yeah...we can walk."

The two walked slowly, hands in their pockets, both staring at the ground. She felt the theater getting closer and closer and wanted to slow down time, as if to know this was the last that she would ever see him. When they finally reached the entrance to the theater, Alex broke the silence.

"This is really sad."

Eva raised her eyebrows as if to prove a blatantly obvious point and nodded at the ground, "Yes, it is." She stepped off the curb to hail a cab that was coming towards them. When it stopped in front of them, Alex opened the door for her to get in.

"Look, Eva, I don't know what's going to happen."

Eva got into the cab and looked up at him. He was leaning on the door.

"I don't want you to go." He said, his face looking like he had lost his puppy.

Eva shook her head; half frustrated, half confused. *Then why are you doing this?* She had so many questions, but her insecurity held them inside.

"Well, I guess...bye," he whispered and closed the door.

Eva put her hands on the glass and looked up at him. "Bye," she mouthed as the taxi pulled away into twilight.

8 STRANGER THINGS

Highline was especially hectic that week. Fashion Week would soon be on the horizon, and the magazine was frantic with preparations. Eva walked through the giant steel doors and into a sea of fashion designers, impossibly tall slender models with European accents, harried makeup artists, and laboring set designers.

Chimes of "Hi, Eva!" sprinkled about her as she made her way through the crowd to get her schedule from the floor crew. She had worked with most of them in the past and they loved her, mostly because she was the most down to earth person in the crew, not to mention the most patient. And let's face it; when working with a bunch of big names in the industry, patience was a precious commodity.

Eva greeted her coworkers with a smile and a quiet wave. She set her camera bag on the end of the break table and picked up the schedule for the day. Suddenly, she felt someone place their hands on the tops of her shoulders. She turned around to see Ramona standing behind her in a Versace suit, pearls, and signature glasses. "Hey, 'Mo," she greeted her mentor flatline.

"Bubba-Lou, if you stare at that piece a paper any long-uh, you're gonna bore a hole in it. And anyways, he ain't on there. Don't think I don't know what's goin' on inside that pretty little head of yours."

Eva blushed and lowered her head; ashamed that Ramona could read her so well.

"Honey, I know what happened. Don't ask me how, but I know. I thought it best to separate you two for a while. Give you time to breath."

"Why?" Eva asked the obvious, but it wasn't obvious to her. She was missing him.

"Honey, it's okay. You ain't done nothing' wrong. I know you're hurting' and I knew it would be hard for you to see him. I thought it best that you take a break from working togeth-uh, at least for a little while. I honestly don't know how you'd be able to after that fiasco anyway. It wouldn't be good for you."

"But Ramona-," Eva started.

"Honey, trust me. I've been married for thirty-four years and even marriages need their breathing room every now and again." Ramona waved her hands around her head. "It's when the man needs to go in his man-cave and clear out the crap in his head. Sometimes they can't do that without hurting us if we're in the way. You know what I'm saying?"

Eva nodded in agreement. "Maybe it would be for the best."

"And listen...if he's got the feels for you as much as he's let on, he'll come around. Give 'im time, Baby Doll. It's only been a week. And men sometimes, they need to go into their caves and 'think'." Ramona accentuated 'think' with air quotes. "Mark my words...he's gonna realize that floozy is no good and he's gonna call you. It may not be today, it may not be tomorrow, but he will."

Ramona's words were reassuring, and Eva felt a new hope growing inside. She hugged her mentor warmly, "Thank you, Mona."

"Anytime, sweetie. Alright, now turn that pitiful frown upside-down and get your booty out there. Big day today and I've already got Peter up my butt wanting to help. I swear, he's like a puppy that can't wait to go bye-byes. I have a half a mind to tell 'im we're goin' for ice cream and then take him to get put up for adoption."

Eva laughed for the first time in a week.

"There's my girl!" Ramona exclaimed placing her hands on Eva's cheeks. "Honey, trust me. A face like that and a heart to match? He won't be able to stay away fuh-long."

***

Eva lay awake that evening; her questions tormenting her. Everything she had wanted to say two weeks before, now doing cartwheels in her brain. She tried to sleep, but she couldn't get her thoughts out of her head.

It doesn't make any sense. Why would he go to all of that trouble to set up a picnic in the park, take me all the way out into the water for Pete's sake? After all of the conversations we've had? Asking me about kids and our future? Telling me he wants to fall asleep with me? All the back and forth, hot and cold? And Amber...where did she come from? Is she the reason he wanted to drop me like a hot potato? Has he wanted her all along? Is that why he's been distant? And the drinking...I've never known him to drink since I met him. When on earth did that start?

Eva tossed and turned, but she just could not get her brain to shut off. Alex had shared enough of his heart to tell her that he was afraid, but she wondered if he would really let his fear sabotage their chance for happiness.

No... I've got to talk to him...I've got to know what's really going on.

Eva reached over, turned on her silk lamp with the crystal beads and grabbed her phone. She pulled up his name to call him. *It's now or never. If you don't ask him now, you'll always be wondering.*

"Alex? It's Eva. Can you meet me tomorrow? I need to talk to you."

***

Alex poured a drink and looked at the clock ticking on the wall of his apartment; the light of the magic hour beaming through his windows.

5:30 pm. Eva would be meeting him in an hour.

He took a drink. It was the only thing that could calm him when it came to her. No other girl had ever made him as nervous as Eva did. He knew she would have questions, no doubt. He knew she would be wanting to know why he was running away from her. And truth be told, he was running.

Ever since the night he told her he couldn't see her anymore; he had regretted it and now he feared it was too late to tell her that he changed his mind. That he didn't really want to leave her. That he was wrong. That he had been afraid and purposely picked fights with her hoping to push her away. Only when she wasn't swayed by his tactics and stood her ground, it made him want to be with her even more.

Eva could see through to him in a way that no one else had ever been able to and it unnerved him to the core. He knew from this point forward; he would need to be completely honest with her; emotionally naked; that she would settle for nothing less.

Although he knew he could trust her with anything, he also recognized that the stakes were nosebleed high for him. This woman easily could be his future and he was terrified of screwing it up, of hurting her even more than he already had. *She deserves better than the crap I gave her. I need to show her I can be the man she needs. I just need to apologize and smooth things over. She'll understand.*

He took another sip. Just a little bit to take the edge off. He looked at the clock again and wondered why he couldn't hear his phone in the other room. *6:00...she usually texts me by now to let me know she's coming.* He sat down on the couch and closed his eyes just for a minute. *She'll let me know when she gets here.*

***

Alex jolted awake and looked at the clock. *9:30...damnit!* He leapt off the couch and ran to the window. *No, you idiot! She wouldn't still be waiting on the sidewalk for you. Check your phone, you moron!*

Alex grabbed his phone to check for messages. It was dead. "Damnit!" he exclaimed with a punch to the table and plugged it in to charge as fast as he could. *Way to go, idiot. She'll never trust you now.*

As soon as the phone was charged enough to light up, he tackled it...one text, one missed call and one voice message...all from her. Her message was a heartbreaking mixture of pain and anger. Alex listened and then promptly threw the phone against the wall in a rage. *I can't call her now...there's no way she'll believe I wasn't blowing her off. It's over.*

Alex picked up the half empty bottle, poured himself another glass, and spent the rest of the night drinking himself into an oblivion.

***

"Charlie? It's me. Open up!"

Charlie went to his door and opened it up..."Eva!" He was surprised to see her. "What are you doing here so late?" Before he could continue, Eva glided through the door and threw herself against him.

"Kiss me, Charlie!"

"What?!"

"You heard me. You like me, right? You've had a crush on me for years, right? Well, now's your chance. Come on...kiss me!" Eva closed her eyes and puckered her lips.

Charlie scratched his head in confusion. He caught a whiff of alcohol as she stumbled through the hall. That was so unlike her.

"Eva...you're drunk," Charlie spoke sternly, but softly and took her firmly by the shoulders and held her away from him.

"No, I'm not." she was irritated. "I've seen how you watch me when we're together! Now, come on, kiss me! I know you want to!"

"Wait, Eves...weren't you supposed to go see him tonight?" Charlie still couldn't bring himself to say Alex's name. "Is that what this is about?"

"Yeah...so what?" she replied defiantly, placing one hand on her hip and her other hand on the wall, barely able to hold herself up.

"Oh, God, what did he do to you? I'll kill him."

"Nothing!" she yelled pounding his chest. "He didn't do anything to me. In fact," she continued, slurring her words and wobbling back and forth, "He didn't even show up. Yeah! That's right! He left me standing there on the street like a dog. No phone call. No nothing!" She emphasized every sentence with a punch to the air.

"Eva, stop. Stop!" Charlie grabbed her arms to keep her from hitting him again. He was heartbroken for his friend. "Eva, I'm so sorry."

"So, come on." she demanded. "Tell me that I'm not completely rejected! That I'm desired, attractive...Come on, Charlie! Kiss me!" And with that, she collapsed in his arms, crying, the pain of the evening dripping down her face. "Charlie...Why am I not good enough?" Her petite body shook in his arms with every sob.

"Shhh, it's okay," Charlie held his friend and cupped the back of her head, stroking her hair, but inside he was livid. It was all he could do to keep from leaving on the spot to go open up a can of whoop-ass on this guy who Charlie, in that moment was certain, was the scum of the earth to hurt someone so precious and tender.

"Why won't you kiss me?"

"Eva, you're three freaking sheets to the wind and you aren't thinking clearly. No matter what I want, I'm not going to take advantage of the situation. You mean way more to me than that. You're special. You deserve the best. Someone who actually sees your value. Not this absolute douchebag who doesn't know his ass from his elbow."

Eva collapsed again, but Charlie caught her before she hit the ground. He carried her over to the couch, laid her down and covered her with a blanket. He wanted to hold her until the pain went away, but he knew he couldn't. These tears were for another man, not him. And he couldn't bring himself to bear the weight of another man's mistakes when it came to her.

Eva cuddled up into the blanket like a little girl and cried into the cushion. Charlie kneeled down beside her and moved her hair out of her face. "You can stay here tonight and sleep it off and go home in the morning," he whispered to her softly, hoping the sound of his voice would soothe her.

74

"Don't worry...it's gonna be okay, Eves." He stood up to go into his own room for the night.

"Charlie?" Eva whispered.

"Yeah," he whispered softly.

"Why doesn't he see in me what you see in me?"

Why can't you see what's standing right in front of you?... "I don't know, Evie."

***

Eva awoke the next morning and the fresh emptiness hit her like a ton of bricks. To say that sleep eluded her was an understatement. At least a few moments of sleep she had managed to sneak in enabled her to forget the deep searing pain of heartache that seemed to have taken root in her stomach.

The moment she awakened, the tears flooded her almond-shaped eyes, immediately remembering the events that had transpired the night before. Worthless, undesirable, unwanted, abandoned, not good enough...these thoughts would plague Eva as she went home and struggled to get herself ready for the long day of work that she knew lay ahead of her.

Eva walked like a zombie through the elevator doors and into the office wondering how in the world she would be able to make it through the day. She took a sip of coffee, looked over her work email and then heard a familiar sound on her phone. She looked down at her phone to find a notification telling her she had a new Profile message. It was from Cyrano.

"I'm sorry, Eva. I can't."

9 MYSTERY HEART

"It's got to be him." Eva had gone down to the Pier that Saturday afternoon to clear her mind. Kate had called her while she was walking. "Who else could it possibly be? What other men do I have in my life that have stood me up recently and need a reason to apologize?"

"But, Evie, he's got your number. Why on earth would he orchestrate a fake person just to contact you? He could have just called you, for goodness' sake. This whole thing just seems very odd to me."

"Well...maybe he's ashamed of what he did. Maybe behind a screen is the only way he can face me to see if I'll forgive him? Maybe if he sees that he can trust me with his heart, he'll fess up. You don't know him, Kate. Something like this would embarrass the crap out of him. He needs to feel safe enough with a person before he'll come around."

"And you don't? Are you kidding me? 'A grown man needs to feel safe with a person.' Eva, seriously...is this really what you want? A guy who treats you like crap and then runs and hides at the slightest mishap?"

Eva didn't respond.

"Okay, so let me ask you this. If you really like this guy, why don't you just go knock on his door and ask him what happened?"

"No... I can't do that."

"Well, why in the heck not? You want this guy, right? You seriously, think he's the one for you. If you really think he's too ashamed of what he did to reach out to you in any other way than by a fake email, then why don't you just go to him?"

"I can't do that."

"Oh, okay," Kate's voice dripped with sarcasm. "And when you see him at work, what are you going to do? Just say, 'Oh, hey, Alex, I got your fake email, thanks for being crazy and making me feel crazy'? I mean seriously." Kate didn't hold back. She didn't want Eva's heart to go through any more pain than it already had. "I mean honestly, I just have a feeling...I don't think you're ever going to see this guy again."

"Why would you think that?" Eva was defensive, she held onto her hope of her and Alex reuniting with everything she had. "And besides, he edits my shoots. He can't avoid me forever."

"I hope you're right, Eva. I hope with everything in me that this turns into what you want it to be."

"Well, I mean you're a praying woman, right? Will you please pray for Alex to get over his fear and reach out?"

"No."

"What do you mean 'no'?"

"I'm going to pray for God's will in this."

"Why?"

"Because you can't go wrong with that. And I'm not interested in begging God for something that might hurt you even more."

Eva didn't understand why her friend would refuse to pray for a specific thing. *After all, isn't that what this God was for? To pray for the things you wanted?*

"Kate, you're my best friend. Don't you want me to be happy?"

"Yes, yes, I do. And that's exactly why I'm praying for God's will for you. If this isn't what God has for you, the best thing He can do is take him out of your life and if he is, then you don't have to worry. Whatever is meant to be will happen in its own time."

***

"Peace pipe?"

Eva was holding an ice cream out to Charlie. She had met him for a walk in SoHo and, of course, had to stop by their favorite ice cream shop on the way.

"That's it," Charlie teased as he took the ice cream from her, "woo me with your wily scoops of dairy."

"Ah, come on, Char. Can't you forgive me for-"

"For what? Practically breaking through my door and trying to have your beastly way with me?" he interrupted her. "Yeah, I guess I can forgive you for that. Besides," he said, taking a bite of his mint chocolate chip, "it was kind of cute...I should have taken a picture."

Eva nudged him.

Charlie looked over at her mid-bite, wide-eyed and innocent. "What?"

"Yes, of course, so adorable. I'm just dying to eternally commemorate the misery of that evening. Let's not and say we did, okay?" Eva replied sarcastically.

"Eva, you know what your problem is?"

"No, but I bet you're going to tell me," Eva replied digging into her ice cream like she was looking for gold. She didn't need anything else to make her feel bad about herself, especially from a good friend like Charlie.

"You don't know your own worth," Charlie stated, emphasizing the 'you' with a dramatic point of his finger and then crossing his arms proudly as if he had just solved an impossibly complicated issue. Eva looked at him, expecting more. "Is that it?"

"Yeah."

"That's my problem." Eva didn't bother to hide her sarcasm.

"Yeah." Charlie looked back and forth between her and his ice cream and shook his head like she was missing the obvious.

"That doesn't seem like a very big problem to me."

"Eves, you're willing to let this guy walk all over you and drag your heart through the mud like he's the only dude on the face of the earth."

"And?"

"And if you truly knew how special you were, you'd have kicked his bi-polar butt to the curb a long time ago."

"So, what's wrong with giving him a chance to dig himself out of the gutter?"

Charlie shook his head. "Dang."

Eva kept her head down. "You don't know how this feels."

Charlie's eyes narrowed. *If you only knew.* "I do know how it feels, Eva. That's why I'm trying to spare you the heartache."

Eva linked arms with him as they walked down a cobble-stoned Prince St. "Listen, I want to thank you."

"For what?"

"For...being a gentleman the other night. I don't know many guys who would respect a girl enough not to take advantage of her when she's basically throwing herself at them," her voice softened. "Especially when it's a girl they're into." She looked at him with an apologetic smile. "Thank you for protecting me."

"Eves, I would never do anything to hurt you. I love you. And not that way, but I mean as a person, I love you."

Eva smiled and squeezed his arm. She knew the depth of his meaning was far beyond what he was letting on, but she chose to let him spare his dignity.

"Hey, listen, I have an idea."

"Uh-oh," Eva rolled her eyes, expecting the usual shenanigans from her friend.

"You and me. In ten years, if neither one of us is married, let's get hitched."

"Charlie, knock it off."

"No, I'm serious. What do you say?"

"I say we'd kill each other."

"It'll be fun!"

"Fun? Is prison a fun concept to you?"

"Oh, come on. We care about each other. We respect each other. We're good friends. The love could grow from that."

"Well..." At the ripe old age of 24, Eva couldn't imagine that she would still be single in ten years. Seems like a safe bet. Surely, neither one of us will not be married by then. Besides, he can't be serious. "Okay," she agreed.

Charlie perked up, almost choking on his ice cream. "For real??"

"Yeah, sure," she replied looking up at him. "Why not? I guess we'll need someone to grow grey with at that point. Might as well be a good friend."

And with that, Charlie picked her up and whirled her around in the middle of the street in the middle of SoHo.

***

Eva sat on her chaise and stared at the screen.

"I'm sorry...I can't."

His words confirmed in her mind what she already knew to be true. It had to be Alex. The message was short but mirrored his recent actions. He'd told her he didn't know if he could be with her. He'd gone as far as to stand her up outside of his own building. If that didn't say *"I can't,"* she didn't know what would.

This has to be his way of communicating with me what he's feeling without facing me in person. Now that the pain of rejection had had time to subside, she was ready to respond.

"I understand if you're afraid to reach out, but it's okay. You don't have to

be frightened or ashamed. I'm pretty sure I know who you are...and this is a safe place."

His response was much quicker than she'd expected. *"Eva, I'm just not ready to come forward yet. But...thank you for not completely dismissing me! Me =)"*

"Dismissing me?" Eva thought to herself. *It's got to be him; he even writes his smiley's the same way as in his text messages. But just in case...*

Eva thought for a minute before she responded. She realized if she wanted him to open up, she was going to have to play along until he trusted her enough to come forward.

"Why do you think I'd 'dismiss' you? Is there a reason I should?"

Eva knew he was assuming she would dismiss him without explanation for standing her up. She continued...

"I mean, your profile says you live in NYC. Which neighborhood is that? You really shouldn't be afraid to just come out with it. Contrary to popular belief, I'm harmless, really. Unless, this is just a game, which really wouldn't be cool. I hate games. What if I said I think I know who you are..."

Eva sat back and crossed her arms.

"As far as you thinking you know, I'd say I think you may be right. But I'm going to guess you have it wrong. By you asking what neighborhood... I'm going to go out on a limb and say you don't know who I am. Sorry, Gorgeous. And as far as this being a game... I've meant what I've said."

Eva was certain it was him, now. She couldn't understand why he felt the need to hide from her. *He must really be ashamed of what he did. Alright...if this is what it takes to win his trust, I'll play the game.*

"I'm sure you've meant what you said, I never doubted that. I'm just wondering where you're going with this. I'm confused here. You have to give me something more to go by...unless you don't want me to know who you are. Why is that so scary for you?"

"Do you think you know who I am?"

Eva sighed, annoyed at the question. *Why is he asking me that when I just told him that I do know!*

"If I'm right, you already know. Let me ask you again, where are you going with this? And, if you are who I think you are, you really should just pick up the phone- unless this is just your way of 'keeping tabs'. Seriously, what are you hoping to accomplish by messaging me on Profile?"

"I don't know where I ever planned on going with this when I started. I first emailed you because I felt like I needed to...because it was the only way I

could reach out to you. I guess I thought I would regret it if I didn't. So, this is where we're at now because of that...And if I had ever been able to secure you as my girlfriend, I wouldn't have ever let you get away."

Eva was more confused than ever now. *Keep me as your girlfriend...not let me get away. But you DID have the chance. You DID let me get away.* Eva felt a pull at her heart. She wanted so badly for him to trust her. But she couldn't stand to wait for him to admit who he was.

"Please...tell me who you are."

10 OLD HAUNT

"Flight attendants please prepare for arrival."

Eva put her headphones in and leaned back into her seat. She had made a point to get a window seat, her favorite viewpoint when she flew, for her short visit home. The late summer sky was a brilliant blue and the shadows from the few, fluffy clouds that it held spotted the ground in various shapes and forms. Eva closed her eyes and listened to the hum of the engines revving for landing. As the plane descending lower and lower, she spotted a cloud casting a shadow that perfectly covered the land of her homestead.

How appropriate.

***

"Evie! Man, is it good to see you!"

Kate ran to her friend pulling up into the driveway, hardly waiting for her to get out of her rental car and tackled her with a bear hug.

"Gosh, have I missed you! I was just telling Collin how much I wished I could see you and now here you are! Come on inside. We've got dinner grilling and we can talk!" Kate took her friend's hand to lead her up to the house. "So, what made you decide to come home so all of the sudden anyway?"

Eva followed her friend around to the backyard; an abyss of green and an oasis of flowers she hadn't seen in so long. "I just needed to get away for a little while. This whole thing has been so confusing...and work has been so busy...I just needed a break."

Collin was at the grill outside in the backyard. "Hiya, Evie! Good to see you! I hope you're hungry."

"Go ahead, Evie, sit down!" Kate offered and walked over to her husband. "Almost done, Honey? I'm starving!"

Collin wrapped his arm around his wife and gave her a kiss. "Yes, my darling."

Eva rested her face in her hands and watched them with admiration. *Well...at least all is still well in Mayberry. Thank goodness SOMETHING is still right with the world.*

Kate came to the table and Collin followed closely behind, bearing cheeseburgers.

"So, Evie, have you heard from Alex?"

Which one...the electronic one or the real one? Eva stared at her plate deciding how to respond. "No, I haven't."

"But you still work together, don't you? Has he been avoiding you all this time? How awkward is that."

Kate shook her head and took a bite of her cheeseburger. "No, he hasn't even been there," she replied. "He's been on assignment somewhere else."

"Wow...all of this time? Geez, I'm sorry. I know that's got to be painful not to have a resolution." Kate empathized with her friend.

"Well, that's the funny thing...I'm still getting messages from him."

"Wait a minute...you mean to tell me that he's still sending you anonymous messages instead of just coming forward and admitting who he is to you? Geez, he must really be terrified of you."

"Oh, thanks."

Collin laughed at his wife's approach. "Wow, Honey, you really go for the kill, don't you?"

"Oh, no, I mean I thought he was testing you at first, but he must really be afraid to face you after what he did."

"Yeah...I mean the whole thing is so confusing to me. I just don't understand it."

"Yeah, we need a guy to help us figure this out," Kate replied, then turned to her husband. "Honey, what do you think?"

"Well, it sounds to me that he was leaving the door open in case he wants to come back," Collin offered.

"Really? Why would he do that?" Eva replied.

"If he didn't contact you after the night, he stood you up to even let you know what was wrong, it sounds to me like he's leaving the door open. It's like saying, 'I don't want to commit, but I don't want to let you go either, so I'm going to not say anything at all to avoid your anger *slash hurt *slash emotion, so that if I do come back to you, you won't be able to throw anything back in my face.' It's a manipulation tactic. If he can keep you guessing, in a sense, he still has your attention."

"Huh. Okay...and the anonymous thing...What about that?"

"Well, that's a bit trickier. He probably feels this is the only safe way he can communicate with you until he's ready to come to you and apologize for what he did."

"See, that's pretty much exactly what I thought," Eva replied, a glimmer of hope lighting in her eyes in the evening summer sun. Kate, being unconvinced that this explanation would excuse such erratic behavior, gave her friend a sympathetic look.

"Evie...I mean, even if that's true, it's still not good. It's totally manipulative."

Eva gave a sad puppy dog pout back to her friend; unsure herself if this was a worthy excuse.

"Well," Kate stated matter of fact and shook her head at her burger, "This guy definitely gets points for creativity, that's for sure."

***

A couple days later back in the city, Eva was tidying up her office to go home for the evening.

"Ping!"

Eva stopped what she was doing and grabbed her phone. *It's him.* Maybe this was the message she had been waiting for. Maybe he was finally ready to talk to her. She took a deep breath and opened the message.

"Eva... I would love nothing more than to be able to tell you who I am... the problem is, the timing just isn't right. Am I going to spill the beans, I would like to think I am. I just can't right now. But I want you to know... the more I talk to you, the harder it is becoming to not tell you. I'm sorry I lied to you before about where I knew you from. That was wrong of me, and I'm very sorry for that. Will you forgive me, please? Eva, thank you for opening up some more about all of this. I'm really starting to enjoy writing to you. Me =)"

Eva closed the message and put the phone down. *Why would the timing not be right? Probably that girl that came up to us in the park. What was her name? Amber.* Eva was discouraged by his statement. Still, she felt it best not to push, but to encourage him as best she could. Perhaps that would break his fear and he would come clean with her.

"Ok, I'm sorry, didn't mean to push. I guess that's just me being persistent. If nothing else, I'm really good at that! I really hope you do someday feel comfortable enough to tell me who you are. I don't know why you say the timing is bad, but I do know that if you don't try...you'll never know. I really believe in taking chances, that's the only way to really live. If I hadn't taken the chance and given up everything I knew to move here, I'd still be back home, miserable and wondering, 'What if?' What a horrible way to live! My whole life in New York has been about taking chances and yeah, it's really been tough to be away from my friends and family and yeah, it's been a huge struggle, but sometimes you have to go through the bad to get to the good AND recognize AND appreciate it! That's the only way you can grow, to find out who you really are. And if I get nothing else out of this experience, at least I have that.

Whatever, you're going through right now, I hope you're not isolating yourself. You need to surround yourself with people who will be there to catch you when you fall, not give up on you when things get a little rocky. It's really important to have good people surrounding you. About saying you knew me from high school...you probably felt that was the only way you could reach out to me at this point. And no... I'm not upset. Lord knows, I've made mistakes, too. I'm pretty understanding. It takes a LOT to ruffle my feathers. (BTW, that's not an invitation to test the waters on that one, lol.) But if you really know me as well as you say you do, you already know that. I just wish you realized you were safe.

I hope you feel comfortable enough to tell me someday and whatever's going on with you, if you need someone to listen, you can always talk to me..."

"Eva, don't worry about being persistent. You have every right to be. The only thing holding me back from revealing myself is the fact that I am in a relationship... So, you can see now my hesitation..."

Eva's heart sank as the confirmation set in. *I knew it...that time away in L.A....it wasn't just for his brother...he's got a girlfriend in California...That's why he stayed away so long... was so cold on the phone. I knew it.*

She couldn't believe how well he'd been able to keep it a secret at *Highline*. No one had heard him speak of any females in his life before, but if his girlfriend was in L.A. and he was living in New York, it wouldn't have been difficult to keep her hidden.

"I'm sorry I wasn't honest with you from the start and I'm sorry I contacted you this way... but I really felt like I needed to. The longer I know you, the more drawn to you I become. I know it's horrible of me given the

circumstances, but I can't help the way I feel. So, I'm writing to you... possibly getting to know you better than I already do. And yes, I do really know you. I'm not just some random guy.

I think it's very incredible what you have done with your life. I love your enthusiasm and outlook on life. And the way you feel about sitting at home being miserable thinking what if... that's exactly why I'm emailing you now.

In regard to my current situation... it's not going the greatest... hasn't been for some time now. And I'm sort of like you, isolated from the good people in my life. So, it's been tough... but it has its bright spots, too. Sometimes I'm just not too happy.

I just want you to know, I really appreciate this last email from you. You have made me feel very safe, thank you! With every sentence you write, you affirm everything I feel about you. Eva, you really are a wonderful woman! Keep that head up and that gorgeous smile on your face. Me =)"

"A girlfriend...so...that's why you're hiding. I'm sorry you're in a bad situation...all I can say is follow your heart. Not knowing the details, I just don't know what else to say. I really wish you would just admit who you are. If you won't do that, then at least answer me this: How long have we known each other?"

"Eva...I really am sorry that this is happening in the order that it is. I'm sure I must look like a jerk to you. But...I can't help the way I feel. You have that effect on me. I light up anytime I know I'm going to get to see you, then actually see you, hear your voice, or hear mention of you. How long have we known each other...? I won't say how long... but I will say that it has been over a year. I'm not saying less than two... it could be more; it could be less."

Eva closed her eyes to allow herself to think. Two years... the length of time she had known Alex. *Why doesn't he just come out with it? She could feel her heart sinking. I don't know how much longer I can play this game.*

"I'm sure you can't help your feelings, but I don't know if this is very fair to the girl that you're in a relationship with...or me for that matter. If you felt this way before and had the chance to say something, why didn't you?"

"Oh, I completely agree that it's not fair to anyone! That's why I'm apologizing to you. I know you deserve to be treated much better! If you'd *rather not talk, I'd completely understand and will back away... What I meant by order... had I met you first, I would have asked you out in a heartbeat and not waited! Unfortunately, that wasn't the case... Which also explains why I never said anything until now... because I've already been involved, and you deserve to know the truth. But, again, I really felt like I needed to contact you. I'm really sorry, Eva, I know this isn't fair... and maybe I should have just kept my stupid mouth shut!"*

Alex wasn't cheating on me, he was cheating WITH me... even if it was only with a couple of sweet words and a kiss. But he still wants to pretend he hasn't asked me out yet. How stupid could he think I am?

Eva was torn...she couldn't decide whether to be angry with him for treating her like the 'other woman' or sad for him; realizing how tormented he was. The only thing she knew was that she wasn't ready to give up on him.

"Thank you for being honest with me. Like I said before, not knowing for sure who you are makes this difficult. It's not my place to judge whether or not it was "wrong" for you to contact me. I don't mind talking to you, but you realize until you admit who you are or the situation changes, this is at a standstill. I'm no man-stealer...I don't even know for sure who you are."

Even though, yes, I do know who you are, she thought.

"...What you said about your feelings...they sound very strong... I'm flattered. But...in your heart of hearts...do you feel that way about her? This is a very sticky situation...and I'm not comfortable now that I know there is another person involved...and I wouldn't want someone doing that to me...I can't tell you what to do...you have to decide for yourself what you feel in your heart is the right thing to do."

Eva waited for his response...
...nothing. A whole day passed. Still nothing.

11 PUSH & PULL

A whole week had passed with no sign of response, Eva began to think he'd regretted his mistake in reaching out when he was already spoken for and decided to withdraw his illicit pursuit. Despite the boundary she's set for herself, she looked for his messages. A month passed. Still nothing.

Fall had begun to shroud the city with its glorious yellows, oranges, and reds. The hot, sticky weather had backed off pleasantly, replacing the buttery-thick humid air with a brisk, light breeze. With each passing day, Eva's heart fell deeper and deeper into hopelessness fearing she had said too much. True to form, Alex disappeared again right after he had begun to bear his patchwork heart to her.

He's got someone else...I have no right to expect anything from him at this point. It never occurred to her that she was worth more than the games he was beginning to play with her.

Then suddenly, it came as quickly as it had vanished.

"Ping!"

It was him.

Dearest Eva...I'm not trying to put you into a position of being a man-stealer. If I leave my relationship, it'll be for me and my happiness. And the way things are going, I'm sure that's going to happen.

To answer your question about if I feel the same way about her, as I do you... honestly, no I don't. I don't know if I have ever felt that way about her. I can't remember a time when I did. Are you saying that you think you might have an idea as to who I am? You may be right... I guess we'll see. I'm sorry it's taken so long to get back to you. This isn't how I would treat you if we

were together, by the way.
    Eagerly anticipating your response,

Me =)

    He thinks this is just one big freaking game. Eva chose not to respond right away. He needed to learn that he couldn't just expect her to be at his beck and call; to come and go as he pleased and treat her heart like a worthless ping-pong ball.

    Eva's heart ached deeply. She wanted desperately for Alex to end the charade and come to her so that they could be together. It hurt her tremendously that he hadn't been honest with her from the beginning, but she didn't care. The trials around their pairing didn't matter to her, she was just ready to create a future with the one who had asked her to trust him one magical spring evening...no matter what it cost her.

***

    Fall had once again turned into another icy, cold winter in Manhattan. And Eva's aching heart was all but turning right along with it. Another month had passed since her last email to her mystery admirer, again without a response.

    Snow piled high along the sidewalk as Eva made her way through the city, bundled up in her North Face and boots, down the salt-sprinkled street towards home.

    The minute she sat down from just getting in the door, *"Ping!"*
Eva looked down at her laptop. *Oh, my God...it's him.*

    It had been over a month since she'd heard from him. She scrambled to open up the message as fast as she could.

    I just wanted to email you real fast to say 'hi.' I know you probably don't want to hear from me, but I really have missed you and I needed to say 'hi' and make sure things are going well for you. I sure hope so! Miss you!
Me =)

    Is he serious? Is that seriously all he is going to say to me after everything I said in my last email and waiting over a month to respond?

    She felt the burn of frustration begin rise within her stomach. He had dragged her into this I-need-to-hide-behind-email-until-I-feel-safe-enough-to-face-you-again game and now it seemed he was turning things around to

89

make it look like she was the one putting him off.

"There's something I don't understand...How can you say you have such strong feelings for me and not act? If I felt that strongly about someone, it would kill me to be apart from that person and I would do everything in my power to be with them. You say this isn't a game, but how can I believe you when you say you wish so many things, but can't even face me as yourself? Are you really that afraid that I'm going to hate you? I just don't understand...if you are really not happy and you really wish you could hug me, see me, whatever, then why aren't you even trying??"

"Eva, it's very complicated. If I were to explain why, that would give it away about who I am. I'm really sorry, Eva. I shouldn't have said anything in the first place. I should have just kept my feelings inside and tortured just me and not you, too. That wasn't fair of me, and that's why I have tried to back off as you asked. This really isn't a game to me, I promise. I just wish I could tell you! I'm so very sorry, Eva. Me =)"

Ugh, I never asked him to back off! Why does he keep saying he doesn't want to give away who he is? Eva thought to herself. *Isn't the whole point of this; a slow rebuilding? He's going to have to tell me eventually...and without another woman.*

"See, this is my whole point... I never asked you to back off! If you really felt that strongly, you WOULDN'T want or try to back off. You would move mountains. This is why I am now having a hard time believing your sincerity. You're acting like you don't have a choice and you do. You are in charge of your own life. I'm pretty sure I've already figured this whole thing out and I'm still talking to you. You do what you want, but don't contact me again until you've made up your mind about what you want and DON'T have a someone else in the picture."

"See... and that's what I'm talking about. You tell me to stop talking to you... and not to talk to you until something has changed... so... I do out of respect for you. How can I move mountains if you tell me to leave you alone? And, I really don't think you have it figured out. I'm sorry, Eva."

"What am I supposed to do when you won't talk to me as yourself? Do you

really think I don't know who you are? I would really like to think that you are planning on coming clean and telling me the truth, when your situation isn't complicated anymore. When I say 'move mountains', I mean, if something is that important to you, you make it a priority."

"I don't blame you for not wanting to talk to me... or me talking to you. And, yes, I really believe 100% you do not know who I am. I can guarantee you one thing, I promise I will tell you who I am when my situation changes. I know you'd probably want nothing to do with me at that time, but I will tell you...I promise."

Eva shook her head in irritation and closed her laptop. She couldn't continue to respond. It was difficult enough that he was not allowing the two of them to communicate in person, but now it seemed he was placing the blame on her for his own indecision. She knew he would have to put aside his pride to face her after what he did, but Eva realized how terribly insecure he must be to think she might want nothing to do with him. Yes, the circumstances were tricky and he had been dishonest with her, but it was nothing that would rule out her forgiveness.

Maybe it was the alcohol that he would need to set aside. Eva wondered if it held more of an influence over him that she had realized. And she began to wonder if there was even more to his relationship than she had considered.

***

The mid-winter snow fell lightly outside of Eva's apartment window that lazy Saturday morning. Not the stinging, powdery kind...the big, beautiful flakes that Eva loved. Eva was gazing out of her window to the streets below, watching the people pass by; on their own missions to who knows what.

Couples were holding hands, some playing in the snow, some holding each other snugly, keeping each other warm as they scurried to their destinations. All of them laughing....and she thought of him. And that night so long ago where he, too, had held her and led her through the snow. She couldn't bear her own vow of silence any longer. She had to reach out to him. *How can I expect him to trust me, if I'm not here to help him through this?*

"I don't mean to shut you out... I just needed to know that there is a purpose behind this. I'm trying really hard to give you the benefit of the doubt because I don't know the whole truth behind this. If you truly are taking steps (that I can't see) to make this better, I don't want to discourage that. Can you

at least tell me when you'll be able to tell me who you are?"
***

"Honey, don't squish ya eyes like that...you'll get wrinkles."

Ramona was referring to Eva's now permanent frown. She was standing in the doorway of Eva's office looking very concerned. "Honey, I need to talk to you." She closed the door, walked over to one of the chairs in front of Eva's desk and motioned for Eva to join her in the chair next to her. "Come ov-uh here. I need to talk to ya woman to woman."

Eva got up and walked over to her mentor.

"Come on, sit down," Ramona directed in a motherly tone.

Eva sat down and looked at the ground.

"Honey, look at me."

When Eva lifted her head, Ramona noticed the reason she had hung her head. Tears filled her eyes, making them an even deeper green. It was all she could do not to let them spill over.

"Honey, what is the matter? Lately, it's been like tryin' to pull teeth to get you to smile." Ramona already knew what was plaguing Eva, but she wanted to hear it from her.

"Ramona...it's been a month and still nothing." Eva cried, now letting it go. "I just don't understand...why would he do this? Share his feelings so strongly and then disappear?"

"Well, he said he had a girlfriend, didn't he? I don't know, Honey, maybe he's confused."

"But he told me he wants to be with me." Eva should her head.

"I know, Honey, but listen...it's been a year and he's done nothing but upset you since then. You need to let it go, Honey. If he truly cared about you, he would not be putting you through this."

"But...I can't...he made promises."

"Eva, listen," Ramona took Eva's hands and stared her dead in the eyes. "You know you're like a daughter to me. And I'm worried about you. You've been walking around here like a lost puppy dog for months now. You've got to snap out of it."

"But I miss him...the real him...and I'm hurting."

"I know you are, Baby Doll, that's why I reassigned him."

"Wait a minute. You? You're the reason he's been gone?"

"Well, of course, Honey. I couldn't very well have him around to break your heart even further. Especially, when you've got a job to do."

"Has he said anything to you? Is this the reason he says he can't come to me?"

"Oh, Honey, no," Ramona swatted the air to emphasize her point. "All I did was get his ass out of here to save you. What he's doing now...that must be his own special brand of jackass."

Eva shook her head in despair and stared at the floor. "Why do you think he is doing this, Ramona? Telling me he wants me and then disappearing for weeks?"

"I don't know, Sweetheart." Ramona's voice was full of compassion. "But...I can tell you this...the sooner you forget him the bett-uh. He doesn't deserve a special girl like you."

"But...I love him. We love each other," Eva said, tears now streaming down her face.

Ramona tenderly put her hand on Eva's back. "I know you do, Honey. But he's not available...or being honest and you need to move on for your own good. Listen, you know I love you, but I can't stand to see you so upset. It's not good for you. If it's meant to be, it will happen in its own time, and you've got to move on with your life in the meantime."

"But...I thought *this* was going to be my life...I mean, he said he wanted it, too." Eva leaned her head on Ramona's shoulder and let the tears flow like a waterfall.

Ramona stroked Eva's hair and did her best to soothe an already broken situation. "I know, honey. I know. But you've got to let this go for now. For your own good."

***

Three months later, the frigid winter weather had finally broken its spell over Gotham and a new Spring had begun to fill the city with its dazzling array of multi-colored blossoms. The heavy atmosphere over the city had lifted along with its winter cloak, but Eva's body felt heavier than ever.

Her days had gone from free and uninhibited to hopeless and anxiety laden. She couldn't even remember what it was like to feel happy. What was once was a comforting promise of love, now held her in shackles as she waited for her ghostwriter to make himself known. Night and day, she waited for a message from the only one who could truly pull her out of the pit in which she had found herself.

Eva couldn't understand why he would choose to stay in a relationship that made him so unhappy. She began to wonder if it was deeper than he had initially led on. If this other woman was giving him something that she couldn't, it would be difficult for him to break away. Or maybe something much more serious had kept him...*maybe she was expecting. Knowing Alex, he would feel obligated to stay with a discovery such as an unborn child.*

Eva's mind drove her nearly to madness as she considered the possibilities. She didn't care what the difficulties were, all she wanted was for the man who had wooed her so long ago to show back up in her life and make things right between them. But his messages were so sporadic, that Eva was left in a constant state of waiting and worrying; waiting for him to come through and worrying that if she by chance said one wrong thing, it would drive him away and she would once again be left wanting.

Finally, one evening as she was getting ready for bed, her laptop chimed with a familiar sound. It was him.

"Ok, so I was reading through my last email to you, and I feel like I should have said more. I'm not trying to play games with you and your heart. The only intention I ever had in contacting you was to tell you that I think you're incredible! I definitely didn't think out the ramifications of what that would do to you hearing it. For all I know, you could be in a serious relationship and my words would be falling on deaf ears. But then, I am in my complicated situation myself, so I don't know where that would have taken me either.

Sorry, I don't know if that was confusing or not. Eva, I just want you to know that I'm very sorry for saying anything and upsetting you. I would have much rather kept my feelings inside than hurt you. But it's too late for that. Hopefully it's not too late for you to accept my apology. Even though you can't see it, I am taking steps to resolve my own situation. I'm beginning to fight for what I want in life. As far as what I'd hope for between us, once my situation has been cleared... I don't know. I have a feeling you wouldn't even want me.

Ok, so I'm sorry I'm rambling on and on, but you're important to me and I felt like I needed to expand a little bit more from my previous email. I just re-read all of what I just wrote, and I still feel like I'm not getting it all right. I've already probably said more than you even wanted to waste your time reading. I'm sorry that I can't reveal myself to you. It's the thing I want to do most! I know, I know... if I wanted it so bad, why don't I just do it? Why not fight for what I want so badly? Those are very good questions! Ones I just can't answer. I'm sorry! If I did, I feel it would give away my identity. Ok, I've probably now worn out my welcome.

Eva, you are a very special woman, and I don't want you to forget that! Do not change one bit! Please!

Thank you for allowing us to communicate up until this point."

But I'm not in a relationship. And you know that. Why does he keep pretending to be someone else??? Eva didn't understand why he was saying so many things to throw her off. *"If I was in a relationship, I wouldn't be encouraging you to open up to me. As you know, I'm not like that. How can you expect anything good to come out of this if you aren't honest with me? I'm glad you're starting to resolve your situation and that you're ready to fight for what you want, but keep in mind that if you really meant that you're starting that fight by talking to me, part of that fight is going to be admitting who you are. You can't just assume I'm going to shut you down without listening to what you have to say. Why are you saying you're sorry you can't reveal yourself to me, when before you promised you would tell me? Pain and regret come with learning what's truly important, even if you have to lose something first to realize what it is. Nothing worthwhile is ever easy, but it is so worth it in the end. Otherwise, you'll never be completely happy."*

"I actually think you will shut me down without listening. I am not trying to disrespect you by not giving you the benefit of doubt, but I just don't see you responding well. But I could be completely wrong. Only you know. Oh, I still promise I will tell you who I am. I just can't yet. I really want to, Eva! I just wish I could call you up and say 'hi' and reveal the mystery! I completely agree with you about it being worth it. That's why I'm talking to you now and taking the steps that I am.

Eva, thank you for not just dismissing me, and taking the time to talk to me. This just re-affirms how I feel. You never cease to amaze me! What a rare gem you are! It's so comforting knowing that women like you are still walking this earth. Even if nothing ever happens between us, at least it gives me hope that they're out there! Again, thank you, Eva, for such a caring heart towards this. I am just grateful that you ever even responded!"

"When you're ready to come to me and talk to me, I promise I won't shut you down. I'm not a cold person. Of course, I'll listen to what you have to say...as long as you're honest with me. I hope you're not letting that fear stand in the way. That's part of the fight.

You said you wanted to fight for us...So... fight!!"

"Oh, Eva, I hope you can see that I get you! Because I really feel like I do. I've felt like that since I met you. Thus, the feelings that I have! I've known for quite some time how wonderful of a woman you are! Like I said before, a rare gem in this world!

I promise I will come to you when the time is right, but I still feel like I'll be shut down! I know that may sound like I don't know you and am underestimating you... but I really think I'm right. I don't know, I guess we'll just see what happens. I am afraid to tell you, yes, but it won't keep me from talking to you. Like I said, you ARE WORTH THE FIGHT! You are SOO worth it!

Would you like to cut off communication again? Just let me know. I want to make sure you're comfortable. But I have to tell you, I've been loving being able to talk to you! It just makes my day every time I have a message from you! But, if you don't want to... just let me know, and I'll walk away."

Eva threw her hands up at the mocking words on the screen. *Like he doesn't know that I still want to talk to him. Geez, he is impossible!*

"I don't feel uncomfortable communicating with you, especially now that you're starting to open up to me. What I feel uncomfortable with is communicating with you under a guise. Like I said before, with feelings that strong, you wouldn't want to back away. And I appreciate that you are taking my feelings into consideration. I just don't want this to become a substitute for something real. And I don't think you want that either. I don't want you to feel like you're 'safer' just emailing me. We can't have a real life over email. You know that.

You promised you will come to me when the time is right, and I am believing you for that. What I don't know is when that will be and I know you don't want to tell me, especially since you didn't answer when I asked you.

Please don't let your fear stand in the way. This has been so frustrating. All I can do is try to put your mind at ease. Just be honest with me, that's all I ask, and I promise I will listen with an open mind. And we'll go from there... I just need you to show me that this is real."

"Well, I'm so relieved to know that you aren't uncomfortable! I really didn't want to pull away! You're right, feelings this strong I want as much as I can get! And, believe me, this isn't going to be a substitute for something real. I would love to be able to turn this into something real. I can't even imagine how wonderful it would be to actually be around you in a different setting. So,

trust me, I do want to move this beyond emails.

I just want to reassure you that I will come to you when the time is right. I really appreciate your willingness to listen and to at least consider giving me a second chance. Is there anything you'd like to know about me?"

Eva shook her head. *Um, obviously, I want you to admit who I already know you are. Why is he playing stupid???*

"It's when you did pull away that I started to question your sincerity. You don't have to feel sorry for opening up to me. I appreciate people who can be open and honest with their feelings. You don't sound 'psycho'. Everything you're saying... pouring your heart out... after everything that has happened between us really means so much to me.

What do I want to know? Obviously, I want you to admit who you are and there's a lot I want to know and I'm looking forward to when you will actually show me in person."

She didn't want to cheapen the connection any further by giving the answer to his question away over something so impersonal as email.

"When are you thinking I pulled away? I only 'pulled' away because you wanted me to not email you. I would have always kept emailing you. I would talk to you every day if you'd let me!

Eva, I want to let you know that I'm very excited about being able to communicate with you! What a ray of sunshine in this dreary life!"

Eva's heart melted for Alex even in her confusion at his making it sound like she was the one who kept him away instead of his own random months-long silences. In all the time she'd known him, she had no idea of the depth of his depression or the severity of his isolation.

It definitely makes sense now...the back and forth, the mixed messages, the weeks to months of silence in between messages...he is hurting. Eva didn't want to be one more cause to his discouraged outlook on life. If the person he was with couldn't make him happy and he had not permanently committed to her, she felt confident that she was the one he was meant to be with, and she wasn't going to let anything ruin that - not even her own doubt.

"I'm sorry if I sounded impatient before. That wasn't my intention. It's just difficult not knowing what the situation is, but I do understand that it must be

hard for you." Eva was completely oblivious to the fact that the situation was even harder on her, than it seemed to be on him.

"You didn't sound impatient before. I just thought about what I've been doing to you, and I know it has to be upsetting to you. So, I backed off. You said you didn't want this to become a substitute for the real thing, and I agree with you 100%. I know I haven't been fair to you, and I'm so very sorry for that, Eva. Contacting you like I have was wrong, and I know it's got to be bothering you. I'm sorry, Eva!

You know, I was reading through all of the messages we've sent back and forth... Do you realize it's been almost a year that we've been talking? Also, I want to make sure you are clear on something... it seems to me, from what you've said, that you think you know who I am, and my guess is you think I'm a guy that broke your heart...Do you think I'm him? I just want to quote to you what I had said before... 'If I had ever been able to secure you as my girlfriend, I wouldn't have let you get away.' I still mean that today. If I am ever so blessed to have that opportunity again, I promise you, Eva, I will not let you slip away! I 100% believe I am not who you are thinking.

I'm sorry I pulled away... I just am torn about what to do here. I want to talk to you, but I just don't know what to do.

I know I told you I knew you from high school, which was a lie... But here's something true... I know you very well, Eva. I really believe I know you, the real you. That's the real reason for all of this... because I can see into that radiant heart of yours! I see the beauty that shines from within. You have the most beautiful soul I've ever known.

I am speaking from within my own heart right now... I always have with you... Always."

Eva didn't know how to respond at first, deeply confused by his insistence on hiding his true identity. It felt like such a jump from one end to the end, and she couldn't see the truth in it. She only felt a want to comfort him.

"I appreciate that you care about the effect this is having on me, but it's important that you understand that what hurts is when you back away after saying you're starting to fight for me and after opening up to me so much... it really does. That's why I was questioning you. Because I don't understand how you would say you want to talk to me every day and then disappear. Even if you pulled away because you didn't want to upset me, I just really

want you to understand that.

I know you said you're torn and I know you must be confused about what to do and I empathize with you, but honestly, if you really want an opportunity to have me in your life, if you really want this to turn into something tangible, I think we just need to sit down and talk to each other. I know you're scared, but it will be okay. I promise I will listen with an open heart. Just like I'm 'listening' to you now. There's no need to be afraid."

"Eva, I completely agree with you. The problem is... I can't do that. I wish I could just talk to you about all of this! It's just so complicated!
I really appreciate you and your understanding. I just can't tell you who I am until things have changed. Nothing more would make me happier than to be able to talk to you. I'm sorry, Eva."

12 HIDING YOU

No sooner had Eva walked into her office that next morning, did she begin to hear panic rising on the open floor downstairs. She ran out of her office to the balcony and looked down to see the cause of the commotion. There was a figure lying on the floor and people were rushing to her side.

Eva gasped, "Ramona!" She ran down the steps as fast as she could. Theo, one of the other photographers met her on the way.

"Oh, my God, what happened?" she asked as she ran across the floor and over to her beloved mentor who was lying on the floor clutching her heart.

"Heart-attack," Theo, replied, running alongside her. "She was fine and then all of the sudden, she collapsed. Paramedics are on their way. I think it's best that you don't go over there." He tried to stop her.

"No!" she insisted. "Let me go. I need to see her." She slipped out of his grip and ran to Ramona's side, kneeling down to see her. Peter stood over to the side with a blank look on his face and his arms crossed, silently watching the scene.

"Mona?" she grabbed her hand. "Hang on! The paramedics are coming. You're going to be okay." She wrestled to conceal the panic in her voice.

"Eva?" Ramona rasped. She could barely talk as she struggled on the cold, tiled floor, fighting for her life.

"Yes," Eva exclaimed with tears brimming. "It's okay! I'm here! You're going to be okay!"

"Sweetie...if I don't make it, take care of yourself.... okay?" Ramona could barely catch her breathe to get the words out"...You got a bright...future....ahead of you," Ramona was increasingly losing strength, her words slow and labored.

"No, Ramona. Don't talk like that," Eva pleaded heartbroken at her friend slipping away on the floor beside her. "You're going to be fine. You're not done yet." Eva tried to encourage her as best she could, hoping that lifting her spirits would be enough to also lift her friend from the floor.

The Highline crew stood away from the two, waiting for the paramedics and watching in disbelief at the scene playing out in front of them; no one said a word.

"Honey...I think it might be my time... and I want you to know...I love you...like you was my own a daughter."

"Mona...," Eva was sobbing now.

"And... there's something you need to know...Peter...he...," Ramona's head fell back against the floor mid-sentence, her arms dropping to the side.

"Peter what?" Eva shouted, shaking her mentor's hands to try to wake her up. "Peter what?" Only Ramona was unresponsive. "No!" Eva cried. "Ramona! Don't go!" She shook her harder. "Please, don't go!"

Just then the paramedics rushed in and pulled Eva off of her mentor and over to the side. "Come on. You need to move so we can do our job." They labored over Ramona's body feverishly until one of them stood up. "She's gone."

"No!" Eva went into panic. Theo held her back as she tried once more to run over to Ramona's lifeless body. When Eva finally gave up, Theo sat down with her and wrapped his arm around her shoulders as she wept.

"I know," he soothed. "It's okay...let it out."

She's all I have here...who am I going to talk to now? She was always there when I needed her. She believed in me. Who's going to be there now?

At that moment, Eva felt herself slipping deeper away, a part of her dying along with her beloved mentor.

***

Eva paced the floor of her apartment, eagerly awaiting Kate and Collin's arrival. When Kate learned of the recent happenings, she immediately insisted that they go at once to check on her and make sure she was okay. Eva heard a knock at the door and practically ran over her friend when she opened the door.

"Have I missed you!" Kate exclaimed giving her friend the biggest hug she could.

Collin was second to walk through the door. "Hiya, Eva!"

"Hi, Collin. So, did you guys find the building okay?"

"Oh, yeah, easy as pie...we took a cab," Kate explained with a chuckle. Kate shook her head and smirked at her friend...a planner to the end.

"Well, come on in and sit down," Eva motioned them over to her cozy sitting area. "You guys must be tired." The three sat down and Eva looked at her friend very seriously. "Okay, so what gives?"

"Gives, what?"

"You guys don't just show up here at the drop of a hat. I find it very hard to believe that you just wanted to take in the sights of the city. So, what's going on? Why are you really here?"

Kate and Collin looked at each other. "Okay, you got me," Kate admitted. Collin wrapped his arm around his wife while she continued. "The truth is...Eva, I'm worried about you. We're worried about you." Collin nodded in agreement as she went on. "Eva, you haven't been yourself in a long time...ever since this guy came into the picture almost a year ago. It's all you talk about anymore. It's like you as a person and your own interests have completely gone out the window; like he's the only thing that matters now. And Ramona dying so suddenly the way she did. I know how much you looked up to her and how special she was to you. I... we...wanted to make sure you were okay."

"Don't worry, guys. I'm fine. Really," Eva replied softly, but her eyes gave away her pain.

"Yeah, I'm not buyin' it." Kate gave her friend a look. "Come on, it's me...who do you think you're kidding here?"

"Okay...so the Ramona thing was difficult, yes."

"And the crazy anonymous guy sending you messages."

"Alex."

"Whatever. Okay, yeah, Alex. What is such a big secret that he can't come to you and admit who he is? If he truly cared about you, he wouldn't be putting you through this."

"Well, he did finally admit that he has a girlfriend."

"I know...and that's even worse."

Collin interjected. "Eva, I know in your heart of hearts you believe it's Alex, but I really don't think it's him. I hate to see you waste your heart on someone who isn't even in the picture."

"I'm not wasting my heart. And besides, who else could it possibly be?"

"Well, you have other guy friends, right? Do you think maybe someone is playing a prank on you?"

Eva sighed. "I don't know who in my life would be that completely cruel."

Kate heard the hurt in her friend's voice and tried to smooth things over.

"Look, Eva, I know you love the guy, but he hasn't done one thing to show you he's got character. All he's done is play games with you and hide from you. Does that sound like the kind of man you want to be with?"

"He's just scared right now, Kate. You don't know him. That night-"

"Yeah, that night a year ago was that night a - year – a-go." Kate enunciated to prove her point. "He hasn't made one single, tangible stride towards you since then."

"He will."

"I hope so. And what can you do about it? Seriously, he's got all the power here. I truly hope for your sake that he does save himself and doesn't turn out to be a complete jackass. Eva, you deserve so much better than this. Can't you see that?"

"I know he can give that to me. I've seen it before."

"Eva, that was seriously so long ago. When was the last time you actually audibly heard from him? And I'm not talking about the sound your phone makes when you get a notification."

Eva stared at the coffee table. "It's getting late. I know you guys are tired. Let's just go to bed and we can talk tomorrow, okay? You guys can have my room. I'll sleep out here on the couch."

"Okay." Kate's voice softened as she realized Eva was trying to tell her she couldn't take any more of her pointed questions.

Collin stood to go into the bedroom. "I'll leave you two to say your good-nights. 'Night Eva."

Eva waved her goodnight; she had no more words left to say.

Kate turned back to her friend, saw the pain in her emerald eyes and took her hands. "Eva, I'm not trying to hurt you. You know I love you and would never hurt you. I have your best interest at heart."

"I know you do."

"I'm just trying to get you to see your worth. You deserve so much better than this. Whatever happens, I know that God has someone for you who will treat you the way you deserve to be treated...I just don't think this is it." Kate administered the last part with care knowing how fragile Eva's heart was at that moment.

Eva hugged her friend. "Goodnight," she whispered.

Kate's eyes exuded empathy. "Goodnight...I love you." She gave her friend another hug, then walked in to where Collin was waiting for her and shut the door.

***

Eva tossed and turned that night as shadows chased her into the night. She felt a dark figure...watching her...reaching for her. She forced herself awake and opened her eyes...*there's nothing there*.

***

Eva was awakened by the tone of her phone lying on the coffee table beside her. She opened it up and looked at her Profile page...*Cyrano*. She sat up slowly; the covers falling off her shoulders, brushed her hair out of her face, and squinted across the room at the clock on the wall... *2 a.m.*

"I just want you to know that things are almost over. I'm not saying that to try and keep you on the hook. I just wanted you to know. Eva, I still feel everything for you and I hope that we will be able to sit and talk together sometime soon. It will be so wonderful to actually be able to sit and talk with the woman I've been crazy about for so long! Eva, I know now that I want to be with you... hopefully you'll feel the same way."

Eva half-smiled at her phone. Every time she heard from him, she longed to break through the text to be with him more and more. For the first time in a long time, she felt hope warm her on the inside. *Finally...he's ready to be honest with me. He's finally going to come to me.* Eva remembered just then that his birthday had just passed. *Well, this will be the test...if everyone is right, and this really isn't Alex, then I'll know by his response.*

"I have a feeling you may have recently had a birthday. So, I'm wishing you Happy Belated Birthday, whenever that may have been. I know things are rough right now, but everything will be okay. And when you're ready I will be here..."

"This email right here is exactly the reason I'm falling for you! How do you know when love is real? I wonder if the passion burning inside of me is also present inside you...Thank you for that wonderful email, Eva! I cannot wait to come running into your open arms!"

Eva was relieved that her test proved valid. *"I knew it was you!...My* feelings for you are very strong as well and I can't wait to be in your arms and tell you in person. We really need to see each other soon. These are things that we need to say to each other in person, don't you think? This is too special to say through email."

Eva had a peace that she hadn't felt in years. Finally, Mr. Man was ready to come forward, to make amends with her and start fresh. Finally, she had the fuel she needed to get her through one more lonely night. She sighed as she stretched lazily and snuggled back into her blanket and entered the most peaceful, secure sleep she'd had in almost a year.

***

The subway roared through the tunnels of NYC taking them downtown to Eva's favorite breakfast place, Coffee Cup. Eva and Kate sat together while Collin stood in front of them holding onto the bar above his head. He gave Kate the most adoring smile that said, "I love you" and leaned down to caress her face in his hand. Kate placed her hand on his and smiled sweetly back up at him. "I love you," she mouthed.

Eva watched them with sad admiration. *Wow...they are so deeply in love...so tender towards each other*. It was exactly what she wanted with Alex and based on the message he'd just sent to her the night before, she hoped that time would prove her desires true.

They enjoyed a savory breakfast that day and Eva showed her friends close to everything that her Gotham had to offer. Just as Eva was saying goodbye to the two and closing her apartment door, her laptop vibrated on the coffee table. She opened it up to find her mystery man's response to her email from the night before.

"Eva, how do you know your feelings are very strong as well? You don't even know who I am! About seeing each other soon... I completely agree! I am considering revealing myself to you despite my situation not being completely over. It will definitely compromise things on my end... so can I trust in you 10000% that this will remain between just the two of us until it's over? I also agree about needing to say these things in person... you can't even imagine what I want to tell you! =) I hinted about it in my last email..."

His word games were starting to annoy Eva. *Why is he still pretending that I don't know him? Maybe this is his way of joking around.*

105

"I know you're feeling vulnerable, but do you really still want to pretend I don't know who you are? After that last email, don't you think it would be impossible for me not to know? I don't know what your situation is, but you know you can trust me. Listen to your heart. And I can't wait to hear what you want to say."

"And see... your email just puts further doubt in my mind that you actually do know. I really don't think you know. I'm really scared you're thinking someone different!"

Eva sighed at her laptop growing more and more frustrated at his back and forth...*Why is he stalling?*

"Why do you seriously still think I don't know who you are? Don't be afraid. I don't know how to reassure you any more than I already am. You know you're going to have to tell me eventually if you want this to go anywhere. It will be okay."

"I just really get the feeling that you don't have it right. I really don't think you know who I am, and that really is scary. I think you have built up all these emotions and feelings and I think you have them for someone besides me."

"I find it really hard to believe that you're anyone other than who I think you are. I know it's you because I FEEL you. I know my heart and my heart doesn't lie to me. There isn't anyone else. You can talk to any of my friends or family, and they'll tell you the same thing. I've known it was you from the start and as hard as it was - and is - to wait until you were ready, I knew I couldn't rush you. I knew you had to realize it for yourself. I feel the same way you do, and I still want to see you and I'm really hoping we can be together soon. I know this is scary, but that's because it is REAL. Please don't give up."

"Beautiful,
What you feel, is me... I agree. You feel the love coming from me, because of the thoughts and feelings I've shared with you. The problem here is I believe that you have always had it wrong from the beginning. I've tried numerous times to tell you that. I have been trying very hard to help you realize I may not be who you think I am, to try and avoid any heartache on your part. Now that you are writing all of this, I truly believe that your heart

will be torn apart if I'm not the person you are thinking I am. That's what is so scary to me. Here I'm falling for you and taking the steps I am taking so I can be with you, and I have a horrible feeling that when I take that last step, you'll move out of the way, and I'll fall hard on my face.

Eva, I want so badly to be with you and for you to be my Eva, my princess. I'm very afraid that I'm not 'him'. The one your heart longs for. My question to you is... if I'm not him... would you truly analyze your deep feelings you have right now and answer honestly if those feelings were because of 'him' or because of me and how you feel when talking to me? How can I prove I'm not 'him'? And if I do, will I lose you forever?

You once told me that if I really felt the way I do about you, that I should move mountains. I want you to know, when you said that to me, I began pushing my mountain. It's been moving now since then, and it's almost out of my way. I took the initial step over a year ago when I first contacted you. When you wrote that to me, I realized I needed to stand up and fight for the woman I know I'm meant to love! Your encouragement and compassion have been absolutely wonderful. I only ask, that if I am not 'him' that you honestly give me a fair shot. You deserve to be treasured like the gem that you are, and I want that chance. I want you, Eva."

"I know you're afraid and I am, too. My heart beats so fast every time I hear from you. But the thing is, you don't know who I'm thinking you are and you can't just assume you're not 'him'. If you truly aren't 'him' then we'll deal with it together, but I wouldn't just run away and leave you hanging. Do you think I'd disappear without an answer and not respond to you again? I wouldn't do that. You know I'm not that cold of a person.

I've been waiting my whole life for someone who actually understands and appreciates and wants to treat me the way you do and who would FIGHT for me. I would definitely answer you honestly about where my feelings came from at that point. I've been nothing but honest with you. I can't even know the answer to that for sure until you admit who you are. I know you understand that.

I want to be able to give you a chance, but I need to know who you are. We have no way of knowing for sure where this can go until you admit who you are.

You've trusted me with your heart and soul up to this point. Now you need to trust me with the most important part of this. If you truly want me, then come and get me."

Eva held her breath and hit send. In her mind, it was the most forceful email she had ever sent to him. She'd been afraid to be so demanding of him before, but she knew she couldn't continue to let this go on. Her heart wouldn't let her. His response came quickly:

"I also get a rush every time you email me back. As I've said to you before, if I had ever been able to secure you as my girlfriend, I would never have let you get away from me! And that's the truth, if I had ever had the chance... I guarantee we'd be married by now! I wouldn't let such a precious treasure just slip by! So, just that alone, if you still think I'm somebody that you've been with in the past and I've been 'keeping tabs' that's not me.

So, what am I afraid of?.. I'm afraid that finding this out you will be crushed that I'm not 'him'. I can tell by the way you talk that you've had deep feelings for this man for a long time, and I think that you're going to need time to get over the fact that I'm not him. I think that puts me at a disadvantage in chances of you wanting to be with me. You will probably think of him all the time because of how we started talking on here. I don't know, I just think you're going to have a very hard time dealing with 'him' not being me. You've gone a year thinking that 'he' was me. So, you've had this year long hope of things to come with 'him'. And recently as I have opened up my heart, you felt that coming from 'him'. So, that's why I over and over again tried to get you to realize that I wasn't him. I didn't want you to have the heartache you're probably having as you read this email. I hate that I've done this to you. My heart aches for you! I wish I could take it all off of you and carry it on me.

Eva, I had deep feelings for you before and now as we've grown closer through here those feelings have deepened by leaps and bounds! I am not scared that you will just stop writing and responding, I'm scared that I won't have a chance because I'm not 'him', the one your heart has longed for, for such a long time now.

With all my love,

Me"

Eva began to worry. The thought that this might not be Alex was trying slowly to seep into her mind for the first time. And she couldn't deal with it. *Could it really be someone else?* The possibility was absolutely terrifying. Eva chased the idea out of her mind as quickly as it came. *No... that's impossible. The way he speaks, his tone and the way he words his sentences. It sounds exactly like Alex. I just need to be as supportive as I can, so he'll trust me enough to drop the charade.*

"It means a lot to me that you don't want to hurt me. If you weren't who I thought you were, we'll deal with it together just like I promised. I wouldn't let myself fall apart over someone who didn't exist. Why do you keep putting quotations around 'him'? I still want to be able to give you a chance and, to do that, I need you to reveal your identity to me. So, like I said, if you truly want me, come and get me. If you know you're MEANT to love me, continue to fight for me! Let me be able to give you a chance."

"I keep putting 'him' to signify the guy you were thinking I am. Are you completely being honest that you will deal with me on this... together? Since I'm not him, are you even interested in pursuing something with me? I know you don't know my identity yet, but are you at least open? And as far as knowing that I'm meant to love you... that is completely true! I do feel that way! 1000% percent! I've felt that way for such a long time! I meant what I said at the very beginning... I've had a huge crush on you for so long!"

Ugh, why does he keep saying he's not Alex? Okay, fine, you're not Alex. Let's see how you respond to that. Eva remembered Alex's pain and his lack of trust. He'd told her before the women who had hurt him to get to his movie-star brother. She believed he was testing her to see if she would even be interested in another man and thus prove her unfaithful. *If this is what it takes to earn his trust, fine, I'll bite. I'll play along.*

"Please don't get upset...Honestly, yes I'm disappointed that you're not who I thought you were. You can't blame me for that. I'm not trying to upset you. I'm being honest with you. But that would also mean that he never tried to make things right. I told you I would only want to be with someone who recognizes and feels everything that you do and wants to treat me the way you want to treat me and who would be there for me. If you were a complete stranger that would be one thing, but you're not. You know so much about who I am, you have my number, etc. I still want to be able to give you a chance, but I need for you to tell me who you are. And there hasn't been anyone else, just so you know."

"Sweetie, why would I be upset with you? I knew you would be disappointed...

That's why I feel so bad... I tried and tried to get you to believe me that I wasn't 'him'. I'm definitely not upset at all... I'm here for you if you need to talk about anything now. Feel free to talk about whatever you need to. And I didn't mean boyfriend... in the true meaning of the word."

"I do want to talk...but in person...Are you ready?"

13 CAPTIVATE ME

"Eva, may I speak with you a minute, please?"

Eva had just climbed the steps of *Highline*, coffee in hand and was headed to her office for the morning when Mr. Solomon called to her from his own office. She redirected her route and stood in his doorway. "Yes, of course."

"Please come in." Eva could tell by the stern look on his face that this had the potential of turning into an unpleasant conversation. When she stepped through the door and into his office, she saw Peter sitting on the couch, with the smuggest look on face that she had ever seen from him. She chose a chair furthest from him and sat down with caution.

"Eva, my nephew tells me that you are responsible for the reassignment of one of this magazine's best editors," Mr. Solomon started.

"Excuse me, Mr. Solomon?"

"Do you mind explaining this to me?" Mr. Solomon laid a picture down on his desk facing her.

Eva reached over and took it off his desk. It was a picture of her and Alex embracing in her office. Eva's mouth fell open in shock. *It must have been taken the morning Ramona first talked to us about our relationship! Who could have done this?* Then it hit her. Peter....

She looked over at Peter in utter disbelief. *How could you?* Peter glared a smug smile back to her, looking down his nose at her as if she was expected to answer to him as well.

"Well," Mr. Solomon interrupted their unspoken standoff. "I'm waiting. What is the meaning of this?" He folded his hands on his desk and waited for her response.

"Mr. Solomon, I can explain."

"Please do. That is precisely what I am waiting for."

"It's true, Alex and I had started a relationship, but only shortly before he left. Ramona spoke to us just that very morning that this picture was taken. She was very supportive of us, sir. In fact, she encouraged it."

"Eva...do you presume to tell me that my sister would condone an illicit affair that could cost the jobs of two top employees?"

"Sir, I feel very uncomfortable talking about this with you, but we embraced in my office only just this once and then we...stopped seeing each other." *Which apparently was enough to give the opportunist enough time to take a picture.* She glared over at Peter and then turned back to Mr. Solomon. "Mr. Solomon, I swear to you. I did not have anything to do with his leaving. It's extremely awkward talking about this with you, but Ramona thought it would be best that we weren't around each other after the fact. She was trying to protect me and she thought it was better to reassign him."

Mr. Solomon didn't say anything but stared at her for what could have easily seemed an hour. Finally, he spoke...very slowly and very deliberately.

"Miss Eva...it is tragic enough that I have lost my youngest sister in a sudden emergency. And Peter, his beloved aunt." Mr. Solomon gestured to his spindly nephew smirking across the room.

"I know, Mr. Solomon. I loved her, too." Eva tried to console him, but he refused to acknowledge her efforts.

"But now you dare to disrespect my intelligence so much as to suggest that my sister is responsible for your complete and irresponsible lack of decorum?"

"No, I-"

"Unfortunately, Miss Eva, your excuses are not valid in this situation. Peter has already told me the whole story, everything. You tricked him into an affair and then when you became disinterested, bribed him to ensure he would leave, and you would not be discovered."

"What?! No! That's ridiculous," Eva exclaimed, shaking her head emphatically. "Mr. Solomon, that is absolutely not true. We didn't even see each other for very long."

"Eva, that's enough. We've already lost our greatest asset. I'm not interested in hearing any more of your lies."

"But what you're saying isn't true. That's not how it happened. I swear to you it isn't true! Peter is lying to you!"

"How dare you! Eva, I will not tolerate your extremely unprofessional behavior at this prestigious magazine any longer! Do you understand? I will not have a staff of dishonest manipulators!"

Peter smirked, clearly aware of the irony.

Eva was devastated that anyone would destroy her character in such a way. "No, Mr. Solomon...please listen."

"Eva, you no longer have a voice or a position here at *Highline*. Do I make myself clear? Peter will be taking your place on staff. Please clear out your office immediately."

Eva sat stunned for a minute, shaking in her chair, too shaken up to move. Finally, she stood up and without a word, turned to walk out the door. Mr. Solomon stood up and walked over to her. Just before she left, he took her arm. Eva kept her body facing forward, but cautiously turned her head up to look at him to see what he wanted, tears streaming down her face.

"Eva," his anger had turned to stern calm as he spoke softly. "I am disappointed in you...I expected more out of you than this."

Eva furrowed her brow in pained disbelief. "Then you should know better. How on earth could you believe that I would do such a thing??" She ripped her elbow out of his grasp and walked out of his office and down the hall to pack up her own.

***

Once inside her office, Eva began to pack. She surveyed the shelf full of awards acknowledging her work. *So, this is what years of hard, faithful work will get you*, she thought to herself.

She began to take things down, one by one...Photo of the Year Award for best photo shot in the rain...An article from New York Magazine crediting her as New York's Most Noted Up and Coming Photographer......the now-dried single white rose that Alex had given her on their first date...and a picture. Eva took it down to look at it. It was from last year's Christmas Party of Ramona and herself, dressed up as Mrs. Claus. Eva smiled slightly, remembering the woman who had been such a support and champion. Her eyes began to brim with fresh tears.

"Oh, Ramona," she whispered to the shiny photo paper. "What am I going to do now?"

"I'd love to sit and reminisce with you, sweetheart, but unfortunately, I'm going to need you out of here ASAP."

Eva jolted from her memories and turned around to find Peter leaning against the doorframe, clearly quite proud of himself. He practically pranced into what was now his office.

"Ooh, I've always wanted a desk like this." He stated proudly as he sat down and put his feet up, crossing them on the top of the desk, crushing the dried rose in the process. Eva had reached to save it, but it was too late.

"Aww, what's the matter sweetheart?" Peter's voice dripped with sarcasm. "Don't you have your mommy here to take care of you and burp you anymore?"

Eva glared at him but didn't say a word.

"Guess you don't have my good old auntie here to protect you anymore, now do you?"

"Peter, I've done nothing wrong, and you know it." Her voice was like ice.

"Oh, but it doesn't matter, Honey...they'll never believe you. Guess you should have thought twice before you messed with me." He pulled a file out of his pocket and was now working at his nails. He stopped mid file and looked up at her with just his eyes. "You can go now."

Eva walked over and stood in front of the desk. "You know Peter, your aunt could see right through you, but she loved you and she always hoped you would grow up into the man that she knew you could be...but you know what? She would be so completely disgusted with you, right now. If this is the way you think you need to maneuver your way through life, you'll never be a man. You'll always be just a scared little boy." Eva said nothing more, turned and walked out the door.

Behind her, Peter's smug smile had faded as he watched her descend the steps of *Highline* for the last time.

***

Eva took a deep breath and stepped through the steel doors of *Highline* for what she knew would be the very last time. Now out into the late afternoon sun, Eva steadily strolled up Madison Avenue towards the park. *Now what am I going to do?* She decided against telling Cyrano A.K.A. Alex...for now anyway. She knew it would just upset him and he would possibly blame himself. Out of the fear that it would add to his shame of his previous faux-pas and push him further into hiding, she opted to give him the news when she could tell him in person.

She rounded the corner to the park and pulled her camera out of her bag. *Well*, she thought to herself. *I might as well make myself useful.* She entered the park and began to take snapshots of the beautiful summer flowers budding all over the southernmost part of the park. *A thing of beauty is a joy forever.* She smiled to herself, remembering her favorite childhood musical.

Suddenly her phone buzzed...*Mr. Man...* Eva put her camera away and headed home to her apartment where she could communicate with him in private without any distractions.

***

Eva slipped into pajama bottoms and a tank top with her home state on the front of it, a heart in place of her hometown. She piled her beautiful auburn waves on top of her head and grabbed the butter pecan ice cream out of the fridge, the only remedy that could tackle the recent events. She turned on her "mood" lighting as she liked to call it and climbed onto her chaise. She opened her laptop and his message from Profile.

"Am I ready to talk in person? No... I'm really, really, really nervous now! Plus... my relationship... But I'm about to say, 'to hell with it' to that!"

Eva typed quickly. *"You're nervous, I understand. That is a very human response. I understand you and I know you're a good man and I know you wouldn't break my heart because you love me. It doesn't seem like anything could change that. I know because I can feel it deep in my heart. I pray every night about this, and you can, too. I want to make you feel better, more comfortable about this, so you can tell me if there is anything I can do to help."*

"You know... you said it perfectly. That is exactly why I would never break your heart. Eva, I feel so incredibly happy right now! I can't even hardly believe what's happening right now. Never in a million years would I have ever imagined I'd have the blessed opportunity to have a chance at being with you after what I've done to you! My heart jumps for joy every time I think about it!
I want to be with you, Eva! I don't want to wait any longer!
All my love,
Me"

Eva's long-suffering heart leaped with joy. *This is it! He's finally ready to come see me!* Eva couldn't wait any longer.

"If you don't want to wait, you know what to do. If you want that chance, take the chance. If you want me to be yours, make me yours!"

"Eva...what if I'm completely not your type?"

Eva smacked herself in the forehead. *Oh, my God. Why is he asking me this?*

"Or, what if you're not at all attracted to me...?? Tell me, what are you looking for in a man? Besides someone who wants to be with you and love you. What qualities are you looking for? What do you want in life? Marriage? Kids? What physical qualities do you find attractive in a man? Who do you find attractive now? Like, which celebrities? Or... any guys you know... remember I am one of them. You don't need to answer that last one. But it'd be wonderful if I happen to be one of them! What if I'm just not your type??? I hope and pray that I am!"

"Geez, it's like he's the girl in a relationship," Eva said out loud.

"I definitely want marriage and kids. One of my goals in life is to have a family. I don't get caught up in celebrity hype. Every guy I've actually considered dating has been different from one another. It's not just about attraction, but CONNECTION, integrity, etc."

"Are you worried at all that I might not be your type?"

Eva threw her hands up in the air and grabbed her ice cream, taking a big crunchy bite. *Oh, dear Lord, how many times is he going to ask me this? Well, maybe if I hadn't screwed up in the beginning and just let him kiss me when he asked me to, he wouldn't think I would be disgusted by him! But I can't just give away the farm here. I've got to give him an incentive to come forward.*

"I don't have a specific type, but I have a feeling that won't be an issue. I can't give you a specific answer until you reveal yourself." There. *You want me to disclose upfront what I think before you'll commit? You'll have to see me first.* Eva could feel herself becoming irritated again at his back and forth.

"Ok, fair enough. Eva, I just want to thank you for being so loving and

supportive through all of this. You are just proving more and more why I feel the way I do! You are such an amazing woman! I feel so incredibly lucky! I can't even begin to express the feelings that I have burning inside me for you! I always feel as though my words are never adequate enough to truly capture that raw true feeling. I absolutely adore you, my princess."

Then why did you leave in the first place? Eva thought to herself but continued typing unwilling to budge from her conditions.

"Show me."

"Ok! I will!"

"What are you waiting for?"

"You told me you didn't want anything to happen until my situation has ended... Trust me, I would come there this instant and pull you in close for a huge hug if I could!"

Oh, dear Lord, he is impossible. How long is he going to torture me like this? Eva felt her hope begin to wane wondering how long he was going to dangle the carrot over her head.
"When you said you didn't want to wait, I thought that meant you were ready. I don't know exactly what your situation is, but I just thought it was the right thing to do to wait until it was over. So, we could start fresh. What do you think? Is it really almost over? Can you tell me when? This is so hard; I feel such a connection to you. I don't want to wait either, but I don't want to force you. I don't want to stop talking to you either. Is there anything I can do?"

*"Eva, you are so incredibly sweet. Once again proving my feelings! Is there anything you can do? I wish there was! I am so relieved to see you have such a connection to me as well. It makes me feel so much more secure. I would love to start fresh with you. Thank you for being so unbelievably understanding about all of this. I really appreciate it! I appreciate you! *Hug* Believe me, the last thing I want to do is wait, but it probably is for the best.
Eva, I really like you... and I just want you to know how wonderful you make me feel! I cannot even believe that you are even entertaining the idea of sitting*

and talking to me and giving me a chance! What a lucky man am I! I would love to continue talking to you through all of this. Is this something you'll consider? I'd love to chat and get to know each other on an even deeper level. I want to be able to study your soul, Eva. Know the real Eva... a side no one has ever had the privilege of knowing.

All my Love,

Me"

"I do want to talk to you. I also don't want this to become a substitute for the real thing. But...my fear is that you'll get too comfortable just emailing. Can you tell me when it will be over? Don't you want to see me and talk in person? Did you mean it when you said that it would be soon that we could talk together? Would you really be satisfied with just emails? I do want to keep talking, but I need to know that it really will be soon that we can sit and talk together."

"I completely understand your concerns, but this won't become a substitute for the real thing. It will be over very soon, and we can just wait to talk until then. And, no, I would not be satisfied with just emails. I don't really ever want to email you again! I'd rather just have the real thing! =)   Rest assured it will be very soon! It's out of my hands at the moment, so I'm just waiting right now. But it is coming really soon. I CAN NOT wait!! Eva, I can't wait to be able to be with you!

All my love,

Me"

Eva was slightly relieved. She had begun to think that their relationship would never move beyond a screen. "That's exactly what I needed to know. I feel so much better! Thank you. You make me feel wonderful, too. When you said you want to study my soul and get to know the real me...what is it that you want to know?"

"I'm so glad you feel wonderful, too! I already feel so close to you! Isn't it wonderful? So, what do I want to know about you? Well... here goes...

... I want to know what little things in life make you smile.
I want to know what makes you cry.
I want to know what things make you laugh out loud.

118

I want to know the things that you blush about.
I want to know your biggest fears.
I want to know your most treasured moments you've had in life.
I want to know all of your dreams for your life.
I want to know what your favorite foods are so I could order confidently for you without fear of picking something you don't like.
I want to see how you see life, feel what you feel.
I want to be able to know you so well I finish your thoughts before you do.
I want to know what you were like as a child.
I want to know your heart, Eva... I want to know what you care about, what touches you, what you find special.
I want to know what makes your heart sing.
I want to know what brings you joy.
I want to know what makes you feel safe.
I want to know how you've been hurt before.
I want to know what it feels like to be loved by you.
I want to know you, Eva.
All of you,
Every breath,
Cherish you,
Adore you.
Respect you.
Treasure you.
I want to know you completely.
Love you completely.
There's a lot more that I want to know, but I'm sure this is a good start...
With all my Love,
Me"

Eva felt her heart swimming in the deep expanse of his love. She could actually feel it. Her pulse began to race. No one had ever spoken to her this way before, or at least since he had spoken to her that night on the rocky Brooklyn shore so long ago. This was a deeper, more intimate side of him than he had shown her before. She could feel the pace of her breathe increasing. The more he began to let his guard down with her, the more she felt it safe to share more of her heart with him.

"*With every word you just spoke, I would feel so very safe! I'm not sure how it feels to be loved by me, but true love to me means giving your heart*

119

and soul completely, being there for the other person whenever they need you no matter what- fighting for that person and not letting anything stand in the way of that love and to work at any challenges that may arise and never abandoning that person when they need you the most. To love someone is to support them, encourage them, build them up, be their shoulder to cry on, adore them, cherish them, etc. That to me is what true love means.

These are just the basics. Spending time with me and learning and seeing for yourself will be the best way to truly get to know me. I'm sure we can learn a lot from each other."

"It appears we both have the same belief in what love is and what it really means to love another. =) Exactly the same belief! That is very encouraging, Eva! I can't even contain the joy that's pulsating through my body right now!

Eva, I can't wait to be with you and learn everything else about you! I am craving more and more! I want to know every detail! Including those blushing items! You know, it'd be less blushie to write them than to say them in person! This way I can't even see you're blushing ;)

I cannot wait to begin this new step in life...

There's only one person I want to begin this walk with...

Will you walk and make sweet dreams with me?"

Eva's hands hovered over the keyboard...she hesitated, torn. On one hand, she felt elated, but on the other, something just felt empty. She didn't like that these conversations were taking place through written word, but neither did she want to draw back and discourage him forever.

"I'm happy that we were able to talk to each other so much today and I hope I've been able to put your mind at ease. I'm feeling more and more that I do want to take this walk with you."

"Oh, Eva...thank you...for opening up with me today. I know how much trust you needed to build in order to do that, and I am forever grateful! You constantly amaze me, My Darling. Everything I've ever felt about you is being proven true over and over again! I knew you were this wonderful woman!

Question to you... in regard to eternity... what would it take for me to fill that first treasured role in your life?"

Eva chose to remind him of her condition that he come forward before she

120

would give any more of her heart to him.

"Being a part of every part of my life and letting me be a part of yours and making me feel without a doubt that you are there for me. Remember all the things I said about love and feeling safe? All of that."

"Then, my love, you needn't fear. For when we are together again, I will be all of that to you and more...I just have one more question."

"Yes?"

"Aren't you even curious as to who I am? You're willing to meet up with me and talk, but you don't even know who I am. What if I'm someone you aren't even attracted to? Then what? All this talking would have been in vain."

Eva's stomach wrenched and impatience sought once more to kill her heart. *Oh, no... not this again, please don't go there again. We were so close!*

"Of course, I want to know who you are! That's why I keep asking you! Are you testing me? Do you really think I'd agree to sit and talk with someone I didn't know? Remember I told you that you'd have to tell me who you are first. Besides you've implied that you have my number, and I don't give that out to just anyone. I'm pretty sure I know who you are and I'm assuming you're going to tell me who you are before we meet. Didn't you promise that before? I don't want to backtrack after all this progress. Why are you questioning me? I've been nothing but straightforward with you."

"I'm not testing you at all, Eva. I just wanted to make sure that we were on the same page. I will tell you who I am before we meet, just like I promised. I sensed a little hostility in your response. Hopefully I didn't offend you with my question. I'm very sorry if I did.

I don't know why you keep saying you're pretty sure you know who I am. I don't think I've given you any solid clues that you could know. Do you want me to prove I have your number? Or do you believe me?

Eva was frustrated that Alex kept choosing to go back and forth with her and pay the hide-and-seek game. Of course, she knew who he was. Why did he insist on pretending that she didn't? Eva was afraid to test him. It had taken him this long to open his heart and she didn't want to chance pushing him away into another months-long hiding session, especially since he felt she was coming across as hostile towards him. That was the absolute last thing that Eva wanted. So, she chose to ignore that particular comment.

"It just seemed like you went from 'I'm crazy about you, I know I want to be with you' to questioning my integrity and I don't like feeling that way. Especially, when it comes to something that serious.

I'm sorry if I sounded hostile. Yes, I believe you that you have my number, I'm assuming that you're going to use it eventually? I'll tell you why I think I know who you are when we talk. I'm sorry if I was too harsh, it's just that this past year has been so hard, so if I'm extra sensitive, that's why. I hope we are going to be able to sit and talk to each other soon."

Eva closed her laptop and set it aside. She couldn't take the back and forth anymore. She'd done all she could to ease his mind and now that he had dove deeper into her heart, she couldn't understand what would hold him back from her when he'd said he knew she was the one for him.

She leaned back, pulled the baby blue plush throw blanket over her, and closed her eyes...and began to wonder if this really was all just a game.

No, she resolved as she drifted off to sleep...*He loves me...he would never play games with me on purpose.*

***

Eva startled awake from the sound of a new message. She looked at the clock. *3 a.m...?* She opened up her phone to check the message. It was from him.

"Eva, I'm not feeling well. I think I need to go to the emergency room."

14 UNDONE

"You gonna finish that?"

Charlie was already taking the last spoonful of Eva's butter pecan when he proposed his question, but Eva didn't even notice. The two were sitting on the grass by the Pier and Eva was long gone, staring far off into space. Charlie leaned over and waved his hand in front of her face. "Hel-*lo*?"

Eva looked at him, but immediately closed her eyes and looked away. She wasn't up for interrogation.

Charlie sighed, unsure of what to do. "Hey, you wanna go to the beach tomorrow? It's supposed to be nice. We can go out to Long Beach for the day...or Sayville. What do you think?"

"No."

"What do you mean 'no'? Eva, you love the beach. The only thing that could keep you away is rabid tourists. What gives?"

"I need to stay in the city. I need to be close in case he contacts me. He said he had to go to the ER."

Charlie sighed and threw his hands up in the air along with his spoon, letting it fall to the ground. "Ah, geeez, Eves! Not this guy again."

Eva looked at him in surprise. "What? I can't leave. I should have gone to every hospital last night. I should have done everything I could to go find him and be there for him," she explained, her tone and expression as if the very notion of her venturing off of Manhattan when he could potentially need her was preposterous.

Charlie pursed his lips and spoke sternly. "Eva."

"I need to be here for him!"

"What, the guy who is never here for you. YOU need to be here for HIM.

Okay." Charlie let out a "shh" and shook his head.

"It's my fault. I got upset. It pushed him away."

"Did you apologize?"

"Yes."

"Okay, Eva. Then, once again, this guy has disappeared and once again, you haven't heard from him in a month."

"He loves me, Charlie. He's just afraid."

"Oh, come on, Eva, wake up! If he truly loved you, he'd be standing right in front of you. He wouldn't keep giving you the run-around. He doesn't love you, Eva. He loves himself. And this whole thing...this whole," Charlie waved his arms around, "back and forth. It's abusive! I mean, look at what it's doing to you! This isn't healthy!"

Eva crossed her arms, clearly annoyed. "Charlie. I'm fine."

"No, you're not, Eva, look at you! You're losing weight. You never smile anymore, and you've been acting like a humongous 'B' ever since this guy came into the picture. I don't know where you went, but I want my friend back because this crap," he said gesturing up and down from her head to her feet, "absolutely sucks."

"Charlie, you don't understand how this feels!"

Charlie sighed and rubbed his brow, then turned to look at her, his face stern. "I'm worried about you. It's like you've completely fallen apart. How much more are you going to let him run you over like this? This isn't healthy Eva."

Eva sighed and tears began to form in her eyes. "I love him, Charlie. Don't you understand that?"

Charlie wrapped his arm around her shoulder. "Eva...I understand that you think the sun rises and sets on this guy. I understand that you think that his demented twisted game-playing version of love is actual love...I'm just not pretty darn confident that he's no way in hell worth it."

***

"Hi, Eva. This is a friend of his. He's been in the hospital with major surgery. He knew you would worry, so he asked me to write to you and tell you he's okay and will contact you as soon as possible."

***

Two weeks later, Eva had just stepped through the door to her apartment and was sorting through mail, when her phone beeped to let her know she had received a text. *It's probably Kate wondering how I am.* She opened the message to find an anonymous text from an email she didn't recognize...*'wonderwhoiam'...?* It was him.

"I thought I would switch to texting you to prove I'm making progress.... Hi, My Love...How are you?"

"How am I? Are you serious? You tell me you're going to the hospital and then you disappear for over a month! Don't you ever do that to me again! You had me worried sick!"

"I'm sorry, Eva. I didn't mean to."

"It's fine. It's getting late. I'm going to go."

"Wait! My Love, I know you're upset, but please don't go. Please?"

"Why should I stay? You seem to have no problem coming and going whenever you please."

"Because I want to know where we will be living when we get married."

Eva's felt that old familiar pull at her heart. He knew just how to get to her to keep her waiting. She tried to resist, but the promise in his words kept her.

"My darling, there is no one else on earth that I'd rather give my last name to. And once I do that, we're going to have to set down roots somewhere. So, I need to know where you'd like to live. I will follow you anywhere."

Eva softened and a faint hopeful as she stared at the screen as she read the words, she'd been waiting her whole life to hear. But she began to feel an empty ache that no written word could soothe...she needed him there. She could not fight the resentment beginning to rise up within her. *"Look...it's getting late...I better go."*

"Please don't go, my love."

"I want the real thing."

"I know you do...and I promise you, I am getting close. But in the meantime,...Please...let me make it up to you."

Eva thought long and hard before she answered. His staying away so long has wounded her, but her heart refused to let her deny him. She did not realize her heart was slipping further and further into a cage that she would never be able to demolish on her own. Finally, she relented. But it felt more like signing her life away than a happier pairing of two people in love. *"...okay."*

"Thank you...my love...are you ready?"

"For what?"

"I want to tell you a story. Will you let me?"

"Okay."

"I walk over to you where you are sitting on the couch.
I stand in front of you and hold out my hand to you. 'Come on, my love...It's time for bed.'
You stand up and take my hand, giving me that beautiful smile of yours.
I pick you up and carry you over to your bed where I lay you down gently.
I pull the covers up over your body and you snuggle down in and look up at me with the most beautiful smile I've ever seen.
I tuck you in tight and then lean down and kiss you softly on the cheek.
'Goodnight, my love,' I whisper.
Goodnight, Eva....I love you."

Tears were beginning to stream down her face in a salty mixture of happiness and sadness. This was the first he had ever told her he loved her. If his tender story was just a small glimpse of how their life together would be, she knew he was the one for her. Her whispers mirrored her response as she returned his text. *"I love you, too.... Goodnight."*

She wanted to be with him now more than ever, but she was beginning to slip further and further into his charade of electronic communication that she had begun to fear that if she once more pressed the issue of a meeting, it would break the spell. He would pull his vanishing act and the magic between them would be gone forever.

***

The next evening Eva rushed home from her grocery shopping in order to get back in time to receive his message. In fact, she was beginning to plan her whole life around his messages. His stories. No longer did her days hold the freedom to let the city take her where it wished, but they were now bound by an invisible electronic schedule to which only he knew the code. She came through the door just in time to hear the familiar ping of his calling card.

"Hello, my love...I missed you today."

"I missed you, too."

"Can I tell you a story, my love?"

"I love it when you tell me stories."

"Okay, sit down and get comfortable...
The sound of ocean waves surrounds you, the ocean breeze fills the air.
The smell of fresh tropical flowers awakens you.
You feel the soft, fragrant petals of a flower trace your body with ever so lightly as your skin tingles in response.
You open your eyes.
'Good morning, my love,' I whisper as I lean down to kiss you full on the lips.
You slept all night as we flew to our honeymoon destination...our own private island.
Our days are filled with sun and fascination and our nights with smoldering passionate, love.
And you become mine...fully...completely...truly."

Eva's heart was pounding yearning for him as she sank into his vision. She could see the aqua blue of the ocean against the powdery white sand. She could hear the waves rippling softly onto the shore and feel the balmy breeze of the tropical air. It was as real to her as if they were there together in person. And she began to cry, not understanding why this love also felt like pain. She wanted so badly for it to be real.

"It sounds beautiful."

"This, Eva, is only a glimpse of what I am going to give you once we are together."

"When? You keep saying that, but nothing ever happens. I don't want to wait anymore."

"I know, baby, soon...it will be soon. I swear to you."

***

"Wait a minute. I thought you stopped talking to him?"

"I did, Kate...for a little while anyway."

"Okay, so why not just tell him to call you? The very least he could do for you is call you. If he can't even do that, then he's not worth it. Just ask him."

"I can't pressure him like that, Kate. It's taken a lot for him just to get passed messaging me on social media to even text me. Do you think maybe he thinks I'm not committed?"

"Oh, Evie, you're committed. The whole world knows you're committed. A pack of wild horses couldn't drag you away from the guy. You're definitely committed...wait a minute...you're afraid...aren't you."

"Afraid of what?"

"You're afraid it isn't Alex."

"What do you mean I'm afraid it isn't Alex? Of course, I know it's Alex. I wouldn't be talking to him if I didn't think it was him."

"Eva, you can't even see yourself...you are so far gone in this. You're afraid to find out who this person is because you don't want the messages to stop."

"Okay, that makes no sense, whatsoever. Of course, I want them to stop! So that he and I can actually do this thing in person and not have to communicate this way anymore."

"And if you find out that it isn't Alex. You'll have to stop. That's what this is really all about."

"Oh, no, I know that it's him. It sounds just like him! The things he says, his way of thinking, everything."

"Okay, fine. But just remember...this is NOT the kind of guy you want to give your life to. It's so unhealthy, Eva, you can't even see it. You will lose

yourself completely."
I already have.

***

Summer was coming to a close and Mr. Man, true to form, had disappeared again. Eva's heart was in chains. Dark circles now shadowed her once bright green eyes. Her rosy cheeks, now sallow and pale. A thin frame now held her once perfectly fit figure, as her stomach held her so in knots, she could barely eat. Eva's life was no longer her own, but now marked by each passing text. Her heart ached for him and despised him at the same time. She longed for him to come and rescue her as he did once on the rocks that night so long ago.

Little had she known in that moment, how literal of a metaphor that night had been. His kiss on the uneven shoreline...love on the rocks. It had now been another two weeks since he had ravaged her heart with more promises of the future, more promises of himself...and then stole away into indefinite neglect. Finally, she decided she could no longer take the silence and she reached through the void in attempt to touch his heart. Perhaps he had gotten lost and it was her duty as the one who loved him to show him the way that would lead her back to him.

So, she sat down to write out her heart in the only way she knew how.

"For the first time in my life, I fully understand what it truly means to FEEL your heart.
But what am I to do when every time my heart breaks to feel you?
It's like subtle abuse when your words draw me closer, an actual feeling of a physical pulling at my heart, but when I look around, you're nowhere to be found.
Those precious words I would have given anything to hear a year ago, now falling so heavily,
I'm buried beneath them,
unable to move, unable to breathe,
for the fear that even the slightest sound would forever reverse this magic as once before.
But a heart can't live on love letters alone.
These written words of love you now so readily confess, so sweet, but bitter at the same time,

129

because these are just words...
and not YOU.
Sometimes I wake up in the middle of the night, my heart so heavy,
it's as if you're standing in the same room,
and each time I feel you slipping away,
it only makes me grow more bitter at your undelivered promises,
as if you're saying, 'I love you, just not enough to be with you'.
So, I looked for your promises to become reality,
but in your place, I found a false name with a false face.
So easy to confess what you say you feel with a turned back.
Too afraid to face the one you say you love, so you choose a facade to hide behind
and once again,
you leave me with an overwhelming feeling of emptiness...
and loss...
and an unbearable weight on my heart that tells me without a doubt,
it's you.
The reverie subsides, now anger in its place when I realize
these precious words are just WORDS
until you decide to come to me and tell me to my face."

"That was beautiful...hello, my love." It was him.

"Don't even bother...Why do you keep doing this? Why do you keep pouring out your heart and then leaving?"

"I'm sorry, Eva."

"No, seriously. I want to know. What is going on?"

"Eva, it's a very delicate situation. I can't tell you what it is, but I am asking you to please trust me. I know you don't understand, but you will soon."

"I don't know how much longer I can do this."

"I will make it up to you, baby...I swear."

"Look, this isn't right. You're in a relationship. You have a girlfriend. I can't keep going through this back and forth. I don't think we should talk to each other anymore until things have changed."

"No, Eva, please...I need you. Please don't go...please. You're the only bright spot in my life. You're the only thing I have to live for...to FIGHT for!"

"But that's just it! You're not fighting for me. You're treating me like I'm disposable. I know you don't want distance between us, and you want us to be together, but this is the only way.

Let me tell you about something that happened with some friends of mine...my friend met the man of her dreams while she was going through her divorce from a very abusive man. Although it was difficult, they decided it was best that they stop communicating with each other until the divorce was final. They knew that God would honor their desire to do the right thing. They waited a year, they didn't talk, they didn't even see each other. They didn't come back together until they were free to do so. And they finally did, their union was bonded stronger than they ever could have imagined. Now they are married, happy, and more in love than ever."

"Wow."

"So...what do you think?"

"I think it sounds like an amazing story."

"Don't you think it will be worth it to do the right thing...do this the right way? Think of how much more special it will be."

"I don't want to lose you, Eva."

"But we can't keep doing it this way, either."

"Eva..."

"I know...please...just go...If we are truly meant to be together...it will happen. But we can't keep doing it this way. You know that...It isn't right...for you...me...or for her."

"I can't stand the thought of not talking to you. Please don't walk away,

Eva. Please stay... I promise you; it will be soon and then we can finally be together."

"How long do you think it will be? We've already been at this for over a year."
"I promise you; it won't be a year. It will be much sooner than that."

"Okay, so how long then? 3 months? 6 months?"

"Eva...I just don't know...and I can't tell you why. I'm sorry."

Eva paused. *"Alright...then I have to go...I can't keep doing this."*

"Eva...please...don't go...I need you."

"One month...we'll know by then."

"I'm going to miss you terribly."

"We have to. I'm sorry...Goodbye."

"Goodbye, my heart...I will come for you soon...I promise."

Eva turned her phone off, crawled into bed, pulled the covers over her head, and let the warm salt of her tears lull her to sleep.

***

A day passed...nothing. Two days passed...still nothing.
Eva was struggling with the absence of his presence through their conversations, but she knew she had to stick to her guns. If he didn't already have a girlfriend, the situation would have been so much easier, but the communicating behind this person's back...Eva knew it wasn't right. She knew that if the situation were reversed, she wouldn't want her boyfriend talking to someone else without her knowledge. She didn't want to touch the situation anymore until he figured out what he wanted, and she didn't want to be the reason for someone else's broken heart. If he was going to make a decision, it had to be his own and not coerced by her.

On the third day, he broke the silence between them.

"I can't stand this!"
Eva sighed as she felt her heart pulled towards him, aching. She felt the very same way he did. Her innate desire was to comfort him, but she knew if she coddled him now, he would never take her seriously. *No... he'll never respect me if I don't stick to my guns.*

She kept her response short. *"Have things changed?"*
"No."
"Then whether it's difficult or not, this is the way it has to be until they do."
"It's not fair! I don't want to be ripped from my baby's arms!"

Eva felt the familiar draw of her heart, but she resisted. *"Look, you have a choice in this. You're not married. If you truly want to be with me and you know that I'm the one, please...come to me."*

"But, Eva, I don't have a choice. It's completely out of my hands. I love you. I need you. I miss you."

"And neither do I have a choice. What I said before still goes. I'm sorry."

15 SEASONS CHANGE

The warm-toned autumn leaves had begun to fall once more. This was Eva's favorite time of year in the city. She would spend hours wandering aimlessly through the park, taking in the vibrant fall foliage bursting all around her- yellows, oranges, and reds. Eva had taken to the park this day to capture the colors on camera.

The loss of her job at *Highline* had found her freelancing her photography skills around the city and although she was enjoying her freedom from the corporate world, it was not enough to make ends meet and Eva was struggling to survive.

As she clicked, couples of all ages passed her by...youth...midlife...senior. She watched as they held hands, the men whispering sweet nothings into their lovers' ears. The giggles. The feeding bites of pretzels to one another. The ice cream nose smudges. Men: clean cut and clean pressed, ready to impress their ladies. Women; adorably robed, perfectly coiffed and gorgeously adorned; the blush of new love on their rosy cheeks.

Eva had long since left her makeup in the drawer of her bathroom cabinet. Her hair once wavy and flowing, now messy and kept pulled up on the crown of her head. No longer did see the point in taking extra care of herself with no one around to pamper herself her for. She had lost her job, her love, and now herself...or what was left of her. Her piecemeal heart had become numb, and she hid behind her armor of the layers of sweatpants and hoodies... feeling unwanted, undesired, unloved...always not good enough. And the carrot Mr. Man had been dangling in front of her face was turning more and more rotten as time progressed with no hint of re-connection. And she had been mourning that death for nearly a month.

As she watched the lovers' banter, she could feel her longing begin to rebirth...the ache she felt deep inside. She wanted so badly for Alex and her life to start together. Eva could no longer take the parade of other people's happiness blossoming before her. She put her camera away and headed for the subway. Half of her craved him, the other half wanting him to be the first to make the first move; to truly pursue her the way she had dreamed about...the way he had promised her. She wanted to be angry at him, but her heart...her heart.

Would he come back? Or had he succumbed to the pressure of his relationship and committed out of fear to something that he did not want to commit to? There could only be one explanation for his fear of leaving someone Eva had not known existed while they were together.

She must be pregnant, Eva pondered...*that has to be it.*

Eva could not take the wait any longer. She had to know the truth. She knew she would be kicking herself for breaking her own resolve, but the thoughts of "what if?" plagued her mind. She could never live with herself if it came to be that they did not find each other again because of her own stubbornness. True to form, Eva once again took the entire blame upon herself. She felt terrible for abandoning him when he needed her the most, when he'd begged her not to go. Although, she couldn't see the irony that he had done the same to her on a sidewalk not so long ago.

"Hi...I just want to know...if everything is okay."

"Eva...I am so sorry. I have decided to stay in my current relationship. Please forgive me."

Eva's heart plummeted to her stomach. Her breath increased, as she struggled to find the words. *"What?! Why?"*

"I'm sorry, Eva...I have to."

"But...why? You promised me! You promised me!"

Eva felt a frustration that she had never before felt in her life. Inside she was yelling, gasping, grasping and desperate; her only outlet, a screen. No one to plead with, no one to listen to her physically speak her pain. Eva felt as though she was in bondage, limited to text on a tiny electronic display. Without him there right in front of her to actually speak with, Eva felt as though she would explode with emotion...all of the pain, rejection, anger, disbelief. The very thing she had feared was now a reality and she could not believe that she had allowed him to do this to her again.

"No! There must be something else wrong...I know you still love me. I know that you want to be with me!"

"I can't, Eva, I'm sorry."

"What do you mean you can't? You had no problem stringing me along for a year! Why don't you just admit it? She's pregnant isn't she? That's why you think you have to stay with her!"

He didn't respond.

"Please don't do this...please. We love each other. You promised."

Still nothing.

Eva was desperate, shaking her head in disbelief at nothing, no one to hear her scream in her head, but her own tortured soul. She waited a day...nothing. Another day...still nothing. Meanwhile, she showered him with love and encouragement in the hopes that something would speak to him.

"Listen, you don't have to do this...you don't have to stay with her just because she's pregnant. I know you're probably getting pressured from both of your families, but that's no reason to get married. Two wrongs don't make a right. Please don't do something we'll both regret! Please, I love you. It's killing me, but it doesn't matter. I would love you and love your child just like it was my very own. You don't have to be afraid. We will get through this together."

The cold silence was beginning to speak louder to her than any of the deeply affectionate words he had showered on her before.

"Please say something."

Silence.

"Please don't be ashamed...I know it's not an ideal situation, but we can work through this together."

More silence.

Eva could feel her future slipping out of her hands. She felt desperate to fix the situation, but without knowing where he was or being there in person, there was nothing she could do. She felt helpless, her heart racing. She had to stop it. She had to do something to make the pain stop. She ran out of her apartment and out onto the street, searching for something, anything that would take her pain away.

***

That night in her darkened apartment, Eva found herself numb with grief

136

on the cold tile of her bathroom floor. She didn't understand how he could have been so careless; how he could have given himself physically to someone else if he loved her as much as he'd said he did, and she hated her own virtue even more because of it. It was the one thing she would not give outside of commitment. She also knew him well enough to know that he was the kind of man that would take responsibility for a mess that he made even if it meant giving up his own happiness. And if there was a baby involved, he would never let it suffer for his own carelessness. He would sacrifice Eva for the sake of doing what he thought was the right thing.

But Eva couldn't imagine a future without him. He had painted her own life as their life together. He'd given her story after story of their future as he saw it in his eyes. He'd told her that she was made for him and that he was made to love her. He'd taken her so deep into his heart that she was far too gone to climb out. She'd dropped all emotional defenses and jumped in willingly after he'd broken down her walls. There was no future without him. It simply did not exist. Eva had come to the end of herself. Without him, the man who knew her seemingly better than she knew herself - the man who seemed to move with her breath - there was nowhere else to turn.

Out of desperation, she turned to the one thing that she thought could help her, not because she trusted it, not because she believed in it, but because she thought it was something she needed to please in order to be happy. *It's my fault. I know it's my fault that You're holding out on me, God. I've never been able to please You before and now I'm paying the price.* Eva put her forehead to the cold tile floor as the tears flowed from her eyes and let everything go, all of the pain, all of the heartache; she let it drain out of her body and splash onto the porcelain tile beneath her.

"God...please...if You're there...if You truly exist...please...show me the answer to this. I don't want to be in chains anymore. I don't want to cry anymore. God, I promise you...if You help me with this...I will follow You...I will give my life to You...I will devote myself to You. Please, God...please help me!"

Eva had no idea where the words had come from. They were definitely not her own as she wouldn't have even thought to pray in such a way. But they flowed from her lips as easily as breathing, almost as if they were being spoken for her. She didn't even know what they meant or what the weight of what she spoke would look like. She knew only one thing - it was her final hope: her last ditch effort. She didn't know this God very well at all, but she knew enough to know that if she were to get any answers at all - any peace at all - she had nothing left to lose.

***

The next morning, as if by clockwork, Eva awoke to a new message. It was from her mystery not-to-mystery man.

"I've given this a lot of thought...and it's not just that I've decided to stay in my relationship, it's more than that... I realized that I don't love you. If I did, I would have to come to you by now. I'm sorry, Eva."

There it was. In all honesty, it was the answer she'd prayed for, but Eva was livid. All of the suffering he had put her through, the waiting, the promises, the stories, the declarations of irreversible adoration...for what? She had given him her heart and soul. She had waited for him because she'd believed somehow, some way, they would come together in the end.
She wanted to yell, but the glass screen between them left little room for human sound.

"What do you mean you don't love me?... How can you say that to me now? You've been describing the depth of your love to me for years now. I felt it. I feel it. I know that's not true."
"I'm sorry, Eva...I don't."
"But...you told me...we were made for each other..."
"Yeah, well...maybe I was wrong."
"If you're saying that now, then you never loved me. There's no way you could have ever loved me and be able to do this to us. And since you won't admit who you are, you get to conveniently and easily disappear again and leave me by myself to pick up the pieces."
"Wait a minute, who ever said this was easy?"
"You just said, you don't love me. Why would it be difficult for you if you don't love me?"
"I'm sorry, Eva, I have no choice. I have to go."
"No... you THINK you don't have a choice."
"Eva, you don't even know who I am. I'm sorry. This is not how I was planning on it turning out."
"Oh, we're still playing the 'I'm a mystery man' game?? Okay, fine. Whatever. Yeah, you're sorry. That's all I ever hear from you is how sorry you

are. Well, guess what, I'm sorry, too. I'm sorry I ever allowed this in the first place. And now you can give me back every intimate word I ever spoke to you because they don't belong to you. And someday you get to watch me walk down the aisle to marry the real man of my dreams. And I hope it kills you. I don't EVER want to hear from you again! You are DEAD to me! Don't ever contact me again!"

Eva threw her phone onto the couch, the silk cushions saving it from the force of the blow. She was absolutely furious...and completely devastated. But despite the pain, she felt a strange hope that she couldn't explain, like a bittersweetness she'd never known before. She remembered the night before and how she had made a plea to a God she did not know. Now that her prayer had been answered, she could not deny the *way* in which her answer was brought about, even though it was a far cry from the answer she had hoped for. That it was a direct answer to her prayer on the floor just the night before. Nor could she deny this new feeling warming the inside of her...hope where she should have felt despair. Eva didn't understand it, but she knew it was from someplace deeper. And for the first time in a very long time...

...she finally felt free. Free from his lies. Free from his grip.

***

"Well," Eva said aloud, "here goes nothing."

She took a deep breath and kneeled on the hardwood floor of her apartment. *Guess it's time to make good on my end of the bargain.* At first, she wasn't sure how this should go. She turned towards her couch and clasped her hands on the seat in front of her. *No. Too formal.*

She turned around and knelt in front of the coffee table but shook her head and stood up. *No. What am I, having coffee with Jesus? Seriously.*

Finally, Eva decided to go back to the very spot she had made her vow in the first place. She walked into her bathroom, turned on the light and sat down on her big fluffy bathmat. *Much better.* And she began to do something that she had never done before.

"God...thank you. Thank you so much for answering my prayer! Now I know you are real. And I meant what I said. I will follow you. I don't know how or what that should look like, but I'm ready. Will you please show me? I don't even know where to start. Will you help me?"

Eva sat for a minute and waited as if expecting some cosmic voice from above to answer. *Well...now what?* She wanted to make good on her promise, but she just didn't know how.

***

"Oh, Evie. Thank *God*! I am soooo glad you finally got rid of that guy! I have been so worried about you. I am seriously relieved."

"Me, too!" Kate heard Collin yell in the background.

"Never mind my silly husband. We've both been praying for you about this for an eternity."

Eva laughed, "Hey, no worries. I know I've been a mess lately. I'm sure you'll be glad to have something else to talk about for a change."

"So," Kate started, "what are you going to do now?"

"Well...," Eva hesitated. "That's actually what I wanted to talk to you about. I have no idea. I mean, how do you even follow God? I mean how do you *really* follow God? What does that even mean? I prayed that after this was all said and done that I would give my life to Him. The thing is I have absolutely no earthly clue how to do that."

"Well, it's simple really. To follow Him is to be like him in every way."

"Um, Okay...but how do I do that...what do I pray for?"

"You can pray for wisdom and start reading your Bible...lots of good stuff in there."

Eva knew exactly where her Bible was...on the shelf collecting dust. "Yeah...I guess that's a good idea."

"Evie, I'm truly sorry this happened to you, but now when the real guy comes along. You won't fall for the same things you fell for before. You'll know the difference. You'll know that it's right."

As Eva listened to Kate, she began to wonder if there was more to life than finding love...that maybe love was not at all the same as what she believed it was. Maybe instead of another human mending her, she was about to embark on a healing process that could only come from something supernatural. And, maybe, no human touch could even come close to the heavenly salve that could mend her broken places.

16 COME AGAIN?

The pale-yellow veil of the glowing sheer sunlight infiltrated the bedroom. Eva awoke from the best sleep she had experienced since she had been involved with Alex; refreshed, and actually rested. The dark circles under her eyes from endless sleepless nights of worry were finally beginning to dissipate. She felt free, like she could breathe. Her life was finally hers again; no longer controlled by emails, text, and time. As much as she had loved him, she couldn't imagine spending any more time in the prison that had become so comfortable to her in the past year. This was the first day of the rest of her life. The possibilities of the fresh new start were so endless.

Eva had lived her life for this man all of this time, she could not even remember what it was like to live her days for herself. Still, she knew she had to make good on the promises she had made during the plea that had ultimately freed her.

Kate's advice echoed in her mind. Something deep within her stirred...a voice she had never heard before...soft, yet firm...it even sounded like her; an older, calmer, more mature version of herself.

Eva...how can you trust someone if you don't know who they are?

Eva knew this voice...it wasn't coming just from her own mind...it was originating from somewhere deeper...

It spoke again. *You can't trust Me if you don't know who I am.*

Eva slid from the comfort of her bed and started getting ready for the day...she knew what she had to do.

***

Binders Bookstore had a personality all of its own. Eva loved the smell of the freshly printed paper and coffee brewing upstairs in Perks, the café sitting area. This was not her first rendezvous with the store. She had perused the paperback-lined aisles many times over the years...fiction, journals, fun little knickknacks. But this morning, her morning mission was quite different.

She took the escalator to the second floor and looked around. *Hmm...Food...Self-Help...there it is!* Eva made her way over to the spiritual section of the upstairs and stood in front of the selection. *So many authors, so many topics...* Eva had no idea that so much variety could be found in this genre of writing.

She looked around and noticed right away the groups of people gathered around the other sections of the store, but the corner she was currently occupying...empty. *Well, at least I'll be able to search in private without anyone knowing that I don't know what the heck to look for...or what the heck I'm even doing for that matter!*

Eva ran her hand slowly over the spines, hoping one would speak to her. *Let's see...Following Him With Your Entire Heart? That looks good.* Eva took it off the shelf. *'Character Restructure'? Definitely need that!* She took another. *Channeling your inner Chef Daniel? Umm, no....Hmmm. Ooh...'Life's Simple Guide to Him'? I'm sure it's anything BUT simple*, Eva smirked to herself. *Still...better start SOME -where.* Eva took it off the shelf and added it to her growing pile. *'Battling the Mind'? Yes, please! 'Ooh, The Secret Power of Speaking Out Loud'!* Eva grabbed her final selection and balanced it her arms with the mountain of books.

Arms full and heart hopeful, Eva began to head downstairs and check out. She couldn't wait to get home and begin her new subject study. Then she spotted it...

'Learning His Heart'? I guess one more couldn't hurt.

***

Once inside her oasis of a home and out of the early October cool air, Eva took off her coat, set her kettle on the stove, and laid her purchases out on her glass kitchen table.

Okay, maybe I overdid it just a little. Where do I start? She picked up *Learning His Heart* and flipped through. It covered the attributes of the spirit and aligned them with real life. *Looks like a good place to start. Well...here goes nothing.*

Eva was amazed as she read. She couldn't believe this was the same God she had learned about growing up. Her god was cold, domineering, and authoritarian, but this God was so foreign to her...compassionate, caring. He had fears just like hers. He had feelings and emotion. Eva felt as though a veil had been lifted; that she was truly learning who God was for the first time in her life.

Why hasn't anyone told me about Him like this before? Eva couldn't believe this God was the same God she'd been hearing about all along. This God held promises she had never known before and Eva began to feel something she had not felt in a long time, something that had evaded her for her entire life up until now. It was a new four-letter word to Eva, only this one wasn't profane...it was hope.

Eva's face shown with the wonder of a child discovering something new as she devoured the teachings. She took another book, and raced through the first chapter, which opened her eyes even more. Who was this strange God who said failure was okay? That she didn't have to be perfect? That she didn't have to kill herself to achieve her dreams or even her daily tasks...even something as simple as letting the dishes go until the next day.

No, this God was not a punishing God. This God understood when she faltered. He picked her up when she fell. And His only requirement was a heart sold out to Him.

Eva began to realize that still small voice she had heard that morning was God wanting to open her eyes to the true things of Him, to break the preconceived religious chains of her past and upbringing. This God was about relationship, and He was drawing her into a new covenant with Him, a covenant that would heal her broken heart and rewrite her future. He had plans for her and they were good. No longer was she destined to a life of depression and hopelessness. No longer did she have to depend on a dream man to make her happy. No... God will fulfill the deepest desires of her heart. And it would not be driven by performance. In fact, it was nothing that would happen based solely on what she did or didn't do. In other words, she couldn't control it. He Himself would see it through to the finish because He Himself was writing the story.

And so, she began to write; a letter to Him - her hopes, her dreams, her fears, her doubts...everything. She bared her heart and soul to Him the way she had to Alex. And that starry night down by the reservoir, she placed them in the water to lay them at His feet; an offering that would begin a dance more beautifully than anything she could ever imagine.

***

"Hiya, Love!" Olivia exclaimed as she gave Eva a bear hug.

"Greetings, my favorite Aussie!" Eva replied.

Eva's friend Olivia was a born and bred Sidney native who had relocated to the states to pursue her dreams of becoming a famous artist. She'd started in L.A., then D.C., and had finally settled in New York City. Eva had met Olivia just shortly after her own move to New York.

Exploring everything the city had to offer and her more creative side, Eva had happened upon an art exhibit in Chelsea where Olivia was the featured artist that week. The two had become fast friends as they talked with each other about their shared artistic interests.

Olivia spoke in a very proper Australian accent and Eva would often ask her to say random words just to listen to her talk; a running joke between the two that had marked their sisterly bond. Olivia was a character to say the least; an undercover private investigator on the side - for the heck of it, as she said - and she only drank her whiskey neat. She would refuse to drink any, but one kind of whiskey and it was incongruously expensive, something that Eva found exceptionally funny when they would go for a night on the town.

"So, listen, darling," Olivia started in her fluid speech. "Now that we've got you away from that dreadful institution that pathetically calls itself a magazine, we can get on to more pressing matters. You know I've been dying to get our little creative heads together to steal some of that artistic magic you've got floating around in that head of yours. What do you say, darling? A little collab-o?"

"Well, of *course*!" Eva teased her friend. "But, hey Liv, I mean, are you sure you want to work with someone who got the can? Aren't you afraid it'll tarnish your reputation?" Eva grinned for the first time in months.

"Listen, darling, pain is art. And we can thank those evil bastards for improving your craft."

Eva laughed. "Well, in that case...it's on!"

***

Winter had engulfed Manhattan in the crystal white of yet another snowstorm. Christmas was fast approaching, and Eva was working tirelessly with Olivia to get the final pieces ready for the show that would launch early that coming spring - "Whither(ing) Rubbish: The Dysfunction of Change," they had decided to call it. Eva was rushing through the tourist-infested crowd, otherwise known as, 'Christmas in NYC enthusiasts', to drop off their work at the framers when her phone buzzed. Eva shifted her bag full of their masterpieces and reached into her pocket. *It's probably Liv calling to see how it's coming.* Eva opened her messages and immediately froze in the middle of the sidewalk.

"Merry Christmas, Eva...I still love and miss you terribly."

***

Eva had to restrain herself from throwing her phone into the snow piled high on the curb in front of her. *Oh, no. I don't think so. Who the hell does he think he is anyway? I'm finally okay. It took me months to be this okay. The last thing I need is more drama. I'm definitely not falling back into this again!*

Eva went to put her phone back in her pocket. *Wait, no, I'm calling his crap on this one. He can't just think he can get away with coming and going in and out of my life like this...especially after that last disaster of a conversation.*

"I thought you said you didn't love me."

"I could never stop loving you. I think that would be impossible."

Eva was irritated. Here come his games again. "Then why in the hell did you say that??"

"I thought it would be easier."

"You thought it would be... 'easier'? Are you kidding me? Easier for who? For me? Or for your own selfish ass?"

"I'm sorry, baby. I know I hurt you."

Eva felt her heart soften against her will as she slowed her brisk pace. He had been the first guy ever to use that term of endearment with her and once upon a time, it made her feel like heaven, like she belonged to someone. But she fought her feelings and fought to stand her much painfully earned new ground of freedom. *No, I'm not going to let him do this to me again.*

"*Look, I'm not a damn toy. You can't just keep me in your pocket until you're bored and then pull me out whenever you feel like it.*"

"*I know you're not a toy, Eva. I don't want to keep you in my pocket. No... where I want you...is much closer. I want you in my arms. Every movement... every breath.*"

Eva was embarrassed to have heard herself sigh softly at his sentiment then caught herself. *No, Eva, stop*, she commanded herself shaking her head as if to shake him right out of it. *You can't let him do this to you again.*

"*No! I won't let you do this to me again. This whole façade is over between us.*"

"*Eva...please...I haven't given up hope on us yet. Please don't you do the same. I still want you. I still need you.*"

"*Oh, yeah? Well, what about before? You practically told me you wanted nothing to do with me, remember?*"

"*I love you, Eva. I've always loved you. You are the love of my life.*"

Eva fought her inner turmoil hard to stand firm and not fall into his clutches again, but she still couldn't deny after all of her progress that she loved him. He was the one her heart and body had responded to even though they had only shared their love through text. She remembered the depth of what they'd shared. The way he'd spoken to her heart in a way that no one else had ever reached. The way he'd known her soul. She had been his and he had been hers...as if they were one person. Eva couldn't fight it anymore. She felt the walls between them disintegrate and the structure of her heart completely melt.

"*Then why did you push me away?*"

"*I don't know...I only know that I can't live without you. I've tried. It hasn't worked. And I'd be willing to bet...you still feel the same, too.*"

146

Eva's heart felt as if it were pulling in two different directions; one wanted to run to him and the other towards her new life free of the pain of waiting for him to decide if she was worthy enough for him to come forward. She did not want to let this man in again to give him another chance to destroy her.

"Yes...I do...I can't deny it...but...I can't do it this way. You can't keep doing this to me. You've got to come forward. You've got to make this real if those are truly your intentions."

"Is it too late?"

"...I don't know."

"What can I do?"

"What can you do...? Really? What do you think you can do?"

"I don't know."

Eva felt the familiar frustration begin to rise within her. *"Okay...so here we are right back where we freaking left off. And what you can do is stop hiding behind this damn phone and come to me and prove yourself! That's what you can do. Until then, I'm done with this conversation."*

"Eva, wait! I'm trying. Please don't go!"

"No, I'm sick and tired of this. I'm done begging you to come to me and I'm done explaining to you the obvious. You figure it out."

***

"You mean you can't find anything?"

"Sorry, darling. Not even so much as a telephone number." Olivia had scoured her undercover resources for any information she could find on the anonymous email address. "Usually, I can find something, but this time, nada. It's the strangest thing."

Eva frowned her disappointment. "So, what do you think of all this?"

"What do I think? I'll tell you what I think...it's just lip service, darling. I don't believe he has any intentions of making good on his promise. It is pretty odd, though. The whole situation. I mean, why come to you now like this through damn email, when he had you in his literal arms? Makes no sense to me. Love or no love, baby daddy or no baby daddy, he just seems like a scared little boy to me."

Eva sighed and pursed her lips.

"So, there you have it. But never you mind your pretty little American head about it. If he's this good at hiding, that means he's this good at deception. Make haste in the opposite direction, darling, and tell him to get on his bike. Quickly.

By the way, have you dropped off the goods yet? I can't wait to see how they turned out!" Olivia was referring to their freshly printed artwork that had been Eva's duty to take to the framers.

"Oh, yes! Just this morning," Eva replied with enthusiasm.

"Wonderful news! Now how should we celebrate? Roo? No. I know just the thing! Whiskey, darling?"

Eva laughed. Liv and her drinking habits were so predictable. "No, I really need to get home."

"Home? At this early of an hour? Rubbish! What wondrous adventures await you at home?"

"Liv?"

"Yeah, darling?"

"You don't really eat kangaroo, do you?"

"Well, of course, I do, darling. Why wouldn't I?"

Eva frowned at the thought. "But they're so cute! Poor little things."

"Ah, they've got plenty of 'em and believe me, they ain't little," Olivia didn't skip a beat. "Menace to the Australian highways they are. See you later, love." And with that she hopped down the street, full-on 'roo.

***

"It'll be different this time, Eva...I promise you. It's just that we aren't together in person right now for me to show you, but I'm coming for you soon."

"I've heard all of this before. And I'm seriously tired of your empty promises."

"Eva, I promise you when we are together, it won't be like this."

148

"I don't believe you. You promised me the world and then you left me. I don't know how I can ever believe you again."

"Baby...I wish we could just get away somewhere and talk everything out face to face. I want to take you away. Just you and me...alone. No one to interrupt us."

Eva was skittish for obvious reasons but had loved it before when he would tell her stories of what their future life would be like together. It made her feel secure, like his stories were locking down permanence in their relationship. She wanted to know what this one had to offer, but knew she had to fight it. She had made so much progress to heal in just a few short months that to let him shower her with a fantasy encounter was just like taking a shower to get clean and then putting dirty clothes right back on. But her curiosity got the best of her, as it so often did. And she wanted more.
"Where would we go?"

"The Islands, maybe. Or a cozy, snow lodge in Aspen. Just you and me in a private state-of-the-art pine cabin sitting by the fire, snuggling with hot cocoa, talking for hours."

Eva knew that travel came at no expense to Alex with his brother being the tycoon that he was, so it came as no surprise to her that he would choose such a lavish destination.

"If you are serious this time...and you really want to talk...Tell me when and we can go."

***

Eva's tender heart slipped slowly back into the despair that had previously held her captive. Mr. Man had once again promised to deliver and had once again disappeared, true to pattern. Each time he left and then came back, he would up the ante knowing that it was the only way she would respond after each disappearance. And it was exactly because his promises were new and more vivid each time, she believed him. She could not even fathom that he would make such serious promises if he did not intend keep them, even if they had to wait years in between them.
She wasn't ready to lose him again. After several failed attempts to get his

attention, she finally decided once again that she had had enough.

"It seems you are having trouble deciding how to move forward. So, let me help you with that decision. I'm taking myself out of the equation. Now you don't have to worry about it. Goodbye."

"See and that's the problem, Eva. You still don't trust me. How do you expect me to be comfortable enough to come forward unless you trust me? Can't you see? I'm afraid because you won't trust me. If you would just trust me, I would come to you." His answers seemed to come much quicker when Eva communicated finality.

"Whose fault is it that I don't trust you? Seriously! You've done nothing to prove yourself trustworthy. Fool me once, shame on you. Fool me twice, shame on me. I'm done with this. If you truly loved me, nothing would stand in your way. So, once again, I'm left empty-handed with this. Goodbye...please don't contact me again."

17 SPRING FORWARD

"Here, love. Space them like that."

Spring had sprung once again in the big city and Eva and Olivia were hard at work preparing for their big artistic debut that was just around the corner. The two had found a quaint little art studio in the heart of the Lower East Side, a white-walled, spacious storefront that set the perfect blank canvas for their creations. Olivia was showing Eva how to strategically hang the pieces in a way that would catch the eye.

"There, done!" Olivia stated with the final pound of the hammer to the nail in the wall. "Whew! Darling, I don't know about you, but I am absolutely famished." Olivia rested the back of her wrist dramatically on her forward to prove her point. "What's say we venture out for some Prefix, oui?"

Eva could hear her own stomach growling. "Yeah, that sounds great. Where do you want to go?"

"Darling, I've got just the place. Follow me!" Olivia grabbed her friend's hand and headed towards the door.

"Wait...they don't have 'roo, do they?" Eva gave Olivia a curious look, pulled back and pretended to be dragged along.

"Darling, don't be silly. They've got something much better than that...eel!"

Eva rolled her emerald eyes as she let her friend drag her towards the door and out to lunch. "I can hardly wait."

***

It was a beautiful spring day in the city. Winter had finally handed the baton over to warmer climates and the early spring sun cut through the still slightly crisp air, warming their faces as Eva and Olivia walked down the streets. Eva stopped dead in her tracks when they rounded the corner.

"What's the matter, love? The thought of eel giving you the heebie-jeebies? Not to worry, they've got cheeseburgers, too."

"No, that's not it." Eva's face drained of color, now pasty pale, as if she'd seen a ghost. "It's...this is his street."

"Who's street?"

"Him."

"What, that ignorant ass who calls himself a man?"

"His name is Alex. And he lives here. I can't walk down this street." Eva pulled her friend back.

"What, are you not allowed to walk down a street just because the man lives on it? That's ridiculous. Are you really going to let that guy control which streets you walk down in New York? Hell no! You walk down and you walk down proud, Eves. Now come on. Let's go. I'm too hungry to deal with this nonsense." Olivia pulled her friend towards the street.

Eva dug in her heels and held back. "No, Liv! Please, I can't. I don't want him to see me! I don't want him to think that I'm checking up on him!"

"Eva, what in the world is the matter with you? We're simply walking down the bloody street. How could he possibly think you're spying on him?"

"I just can't. Please understand!" Eva was terrified. The effects of the situation had been much more traumatic than she had realized. Although she had found facets of freedom, a new threat was beginning to uncover itself. Invisible ugly roots of fear had entwined themselves so deeply into her system and threatened to choke her lifeblood if she did not fight to break free.

"Eva, be reasonable. The restaurant is on the opposite corner. Are you truly suggesting that we walk all the way around the block when we could easily get there in 2 minutes by walking down *this* damn street?"

Eva was unreasonably panicked. It didn't take Olivia too long to realize her friend was serious. She sighed with sympathy. "Alright. Come on. Let's go," she said softly. "Eva...I had no idea how much this situation affected you. You can't even walk down the same street. Man, if I ever run into that guy..."

***

Back home in her apartment, Eva had just finished dressing for the evening. It was the first event in almost two years that gave Eva a reason to doll herself up. Only this time, she was not limited to the confines of conservative work attire. This time she could be herself, express herself. No longer was she required to fit the mold of the oppressive. She chose a little black satin pencil dress with a fluted back-hem and a plain white tank top, champagne-colored strappy heels and a black sequin sash tied around her waist. A tiered, beaded necklace and clutch purse and she was heading out the door when her phone rang suddenly.

"Oh, my gosh, if that's even him...," Eva said to herself as she rummaged through her purse to find her phone. Finally, she located it. "Hello? Oh. Hi, Dad. Listen, I'm just about to head out the -"

"Eva Rose, I need you to come home right away. It's your mother...she's very ill."

***

Eva's heart raced as she ran through the terminal, her carry-on trailing behind her. Living in the city had made her a pro at running in heels and with good reason. She had only enough time after her father called to pack a small carry-on, no time to change. She noticed the stares of others, no doubt questioning her very un-Virginia-like attire as she sprinted towards the pick-up area, where her father would be waited for her. She was just coming out of the airport to look for her father when her phone rang. Oh, good gracious, if this phone rings one more time, I'm seriously going to flush it down the toilet!

"Hello?!"

"Well, darling, I know it's fashionable and all to show up late to your own party, but two hours?" It was Olivia. "No offense, love, but where in the hell are you? I've got New York's finest critics up my bum asking me questions that I can't answer without you, and I need your expertise. Were you planning on coming or..."

"Oh, Liv, I'm so sorry!" Eva interrupted. "My Dad called right as I was about to walk out the door. I had to come home. I'm sorry, I was so busy packing to make my flight in time that I totally forgot to call you."

"...Darling, the party's in New York, not Virginia."

"It's my mother. She's sick."

"Oh...oh, dear. Oh, Eva I am terribly sorry. What's wrong?"

"I don't know. I just landed. I haven't seen my dad yet."

"Rats. Well, keep me posted, yeah? And don't you worry about things this end, love. Holding it down, ten-four. I'll fill you in when you get back."

"Thanks, Liv." Just then her father honked his horn to get her attention.

"Hey, I've got to go. That's my dad honking."

"Alright, well, take care of yourself. I'll see you when you get back in the city, yeah?"

"Yeah, I'll see you soon. Thanks, Liv."

Eva lifted her arm to shield her eyes from the blinding headlights emanating from the cars lined up to pick up their respective beloved travelers. She threw her bag in the back of her father's car, got in the passenger seat, and buckled her seat belt.

"You look...different," her father greeted her.

"Hello to you, too," Eva replied annoyed at his jest. "What's going on with Mom, is she okay?"

"You look like you're dressed up to go to some artsy disco prom or something. Where'd you get that belt?"

"Dad," Eva interjected, putting him back on subject. "Mom?"

"Oh, yeah, your mother. She's...well...you'll see. Let's go home first and get you comfortable and then I'll take you to see her."

"Take me to see her? What, isn't she home with you?"

"No, honey. She's not."

...

"Evalyn? Is that you?" Eva's mother strained her neck from her hospital bed to see her daughter.

"Hi, Mama." Eva stood in the doorway, her father behind her in the hall. "Go ahead, honey," he encouraged and gestured for her to walk in. Eva hesitated. The room was dark, and she barely recognized this frail woman who supposedly was meant to be her mother. *Mama was strong and round. This weak, stringy-haired woman is practically emaciated.* No, this was not the same woman Eva had known when she left home.

"You've changed, honey. Come here. Let me get a good look at you." She struggled to push herself up into a seated position but fell back from weakness.

Eva hurried through the door to help her. "Here, Mama. Let me help you."

"Ah, that's better." Her mother announced after Eva had helped her to sit up. She observed her daughter while Eva was still close. "Well, honey, you're just as pretty as the day you left. Prettier!" she enthused.

Eva held her stare for a moment before she stood up, quite taken aback. She wasn't used to such kind words from her mother. Harsh words filled with criticism had once attacked from a shrill voice, but there was a softness about her now, broken down by her weakness.

"Thanks, Mama." Eva replied softly, almost in a whisper.

"So, Daddy tells me you're doing real well out there in the big city. I'm sorry you had to miss your big show, honey."

"It's okay, Mama. There will be others." Eva sat down on the chair next to her mother's bed, her father stayed standing in the doorway.

"And it about boiled my blood to hear what they did to you at that magazine. Boy, if I wasn't sick, I'd have half a mind to go up there and read those boys the riot act, messin' with my daughter like that. Who do they think they are anyway? They're no better than you, Evalyn."

"Oh, mama, I know. It's okay, really. It worked out for the best really." Eva wasn't used to her mother being so supportive. It was so contrary to their normal relationship routine. The softness almost embarrassed Eva, as if her mother would suddenly come to and realize how pleasant she was being to her daughter and Eva would have to pay for that, too. Deflection would always soften her mother's anger. But there was no anger here first the first time that Eva could ever remember.

"And all over a good-for-nothing guy, too. Did you ever hear from him since that night he stood you up, honey?"

"Oh...no, mama." Eva shook her head quickly. She wasn't ready to tell her mother all that had transpired after that night, the emails, the texts, the promises, the disappearing acts. She feared that it would only fuel her mother's previous disapproval of her choices. Her mother had disapproved of almost everything Eva had done since she was an adolescent.

"You deserve better than all of that nonsense."

Eva gave a faint smile. *If only you knew.*

"Come. Come here." She waved her daughter over closer to her. Eva moved closer to her and kneeled down by the side of the bed.

"You know something, sweetheart?" Her mother asked, taking Eva's hand.

"What, mama?"

"I'm real proud of you."

Eva was shocked. "Oh, mama-"

"No, listen. I am," her mother interrupted. "I'm real proud of you. Not many people in our family could do what you've done. Movin' to the big city like you did and making a go of it. Not knowing anybody, not having yourself set up jobwise. Truth be told, I was not happy about it even in the least, terrified even. I didn't think you knew what you were getting yourself into. But the more

I saw that you were okay, the more I realized there was nothing to worry about. You did it. And I am very proud of you."

Eva let her tears flow, dripping onto the bedsheet in front of her. It was the first time she had ever heard her mother say she was proud of her - nothing could have meant more to her in that moment than those words.

"Thank you, Mama."

"Well, Eva Rose, we better go," her father spoke from the doorway. "I don't want to wear your mother out with all of this mushy stuff."

"You hush now, Frank. Can't I have a moment with my daughter?"

"Honey, it's getting late," Frank spoke softly to his wife. "You need all the rest you can get, so you can get your strength back up."

"He's right, Mama. We'll come back tomorrow. And maybe we can bring you some ice cream. Remember the ice cream parties we used to have when I was little?"

Her mother smiled as if she were remembering a time long passed. "Yes, sweetheart, I could never forget that."

Frank walked over and leaned down to give his wife a kiss. "Bye, sweetie. We'll see you tomorrow."

Eva was next. "Bye, Mama," she said as she leaned down to give her mother a kiss on the cheek.

"Bye, honey. I love you." she replied, giving her the biggest hug, she could muster although she was shaking from weakness. That broke Eva's heart.

"I love you, too, mama. We'll see you tomorrow, okay?"

"Evalyn Rose," her mother called to her just as she was about to walk out the door.

Eva stopped and turned, "Yes, mama?"

"I've missed you."

The corners of Eva's mouth slowly turned up into a smile. "I've missed you, too, Mama."

***

Back home, Eva sat down on her old canopy bed and looked around. Nothing much had changed about her old bedroom. The walls still painted pink, her former favored color, which she later had sworn off for all of eternity due to its "little girl" connotation. Old pictures and knick-knacks decorated every shelf, wall and corner. Her riding medals still hung from the post of her bed along with her black English riding hat. A glimpse of silver caught her eye; her tap shoes on the shelf where last she left them. *Now there's something I haven't seen in a while.* Eva stood up and walked over to get a closer look. A trophy, some pictures, dried corsage from her senior prom...all reminders of the former life she had tried so desperately to leave behind when she left to chase her dream.

"Was it worth it?"

Eva turned around to see her father standing in the doorway. "Huh?"

"Well, your mother wanted to clear out all your old stuff and turn this into a guest room, but I wouldn't let her. Didn't seem right giving up your room and all. How does it feel being home? Are you glad we kept it?"

"Oh, Dad, you know I don't care what you guys do with it. It's your house. I don't live here anymore anyway so what difference does it make?"

"Well, holidays and-"

"I can stay with friends," Eva interrupted.

"Yeah...I suppose you could."

"Dad, what is going on with Mom? And why didn't you tell me sooner that something was wrong?" It was true that they had their differences, but Eva did not like being kept in the dark over something so serious.

"Well, honey, I didn't want you to worry."

Eva gave a sarcastic laugh. "You didn't want me to worry? Are you kidding me? So, you call me up and demand that I come home immediately because my mother's sick and when I get here, she's skin and bones and you think that's not going to make me worry?!"

"I'm sorry, honey. Well, you just seem so busy and all. I honestly didn't think you'd come."

"Oh, don't even pull that card with me, Dad. You and Mom know that I love you. Going off to live my life and pursue my dreams has nothing to do with whether or not I care about you. What was I supposed to do, stay a kid forever? Stay here forever? People leave home all the time. It's the normal thing to do...It's the healthy thing to do. And you've got everyone thinking I'm some horrible daughter when it's not about them or you or anyone else...it's about creating a life...the same as you created one for yourself. Did anyone call you selfish then? I didn't do it for you or anyone else. I did it for myself. You don't see me going around criticizing anybody else for their life choices. You know why? Because I have a life. Maybe everybody else should get one, too. I don't give a crap what other people do with their lives."

"I'm sorry, honey."

"Yeah, a lot of people seem to be sorry lately." Eva replied shortly.

Frank had been looking at the floor with his hands in his pockets but looked up sharply with her last comment. "You okay, honey?"

Eva paused for a moment, fighting back the tears. Finally, she relented. "No, Dad...no I'm not."

"What is it?"

"Nothing, look I really don't want to get into it right now. I want to know what's wrong with Mom."

"Cancer." He blinked a few times blank-faced, as if he'd been preparing himself for this conversation and trained himself not to show emotion, lest it should trigger undue worry in his daughter.

Eva stared at her father dumbfounded.

"Yeah, we tried to fight it, but that darn sucker is a doozy. Real nasty, this one."

Eva closed her eyes. "Mama," she whispered. She opened her eyes and looked at her father. "How long have you known." It was a statement, not a question.

Her father shrugged his shoulders and scratched his head. "A while."

Eva shook her head, "And you said nothing...? How bad is it?"

Frank frowned at the floor, but Eva wouldn't let him escape the question. "Dad?" she asked, raising her voice. "How bad is it?"

"She doesn't have much longer, Eva Rose."

Eva wanted to shove the words back into his mouth the second he spoke them, but she let them sink in, feeling helpless to stop them.

"And keeping it from your mother has been damn near exhausting."

"Wait a minute. You mean you haven't *told* her yet?"

"What am I supposed to do, Eva Rose? Tell the woman who has become more positive than I've ever seen her in my life that she doesn't have a chance in hell? I can't do that to her. It'll kill her faster than this poison is."

Eva let out a deep breath, feeling the weight of the situation, unsure of how to respond.

"Look, I need you to come home."

"What?" Eva opened her mouth and shook her head in disbelief, but her father continued.

"I want to bring her here, so she can live out her last days in peace. I can't bear the thought of her dying in that cold, dark room. But I'm not going to be able to do it alone. I need you to help me."

"And what am I supposed to do, just give up my entire life to come back here to help you? Give up my dreams? Dad, you guys were always needing

158

help because you refused to do things for yourselves. Where were you when I needed your help? Now you want me to give up my life, too? I've got a life there now, and friends, and opportunity-"

"Eva, I know your mother and I have made some bad decisions. I know you have a life you've built all your own. But your grandparents aren't strong enough to help. You're my only hope."

"And you don't think she'll be suspicious and wonder why I'm here?"

"Well, we can tell her you got sick of the city and wanted a change of pace."

"Oh, great, so we're going to just keep lying to the woman?" Eva shook her head and muttered, "She'll never go for that. We don't have to manipulate her into a different plan."

"Please, Eva Rose. I realize what I'm asking you. But you have the rest of your life to live. Your mother only has a short time left and I want her to be comfortable and happy. Please, will you help me make that happen for her?"

Eva sighed. Although she had regained much of her emotional strength, she wasn't strong enough to go up against her father, especially in his moment of weakness.

"Alright, Dad...I'll help you."

***

The rain fell steadily that afternoon. A mist fell over the ground shrouding the gravestones in ethereal white. Eva stood in front of her mother's casket under her black umbrella, numb to the world. She stared at the intricate gilded detailing as if it were the only thing to look at. She was there, but not really. Her eyes fixed ahead of her, but not really taking it in. Her feet planted firmly, Eva's shock did not allow her to make even the slightest move, nor any facial expression other than blank. All she could hear was the pitter-patter of the soft late-spring rain falling on the soggy, spring-green ground around her.

No, she had not anticipated this. It was too soon. She could not have known that the first time she had seen her mother in almost two years, would also be her last.

"I'm sorry, Mama...I didn't want it to end like this," she whispered; a fresh, hot tear finally betraying the flint in her face as it rolled down her cheek.

"You know...your mother loved you, Eva Rose." Frank came up beside her and wrapped his arm around his daughter's shoulders.

"I know." Eva let herself rest her head on her Daddy's shoulder like a little

159

girl again. It felt good to let someone else hold her up for once.

"She didn't say it much, but she was real proud of you. She always wanted the best for you. I think she was starting to realize the importance of letting go, so that you could be free to blossom in your own right."

"I wish she could have seen..." Eva let her voice trail off.

Her father picked right up on the nuance. "I know...Well...I suppose we better get going."

Eva was reluctant to turn around as her father took hold of the umbrella and guided her away from her mother's final earthly resting place. Over her father's shoulder, her eyes held her mother's bronze-colored casket as she turned until they had turned away so far that she could no longer look back.

There out of the rainy mist came the drawn faces of her relatives, scowling as she and her father walked by. Eva heard the whispers.

"Surprised she could even make it in for her mother's funeral."

"Who does she think she is parading around like she's even still a part of this family?"

Eva knew the words were spoken out of ignorance, but they still pierced her heart. She had been the first to break out. The first of her family to leave her sleepy hometown and she had been met with blind resistance from the beginning. She peered out at them from underneath the umbrella, fighting her shame which had become so familiar to her now. *Hello, old friend.* Her father firmed his arm as he held her and gave the relatives a stern look as he and his daughter continued to their limo. "Don't you pay them any mind, Eva Rose. You know where that's coming from."

Eva knew. But the knowing did not help her to understand why lack of brave action in their own lives would require the expectation of her to give up on her own.

Suddenly, her phone went off. Eva was expecting to see a message from one of her friends. She had left word with her contacts in New York, and they would no-doubt be wondering how she was. She looked down at her phone.

It was him.

"Eva, I just want you to know how sorry I am to hear about your mother's passing. I wish I was there so I could hold you."

Eva ignored the message and turned her phone off.
No... not anymore.

***

The hot afternoon sun began to sear through the fog as the rain clouds dispersed. Eva sat on the front porch in an old yellow flowered sundress, sweet tea in hand. Buster, her old golden retriever, lay on the floor at her bare feet. Eva closed her eyes and leaned back in the rocker, breathing in the freshly dewed country air. It felt good to slow her pace for a change and forget about the hustle and bustle that no-doubt awaited her return in the big city.

Eva looked out over the rolling hills and remembered her childhood. Those carefree summer days running through the grassy fields. Her mother yelling at her for returning home in a dirty dress. "Honestly! You'd think I raised a pig, not a lady!" Eva always grimaced at her mother's disapproval; never, ever feeling that she could please her.

The black screen door creaked as her father came out to join her. He sat down in the rocker next to her and leaned down to give Buster a scratch behind the ear. Buster closed his eyes and gave an approving whimper. "Bet this is quite a different landscape from what you're used to...all that concrete and what-not."

Eva smiled at her dad and gave a little chuckle. "Yeah, well, this is definitely more nature than I'm used to. I'll tell you that much!"

"I know it's bittersweet for you."

Eva's smile turned to pain. She turned her face away hoping her father wouldn't notice.

"Eva Rose, don't hide from me. You know I can read you like a book."

Eva looked back at her dad, an almost helpless look in her eyes. "It's just a lot to take in, Dad," she said softly, "Memories...Mom...everything."

Frank let out a loud chuckle.

"Thanks, Dad...I'm glad somebody finds this amusing."

"No, no!" Frank swatted at the air as if it held the memories in plain sight, still chuckling. "I'm remembering that time when you were a little girl," He could hardly get the words out for the laughter. "And the neighbor boy chased you around on his horse and you ran and ran! Well, when you were almost to your grandparents' house, you climbed the fence and had to jump down. Well, you landed in a pile of manure so tall, it about came clear to your nose!" Frank was really roaring now. "I'll never forget the look on your mother's face when she saw you...new Easter dress and white sandals no-less! She made you stand outside and hosed you down with the garden hose! It was so cold, you screamed for about 30 minutes! I'm sure the neighbors must've thought we were switching the hell out of ya!"

Eva smirked at the memory. "Oh, yeah. Super fun."

"Oh, man, we had some good times. Those were the days." Frank looked off into the fields as he reminisced. He looked over at his daughter. "What are you thinking about Eva Rose?"

Eva took a deep breath in, not ready to come back down to reality. "I'm thinking about how I've got to trade in all this beautiful scenery in a couple of days for all that concrete and 'what-not'." She nudged her dad with her elbow.

"Well...what if you don't?"

Eva looked confused at her dad. "What do you mean?"

"I mean, what if you don't?"

Eva kept her eyes on him almost suspicious. "What do you mean, what if I don't?"

"I mean what if you stay?"

Eva sighed and looked back out over the fields. "Dad, Mom's...gone..." The words stuck in her throat. It pained her to say it, but also realizing it was the first time it had been spoken, solidifying the inevitable. "...there's no reason for me to stay here anymore."

"Eva, I just lost your mother. I'm not ready to be alone yet."

Here we go, more expectation.

"And you...perhaps it would do you good to have a break. Take the load off for a while. Losing your job and everything, you must be stressed out."

"Dad, there is no 'for a while'. The city doesn't wait. If I leave, I'd have to leave for good. What could I possibly do here?"

"Keep your old man company." He gave her a smile. "Eva, I'm alone now. You're all I've got left. And you know I'm not looking forward to cleaning out your mother's things. I'm not ready to face that alone. You could help me. Well...keep what you want. We'll get rid of the rest."

Get rid of the rest. Eva didn't like that last statement. She didn't like the idea that anyone could get rid of a person, which to her was what her mother's things represented.

"So, what do you say?"

162

18 SAYING GOODBYE

"Wait a minute...you're *leaving*?" Charlie's mouth hung open like he was catching a fish after the words left.

"Yeah."

"But...you just got back here!"

Eva smiled sweetly at her friend and shrugged her shoulders. "I have to go, Charlie. My father's expecting me."

"Well, you better hurry back. 'Cause summer will be here soon and all this ice cream ain't gonna eat itself, I'll tell ya that much." Charlie went to take a bite of his ice cream, but Eva hit his arm causing it to fly off of his spoon and splat into a creamy puddle on the ground as he tried to chase it with his tongue.

"Noooo, Charlie! Listen! I'm leaving... as in... I'm moving back home. I'm not coming back."

Charlie stared at her in disbelief. His face had completely dropped, all signs of jokester going with it. His eyes were full of confusion. "Are you serious?"

"Yes."

"But...why?" Charlie had to fight to hold back the tears. He didn't want to let her see just how deep his feelings truly were for her. He couldn't lose control in front of her. He was the one who was supposed to make her laugh, not cry. He didn't ever want to be responsible for that. He didn't ever want to be in the same category as Alex.

"Well...I just think it's time. I need a break. I lost my job, my mother just died, the whole thing with...Alex. I just...I just need some time away."

Charlie didn't say anything.

"And that's not to say I won't be back."

Charlie frowned and shook his head at the ground. "You're not coming back."

"What do you mean I'm not coming back? Sure, I'll come back. I just need a break, that's all."

"Eves...you're not coming back. You'll go back there, find some guy, get married, and squeeze out some babies. You're not coming back...I know it. And don't think it makes me happy in any way, shape, or form to say that." Charlie pointed his finger emphatically at that last point.

Eva gave an apologetic smile to her friend and rubbed his arm. "Well...I have no idea what's going to happen. It's not like it's goodbye. I'll still be back to visit."

Charlie turned and grabbed her hands. "You know something? You're right. We don't know what's going to happen. But we can 'not' know together! And I'm coming with you!"

"What? No! Charlie, you're not coming w-". But he had already cut her off with a kiss as he leaned in to stake his claim.

Eva pulled back and slapped him one, hard on the cheek.

"Owwwww!" Charlie's hand shot to his face, giving her a horrified look. "What did ya do that for!?" he exclaimed through a muffled cheek.

Eva glared at him. "Charlie, what in the hell are you doing?"

"What does it look like I'm doing? I'm kissing you! I'm kissing my woman! And I'm not letting you go without a fight!"

"Charlie," Eva gave him a look. "Listen to me like you've never listened to anyone before in your life. You need to catch this because you don't seem to get it...I am NOT your woman." The words came out of her mouth slowly and deliberately to prove her point.

Charlie felt his heart slip to the ground and turn into a black puddle. For the first time, since she'd known him, he'd let his sincerity show. His eyes narrowed in on hers with a softness she had never seen from him before. Before she could take back the last few seconds, she knew she had broken his heart.

"Eva...," he spoke softly, searching her emerald eyes. "I'm in love with you." His head shaking in disbelief as he searched her eyes. "I'll be everything to you. Anything you want."

"I know, Charlie." Eva softened. "But I can't love you back the way you want me to. You know that. I know it hurts you...but I just don't feel that way for you. I've always loved you as a friend...a brother.... but nothing more. I'm sorry."

Charlie let her hands slowly slip from his and stood up. He couldn't look at her.

Eva stood up and took him by his shoulders. "Charlie..."

He looked back over his shoulder at her almost disgusted. He knew this may be the last time he would ever see her.

"I do love you...and I will always be your friend."

Charlie sighed, rolled his eyes, and pulled her in for one of his signature bear hugs. "Come 'ere."

Eva held on tight as she whispered into his shoulder. "And that won't ever change."

***

"So, you're skippin' town, eh love? I thought as much."

Eva stood with Olivia in the center of what had been chaos just a few weeks before. Tags marked "Sold" hung off of their own framed masterpieces all around the studio proving that the opening exhibit had been a success.

Olivia sighed. "Well darling, it's a shame to let all that raw, beautiful talent go to waste just when you're getting started. You know, artists aren't supposed to disappear from fame until after they've kicked the proverbial bucket. Unless, of course, you're going for the eccentric route, which would be a good change for you, Darling. So, what are you going to do now?"

Eva crossed her arms and looked at the floor. "I don't know, Liv." She looked up at her friend. "I mean, I'm not really worried about it. All I know is that I need to do this. I need to be there for my father. He's not strong enough to handle this on his own. As for the rest of it, I have to trust that whatever is meant to happen will happen."

"You know, friend, I admire you. It takes a set to do what you are doing, to walk away from fame when you're right there at the threshold. It's brave. Your mama must have really been something and I have a feeling she would really be proud of you for doing this."

Eva crossed her arms and looked away towards the window, not wanting her friend to see the tears starting to form in her eyes.

"Don't you go hiding from your fabulous friend now." Olivia walked over to Eva and wrapped her arms around her friend. "You're a good person, Eva. Your heart is good, despite what you may think about yourself. What you're doing is noble. Don't let the monsters in there tell you otherwise." Olivia tenderly pointed to her friend's forehead. "They don't know what they're talking about anyways."

Olivia walked over to her bag and pulled out a paper check. "Now, you're going to need a little nest egg to get you started. I believe this will do quite nicely and then some." She walked back over to Eva, took her hand, and placed the check in it. "Your share of the spoils, Darling."

Eva looked down at her hand and her eyes went wide. "For real?"

Olivia laughed, "I know not bad, eh? I told you the show would be a smash! Now listen, you go back to your hometown, and you face this new chapter with fresh fervor."

Eva looked up at her friend. Knowing she was in a safe place, she finally let the tears flow. Everything that was built up inside finally spilled over, anger, pain, defeat. Olivia held her friend and just let her cry out her emotions; all of her pain, all of her fears, everything.

"I know, hon," Olivia said. "It'll be alright. Sometimes you just need to press the reset button. And you'll be all the better for it. Just don't you be a stranger now, you hear?"

Eva held her breath as the reality of the situation hit her. Tomorrow she would be boarding a plane, another one-way ticket this time, and she would leave this sparkling city behind not just for a visit, but for good. She sobbed and held on to her friend as if she were the last bit of New York that her eyes would ever behold.

***

Eva walked as slowly as she could down the twinkling tree-lined streets of upper-Manhattan one last time as twilight overtook the city. Tomorrow, she would be boarding a plane that would take her back to her former prison; and back to the place where her dream had born itself so many years ago.

Eva made her way through the city that evening almost strolling; stepping as lightly as she could for fear that if her feet fell too firmly, she would forever be glued to the pavement and to the dream that had shattered into a million pieces. No. If she stepped delicately, she could remain in her trance-like state and hold at bay the pain of the reality that loomed before her in just 12 short hours.

The twinkling lights that swirled around the trees that lined her neighborhood streets, the sharp contrast of stone versus tree where the buildings ended and the park began, the patios of cafes bustling with the activity of excited New Yorkers taking advantage of the warm almost-summer air to enjoy a fabulous outdoor meal with their friends; the excitement of it all.

Eva took it all in. The corner where she had first met Tony and her first true New York breakfast from a street cart; the corner deli which fueled her through many late working nights; the coffee shop which held her weekend reprieves...*burn it...burn it into memory so you don't forget.*

People whizzed by, but Eva seemed to be moving in slow motion. The city held such an energy, such a power; it had once given her the wings to fly, and she was absorbing every last bit as if to keep a reserve; not knowing when she would be back again...not knowing *if* she would be back again.

Eva stopped suddenly. Night had fallen hours ago. Her daze had led her, without realizing it, all the way to Central Park South on the West Side, where the fountain guarded the bottom-left corner of the park at Columbus Circle. She made her way over the walkway and sat down in front of the fountain, hugging her knees into her chest. Eva rested her head on her knees, sighed and looked up, gazing into the night sky glowing with a halo of electricity emanating from the concrete and steel below.

Then she spotted him...a tall dark figure watching her from across the street. Eva slowly sat upright and froze in astonishment. Was it really him? It had been years since she had seen him. Perhaps the passage of time had dulled her memory of his features. But she knew by the look, walk, and demeanor that it was definitely him.

Alex stood on the opposite street corner. On the traffic sign, an electric man lit up in white would soon lead him across the street in her direction. Eva looked at the light in expectancy and then back at him. His expression just as astonished as hers; slowly he lifted his hand towards her and opened his mouth ready to say something to her, but then stopped. He tried again, mouth open to call to her, but no sound came out. He ran his finger through his hair in frustration.

Eva's heart filled with compassion. Sensing his urgency, she stood up ready to go to him; not taking her eyes off of him. She hurried forward. *Dang it, my jacket!* She turned back to grab it.

When she turned back around, he was gone.

***

Rivulets streamed down Eva's face as she watched the jagged skyline of the island disappear into the pale pinkish-orange sky until it was finally engulfed in the early morning mist and out of sight. She felt imprisoned against her will as the plane took her further and further away from Manhattan. She remembered the night before and how Alex had appeared so unexpectedly after so much time and correspondence had passed between them. She remembered how once again, just as quickly as he had reappeared, he had disappeared again before she could be reunited with him. She didn't understand. And she was angry at God.

What was the purpose of all of this? Why did I have to see him? Why now when I'm leaving? Why did he run away again? Did I even really see him or was it only a piece of my imagination? Will I ever see him again? Will I ever see this city again?

For all of her former frustration, one glimpse of her former love's sorrow had erased all bitterness and she had been ready to make amends, until he vanished again, once more tearing a gaping hole in an already tender heart that was still healing. Eva realized that night that no strength of anger could erase her love for this man who had eluded her far too many times. She was captive and a willing prisoner. She never knew she could hate someone so much and love them so deeply at the same time. He was not in her life and yet, she could not imagine her life without him.

Her mind swirled with what-ifs...Was it too late? What would happen now that she was leaving? How could he come to her now if he didn't know where she was or that she had left? And why did he turn around and walk away when they were so close to reconciliation? And what was to come? What would the future bring? Would she ever truly know for sure that it was him who had written his love to her in so many emails and text messages? Or was it her worst fear...was it truly not him, but someone else? And imposter? The ramifications of that possibility were far too scary for her to consider too deeply. Because if it wasn't him...who the hell *was* it?

Finally, out of her own mental exhaustion, Eva fell asleep. She dreamt for the remainder of the flight that she was running, but from what she fled was not clear, running from something both behind her and ahead of her. No matter where she turned, she couldn't escape...pain of the past...fear of the future...all closing in on her. Ahead in the distance, God beckoned her gently, "Come, My love. It's time."

Eva cried out, "Time for what?"

Behind her, evil laughed in shrieks, "Turn around, you're a failure! You'll never make it! Who do you think you are anyway? You'll never get any further than your past! Why don't you just give up?"

...And Eva was caught in between; crying, frightened, and running. She didn't know this God well enough to be comforted by Him and evil's arrows were all too familiar.

Above her and all around, angels and demons were fighting for her for different purposes - the angels, to lead the way to new life - the demons, to pull her back, ready to attack should she trip and fall.

And Eva running, gasping for breath, and sobbing. Nowhere was she safe, her only escape to stay in motion...to run.

And she was always running.

Always.

19 NEW LEAF

Eva tossed the last of her stilettos into a pile in the corner of her closet with a final 'nope.' She'd spent most of the night unpacking the last of her clothes, making a point to sort through 'urban' and 'suburban'. Now that she was back home, she could relax herself and her style.

"And you," Eva picked up her camera and ran her hand slowly across the viewfinder as if to put it to sleep. "Guess I'll be saving you for a rainy day."

She carefully set her camera into its case, buckled it closed, and set it on a shelf in the corner. "Time for a new chapter," she sighed. She turned around just in time to see the sun rising over the rolling green hills through her bedroom window. Eva wrapped her faux fur bathrobe tighter around her shoulders, walked over to the window and leaned her temple against the window frame to take in the view.

"Eva Rose, you awake yet?" her father gently called through the door. Eva shuffled sleepily over to the door and opened it to see her father standing there with a fresh, hot cup of coffee. "Mornin', Sunshine. I thought you could use a little 'jo to help get you going your first morning back."

Eva reached out and took the cup, yawning. "Oh boy, Dad's special brew," she yawned, taking a sip. "Thanks, Dad."

"Yeah, I figured I'd be able to coax you out of that room with caffeine. It's not New York, but it can hold its own."

"Yeah, well yours is still the best, Dad." Eva gave him an appreciative smile.

"You flatter me, kiddo," Frank replied, rustling her already sleep-tousled hair. "Hey, listen, now that I got you to open the door, can I get you to put on a pair of shoes, too?"

"At 6:30 in the morning?"

"Got something I wanna show ya and it ain't here."

"Ah, Dad, can't I just relax for a while? I mean, I just got back. And I need some time to sort through everything."

"Honey, all that stuff will still be here when we get back."

"Well...not all of it is tangible...and I really don't feel like dragging it around with me to some mystery place this early in the morning."

"Trust me, Eva Rose, you're gonna want to see this...may even help you clear your mind."

"Okay, Dad...you win. I'm game."

Frank kissed her on the forehead. "Finish your coffee and meet me downstairs."

***

"Okay, kiddo, wait here." Frank ran up ahead to open the barn doors. "Oh, and close your eyes!" he called back. "And hold out your hand!"

Eva hesitated, but then closed her eyes...then it came...the reason she hadn't wanted to close her eyes...a flash-back...and the last time someone had asked her to close her eyes and asked for her hand...nighttime on the rocky shore in the middle of the bay...the stars and city lights throwing a thousand sparkles all around her...and her love...leaning in to kiss her. A single tear escaped the corner of her eye as she fought to kill her emotions.

The touch of warm, bristled fur against her outstretched hand broke the spell. Eva opened her eyes to see the most magnificent creature standing tall and strong in front of her. Shiny dark, tan coat, muscles rippling in the morning sun; beautiful long black mane, tail blowing in the breeze; and chocolate eyes.

Eva gasped as the horse whinnied softly and nuzzled its nose against her cheek.

Eva slowly reached up and placed her hands on either side of the equine's face. "Arabia!" she whispered, looking into the horse's eyes.

"No, Hon, it's not Arabia. But not a bad second if you ask me. Her name's Madonna."

"Madonna? Seriously, Dad?"

"Well, I thought an ode to your favorite recording artist might be nice."

"Wait a minute. She's for me?"

"Well, she sure ain't for me, I'll tell ya that much."

Eva gave him the biggest hug she could. "I think I'll call her Madge. Thanks, Dad!"

"Eh, it's nothing. I knew I'd have to find some way to keep you entertained, coming to the country from the big city and all. Now, I know it might take you two some time to warm up to each other, but-"

Eva had already climbed up onto the horse and was off; laughing as they galloped over the rolling green hills of her grandparents' old estate.

Frank smiled as he watched his daughter until the last bit of burnt auburn disappeared over the hills, lost in the joy that had for so long been a stranger to her.

"Or not!"

***

Eva walked the beaten path back home that evening. She made it back to the warm light of the porch just in time to see the pale blue fade into navy, the first of the evening stars twinkling their crystal faintly against the ombre sky. A steaming cup of black tea was waiting for her next to the swing along with Buster, who's tail promptly began to wag as he spotted her walking barefoot through the grass and up onto the porch.

"Hey, boy." Eva cooed to him and scratched his ear. She took the teacup and climbed up onto the swing, Buster jumping up alongside her. Eva stretched out long-ways on the swing, which Buster took as his queue to rest his chin on her feet.

"Well, buddy, guess we have some serious thinking to do, huh?" Buster looked up at her out of the corner of his eye with an inquisitive look, not moving from his spot. Eva reached down to scratch his soft furry ears. "But...," she paused to take a sip of tea, looking out over the night sky now brimming with shimmering stars, "I could get used to this quiet." Buster let out a contented sigh as if to answer her; simultaneously sending a light sneeze of puppy snot over her feet.

"Thanks, buddy."

The screen door opened with a creek. "I thought that was you." Her father walked over and sat down in the weathered rocker caddy-corner to where she was sitting.

"So, kiddo, how do you like your new muse? I'd venture to guess pretty well, since I'd hardly said two words before I turned around and you'd already high-tailed it outta there."

"I love her, Dad. She's great. Really. You knew it would make the transition easier."

"Yeah, funny...parents have a way of knowing those kinds of things. No matter how old their kids get. So, listen, tomorrow I was thinking we could start going through your mother's things. No sense in keeping that stuff around here anymore. Besides," he said looking down, "it's too hard lookin' at it every day. Like a constant reminder that your mother's not here. That she's...gone."

Eva furrowed her brow and looked at her father with compassion, realizing she could sense what he was feeling. "I know. Dad, I'm so sorry."

"Eva Rose, I want you to know how much I appreciate your coming back here. I know it wasn't easy for you."

Eva smiled and shrugged her shoulders, looking away as her forest-colored eyes brimmed with tears.

Frank reached over and took her hand. "You can't fool me kiddo. You put up a tough front, but you're just one giant heart on legs. Don't be afraid to let it out."

Eva turned her head towards her father, tears now falling. "It's just...a lot, Dad."

"I know, cupcake. It'll get easier...for you and for me." He leaned over to give her a peck on the forehead as he went to stand up. "Get some good sleep tonight. I know you hardly got any rest at all last night tinkering away up there. Exactly how many pairs of shoes do you own anyway?"

Eva gave her Dad a look before dismissing him, "Night, Dad."

"I'll leave the storm door open for ya." Frank walked into the house; the screen door swinging slowly shut behind him.

Eva watched her dad walk into the house, smiling sleepily after him and reached down once more to scratch Buster's ear again. "Well, Buster, looks like it's just you and me again." Buster let out another soft sigh and licked her hand as she laid her head back against the swing pillow and slowly drifted off to sleep in the fresh summer's night air.

***

"Ping!"
Eva awoke with a start at the sound of her phone. She rubbed her eyes

and sat upright, reaching for the phone on the little table next to the porch swing. *Dear Lord, who could it be at this hour?*

It was him. Once again, he had found a way to creep in just when she thought she was safe.

"Eva...I know you moved back home to Virginia...I will miss you terribly...but I want you to know that doesn't change the way I feel about you. I still love you. I still want you. I haven't given up on us. I will do whatever it takes to hold onto the hope of us. Nothing can change my love for you...no amount of distance can separate my heart from you...nothing. I love you, Eva."

Eva pursed her lips as she read the message. Her resolve was stronger than ever. *No... Not now. I'm not doing this again. It's over.* She turned off the phone and smiled proudly through closed lips at her new-found strength, almost a defiance. Never before had she rebelled against him. The rush of empowerment gave her a confidence she hadn't known in years. She turned her phone off and gave a contented sigh, letting herself fall softly back on the swing, slipping once more into blissful slumber.

No way am I going to let him do this to me again. No, this is going to be a whole new chapter...

***

"Needs some fixing up, but nothing a fresh coat of paint couldn't fix."
Eva and Kate walked up the brick path that cut through the yard to the very quaint looking structure ahead of them. A spontaneous adventure that morning through the winding country roads and rolling green hills had led the two friends into town and to a find that Eva couldn't refuse. She had fallen in love with the cozy little place the minute she'd set eyes on it. It was a small, white building with charcoal grey shutters and a beautiful wide-open front porch. It seemed an odd independent placement among the other unique little cafes and storefronts on the intersection. This one stood alone; set back from the road a bit on its own very lush green plot of land.

Inside the walls were white and windows lined every wall all around the room letting in brilliant streaming veils of sunlight. The windows seemed like eyes to the room, giving view to the most beautiful scenery outside; rose bushes of coral, crimson, and blush surrounded the little cottage-esque building.

"Ooh, look, Eves!" Kate peered through one of the back windows and waved her friend over. Eva strolled slowly over to the window as she pondered in her own mind the inspiration that was coming to her. She bent down to see what Kate was looking at. It was the only building on the street that gave way to its own backyard, which gradually spilled down into a private pond surrounded by the flowing green hills of Virginia.

"C'mon, let's go check it out!" Eva grabbed her best friend's hand and ran to the front door and back onto the porch. They followed the private brick path around the side of the converted cottage; passing magnolias and dogwoods; rose bushes, tulips, and pine until they were in the back.
"It's like an oasis," Eva whispered.

"It is really pretty back here, Eves...like your own private getaway."

The two walked down the hill and looked out over the pond. To the left of the yard, a white picket fence engulfed in greens and coral flowers cascading down in spots. And the yard a sea of lilies of every color. Weeping willows brought shade to the outer corners of the land.

"Okay, Eves...I haven't seen that look on your face in a long time, but I know what it means. Sooo, whatcha thinkin'?"

Eva gave her friend a smile in a sideways glance. "I'm not sure yet."

"What a minute. What's up there?" Kate had turned away from the pond and was looking at a stone back patio porch lined with ivy of deep green with what looked like a private entrance to the rest of the building. The ivy drew Kate's eyes upwards to the classic colonial windows lining what looked like a second floor.

Eva shielded her eyes from the sun to follow her friend's gaze. "Looks like we missed a spot in our exploration. Let's go check it out."

The back door opened into a small foyer with a staircase to the right. "I didn't see that door when we first went inside, did you?" Bella questioned, pointing to an aqua-blue painted wood-paneled door in front of her, which no doubt led into the main room they had been in prior to their backyard adventure.

"Nope. Let's go see what's hiding up there."

Eva started up the staircase first, eager for more discoveries, while Kate followed closely behind.

"It's a separate apartment!" Eva looked around the cozy space to see a small, but modern kitchen with an elegant dining area just off of it. A living area with the same colonial windows looked out over the front of the building and included a small second story screen-in sunroom in a classic beach theme. Eva walked past the kitchen, down the hall, and into a Victorian bathroom complete with claw-footed tub, oil-rubbed bronze fixtures, and mother-of-pearl tile.

The next door in the hall held another surprise; a small, but luxurious bedroom complete with flowing sheers hanging haphazardly around a lushly dressed queen-sized bed.

"This place is freaking awesome!" Eva followed her friend's call back out into the main room.

"Are you thinking what I'm thinking?"

"Yeah, I am. It is really something, but it looks like somebody already lives here."

"Nope, free and clear." A third voice had entered the picture. Eva and Kate looked up in surprise to find a short, but sturdy looking old woman leaning on the stairwell peering out at them from underneath her sunhat. "I thought I heard some voices up here," she stated, taking off her hat and giving a finger-comb to her smart white bob, which held a sharp contrast against her sun-tanned, weathered skin. "Well, what do you think?" she asked in a voice that was surprisingly gruff for her small stature. "Like it?" The question was specifically directed to Eva. The old woman looked at her with a knowing twinkle in her eyes.

Something seemed oddly familiar about the old woman's stare, but Eva quickly looked away. "It's beautiful, but why do you have it decorated if no one lives here?"

"Truth be told, I used to live here back in the day. But it's sat empty for years since then. Was looking pretty sad and lonesome, but I had an inkling someone might be coming soon to give it life again. Thought I'd better spruce it up for the right person." A glint of familiarity sparkled in the old woman's bright blue eyes once more, as if she had something up her sleeve. As if she had known that Eva was coming.

"What do you say?" The old woman wrote something on a piece of paper and slid it across to Eva who was leaning on the other side. She looked at the paper for a while before slowly reaching out to pick it up with the same motions with which she had once taken a white rose from Alex. Would this be another offering that would later be taken from her in the same manner?

"The right price for the right person."

"Indeed." Eva looked at the paper in disbelief, the offer seemed way lower than what she would have estimated the value of the property. "This is just for the apartment?"

"Heaven's no. What good would selling half a building do me? It's for everything; the upstairs, the downstairs, the entire building. That and the outside, too, of course."

"Why so low?"

"I have one condition. I give you a good price and you let me come and tend the garden. I imagine you'll be busy with getting the downstairs in order and I do enjoy taking care of growing things."

Eva smiled at the woman and took out her checkbook. "You got yourself a deal."

"Wonderful. Name's Rose Truman by the way," she stated nodding to Eva's hand paused on the checkbook where the recipient's name would go. Eva held her surprise at their similarity in names, but chose not to comment on it, grateful for Rose's kindness, but not quite ready to let anyone new in.

She tore the paper from its casing and handed it over to the tiny, but strong-looking woman. Rose took it without breaking Eva's gaze and shook her hand. "Thank you, Eva."

"How did you know my na-"

"I'm sure I'll be seeing you around here," Rose cut in before Eva had the chance to finish her sentence and was already heading back down the stairs.

Eva looked at Kate. "What the heck was that?" The two pranced down the stairs to follow the old woman and opened the door to the large, open downstairs floor.

"She's gone. How the heck did she know my name?"

"Well, she must have seen it on your check."

"No, she said it before she even looked at it."

"I don't know, Eva, you must not have noticed her look."

But Eva knew differently, she specifically remembered the old woman holding her gaze, not once peeking down even to see if the amount written was correct. Eva could have filled in the box with a big fat zero as far as she was concerned.

"So anyway, that's not important. What is important is-s-s," Kate held out a long dramatic pause to punctuate the anticipation.

Eva, still preoccupied by what had just transpired with the old woman, snapped out of it long enough to humor her friend. "What?"

"Well, the upstairs is pretty-much move-in ready. But this place..." Kate let her voice trail off and let the gesture of her hand continue the thought, drawing attention to the barren room. "If I know you, you've already got some tricks up your sleeve."

177

Eva smiled, more at the room, than at her friend waiting anxiously to hear Eva's big plans. "Oh, I've got some ideas, alright...guess you'll have to wait for the Grand Unveiling!"

"Spoken like a true art-eest. Okay, so onto the next order of business, can we grab some lunch now? I'm starving!"

"You bet. My treat!"

"Look at you, writing big-money checks like it's nothing. Throwing that wallet around. Since when did you become Miss Money Bags?"

"Since my show in New York became a spectacular smash, my friend!" Eva teased.

"Ah, I forgot about that. Must suck to leave all that behind when you're just getting started, huh? Guess you can't have it all."

Eva detected a bit of sharpness in Kate's response and gave her a look. "What's that supposed to mean?"

"Oh, nothing. I just-"

"And anyway, who says I can't? I'm not dead yet. And besides, I don't think I had much choice in the matter, considering the circumstances. And now this," Eva paused, hopefully surveying the new space, "This is a chance to start over...or continue what had started. I'm not exactly sure yet. And I really need your support. It's like I'm from here, but I don't even feel like I belong anymore. I feel like a complete fish out of water here. I don't know anybody anymore. I left everyone I was close to back in New York and I have no clue if I'll ever see them again. Hell, I don't even remember how to get to places around here!"

Kate scratched her blond head and patted Eva on the shoulder. "I know. It's hard. I'm sorry. I don't know why I said that."

Eva put her hand on where Kate's had rested on her shoulder. "It's okay. I think there's a lot of emotions going around for all of us. Just be nice, okay? I just left the Land of Attitudes, and I seriously don't need any more right now, least of all yours. I mean, it'll be hard enough to get rid of my own!"

"Eh, maybe you should keep a little bit of that New York edge."

"Yeah?"

"I think people think they can get away with being nasty to you because you're so darn sweet. You could do with a little bit of a protective fence right now. Just make sure it's crossable for those worthy."

Eva breathed out a laugh and nudged her friend.

"By the way, I've been meaning to ask you...how's your mystery stalker doing? Have you heard anymore from him?"

Eva caught her breath at the question, the smile fading from her face. "No," she lied soberly. "That's over...Long over."

***

"Eva, please...answer me. I know you still hear me. I know you can still feel me even miles apart. I know I've hurt you deeply and I am sorry. Please give me a chance to make this right. Please give us a chance. My heart bleeds for you. You're my one and only. I'll never love anyone the way I love you. Please respond to me, Eva. Please."

Eva looked at her phone and rolled her eyes...*what part of 'screw you' don't you understand?* She took her coffee cup, stepped down off the porch and walked barefooted down through the early morning dew-covered grass with Buster following closely behind. The sun rose over the hills, sending soft yellow streams of light pouring over through the trees and over the green of the slopes; the new day a symbol...as if to beckon her into a new life. Each step a rejuvenation, as her feet met the soft cool earth again and again.

New life, Eva thought to herself, *...and nothing old is coming with it...*

***

"It's gonna take a lot of work to get 'er up to speed. Are you sure you know what you're gettin' yourself into?"

Eva took the contract out of the realtor's hands and signed her name with a flourish. "Don't you worry," she declared with a smile. "I have a few tricks up my sleeve. A little love and a few personal touches will breathe new life into this place before you know it."...*May just be my second wind, too...*"So, where is Rose anyway?"

"Ah, she doesn't get into the legal side of things. She lets me handle that."

"Who exactly is she?"

"Not really sure. I just do what she tells me."

"Yeah, I got the feeling when I met her that she's not one to take 'no' for an answer."

The realtor shook a hearty chuckle. "You got that right. Well, that should do it. Good luck kiddo. You've got yourself a real find here." And with that, the man picked up his crocodile leather briefcase, set his tweed hat on his head,

179

and strolled out the front door.

***

Later that evening, Eva took Madge on a ride through the lush country trails behind her grandparents' house, contemplating her new project. After speaking to Frank the night before to ensure he was ready for her to leave the house, she had a deeper peace about the move. The signing of the lease on the building marked a new chapter for her, and with that, the need to lay down her own roots; away from the familiar, so she could begin her own healing process.

The evening moon began to rise over the wavy horizon throwing a bluish glow over the countryside. It was as if her Father in heaven was lighting the path for her. And for the first time since that fateful night in New York, when she had come to feel that He was real, she began to hear that quiet voice deep within stir once more.

"See, my love? I paint the twilight sky for you. Do not go back to what was before. For I have set a new path before you. Do not look back, my love. The old has passed and a new life has come. Do not be afraid to step forward boldly."

Eva peered up at the sky as her equine strolled lazily through the field, growing even more awestruck at this voice that had begun to quiet her soul. It was a familiar voice, like her own, only solid like a rock, steadfast, as if nothing could penetrate or shake its foundation. It was to her like the coo of a newborn to its mother's ear...soothing, secure.

Just as the pair were turning the tree-canopied bend to come back home, a familiar ping of her phone shot through the night air, killing the silence and startling her peaceful repose. She opened her phone with hesitation.

"Okay, so this is the 3rd time in a week I've tried to reach out to you without even so much as a response from you. That has to mean something to you, Eva. Look, I don't blame you for being upset, but I promise you...my situation is almost resolved. Then we can begin to build a life together...our beautiful life together. You haven't forgotten...I know you haven't forgotten. All of the dreams we shared. I know you still want everything as badly as I do. You might have everyone else fooled, but you can't fool me. I know your heart...and I can see the pain in your eyes without even being in the same vicinity as you. Don't deny what's in your heart. Don't deny your one true love.

I could never deny you. You are my life. My everything. Please don't give up on me. I have nothing without you. Please, Eva!"

Eva felt a familiar ache begin to rise within her heart. *After everything...and all this time...I'm not even in the same state as him and he still wants me.* But she couldn't forget his come-and-go approach, and the way he'd so cruelly denied his love to push her away. So easily. As if she meant nothing to him.

She shook her head to snap herself out of it. *No... he'll never take me seriously if I cave to him now. If he's serious, he'll come forward.*

"Yeah, you love me so much all you can do is hide behind a screen instead of coming forward like a man. I'm not doing this again. You've had two years to make this right...two years! Now I finally have the chance to start my life over and you want to come in and ruin it all over again? NO! I'm not even in the same city as you are anymore! Either come forward or leave me alone and let me have some peace for once in my life! How in the world do you expect me to take you seriously when all you do is send texts and never actually physically DO anything??"

20 GALA

Eva watched the brush glide across the last corner of the wall, transferring the final touches of warm-colored paint. Blue like water, but with a hint of green. Warm, not cool. Muted, but light. It was a color that reminded her of the sea, the only other place that could come close to holding a candle to her beloved Big Apple. And she wanted to immerse herself in it.

"Feels like you could dive right in from this viewpoint."

Eva startled at the deep, husky female voice coming from across the room and looked up to see Rose leaning in the doorway on the frame, trowel in hand. She pointed at the wall with it, "it's a good color. Brightens up the place."

"I'm glad you like it."

"Well, I'm glad you're making it your own. Place needs young blood to give it some life again. What do you plan to do with it?"

"Oh, I've got some ideas." Eva's eyes twinkled. "I was a photographer for a magazine in New York and I'm really starting to miss that creativity."

"So, you're an artist." Rose smiled knowingly.

"Yeah. Yeah, I guess you could say that. I never really thought of it that way because it was geared toward a corporate setting and didn't leave much room for artistic license. Lots of rules, regulations, that kind of thing."

"I figured as much."

"But I think I want to take it into a different direction. I've been using pictures to say what's on my heart for the longest time. It felt safe on the other side of the camera, like a buffer. If I could say what I needed to say through image, it was like it wasn't really coming from me. I could be as real and raw as I wanted to be without the fear of getting "too close"...because it was a just a picture, for all intents and purpose...not technically my own words. I didn't have the risk of hearing anybody tell me that I was wrong in what I was saying. Because they would never know the story of the pieces of my work. You know what I mean?" Eva asked, turning back to Rose.

"I know exactly what you mean, dear."

"So, I want to give other artists the opportunity to take it further. To create a story through image and have the freedom to interpret other's images, as well. To have writer's come to write or write the story behind what they see through the eyes of another artist's pictorial work. Paint, sculpture, other modes of creativity. I want a safe place for people to come to work out their grief and stress through art. And I want to help them through it.

"So...an artist's retreat."

"Right...but more like an artists' grief-share. Not a lot of people know this about me, but photography was my minor. I actually majored in psychology. What I want is for this place to be a place where artists who are hurting, for whatever reason, to come and work out their stories and feelings through their own mediums. And help talk them through the process. Encourage them. Be a listening ear."

The blue of Rose's eyes deepened as she smiled back to Eva.

"So, that's what I'm hoping to do anyway. Have coffee or tea. Treats. Things like that. Maybe some support groups, too, where artists can come and just talk." Eva turned the focus back on Rose. "What did this place used to be, anyway?"

"Well, you might be surprised to know not too far off the mark of where you're coming from. It was an artist's retreat."

Eva's deep green eyes lit up with surprise. "Seriously?"

"Well, of course, my dear. Well... painting and such. I'd work on things of my own while my husband was off to work, and I'd have classes and things like that. Although, I'll tell you, I didn't need to do much teaching given the talent that came through those doors. I kept the upstairs open for any transient who needed a night or two to rest from their travels. Met all kinds of people. It was really a lovely time."

"So, what happened?"

"You mean why did I stop? My focus shifted after my husband fell ill. Didn't have much time for anything aside from taking care of him, God rest his soul."

"Oh, Rose I'm sorry." Eva could relate more than Rose knew at this early point in their knowing each other.

"Don't be!" Rose's voice went from nostalgic to fresh fervor. "Listen, you're doing me a favor. The place has been sitting empty for years and I was afraid whoever I ended up selling it to was going to turn into another one of those damn corporate coffee-houses. The last thing we need is more idiot hippies running around overly caffeinated."

Eva laughed.

Rose gave her a proud smile that reminded Eva of that look Ramona would so often give her. "Glad to know this place will be following in its own artistic footsteps...2.0 version."

***

The Artist's Reprieve was well underway, and Eva basked in all of her hard work as she strolled through the room teaching her creative techniques emphatically to her evening group. It had taken her the better part of a year to get it up and running; requiring much more than the fresh coat of paint she originally had intended. But now a year and many cups of coffee later, Eva was ready to enjoy the fruits of her labor.

Artists of all mediums were discovering Eva's little creation-hideaway and were coming regularly to create, to sit and talk with Eva over a steaming cup of tea or coffee or enjoy the company of other artists who were struggling in some way, shape, or form just like they were. The only rules were that they respect each other. Pointed criticism and gossip were not allowed as Eva had made very clear the first opening night.

That warm, summer evening had been a beautiful crystal clear deep, navy. A blanket of fiery-white stars dotted the blue as if the sky also had been elegantly decorated just for the event. Eva had gone so crazy with twinkle lights that one could hardly tell where the sky ended, and the lawn began.

Guests were bathed in light as they walked up from the sidewalk. There must have been thousands of twinkling strands of light in arches over the brick pathway up to The Artist's Reprieve. Tables draped in white dresses of tablecloths were placed about the yard among golden veils of candlelight for guests to enjoy themselves outside if they wished. Sheers of pale aqua-marine gossamer danced in the evening breeze around the yard, hanging from overhead and coming together to make a breathtaking entrance to the candle-lit porch.

This evening was truly special and she'd wanted for her guests to feel the same sentiment for themselves. It was for that very reason she'd chosen to put on a Gala rather than your regular run of the mill opening party. *"Petit a petit, l'oiseau fait son nid - Une affaire de la Coeur: an evening of new beginnings"* had been printed on satin cardstock and distributed far and wide throughout Virginia Beach to almost every business Eva could think of. She'd even invited her former colleagues from the city, although she'd doubted their attendance.

Eva finally had an excuse to get all dolled up as once upon a time she had so much loved to do. To offset her dark reddish-brown hair, half-pulled up in flowing waves, she'd chosen a special champagne and blue ombre. It was not quite navy, not quite bright blue, but somewhere in between. Her deep green eyes picking up on the green tones in the blue. The shimmering champagne-nude material draped across her neck from over one shoulder to underneath the other, tight through the satin bodice, then light and almost sheer sparkling gauze in the same color flowing from her hips, fading slowly into the blue just to the floor in a loose column. As she walked, the breeze revealed a slit on one side, showing off a very well-toned leg, then closing modestly as she stood still.

"Darling here, have some bubbly. It is a celebration after all."

Eva turned around to see Olivia standing there in a daringly short mini holding out a flute of Armand de Brignac. "Olivia?! Where did you...I mean how did you?"

"Darling, you invited me, remember?"

"I know, but I didn't think you'd actually come! I mean it's so far from New York and you've got so much work-"

"Are you kidding?" Olivia cut her off, "I wouldn't miss your big night for the world! Listen...it's been a long time coming and I can't think of a person more deserving than you." Liv held up her glass. "To you, my friend, and your fantastic new endeavor. May the muse of success and happiness always be at your door. Cheers, darling!"

"Cheers!" The two clinked glasses and took a sip.

"Oh! I just can't believe you're actually here." Eva squeezed her friend, jumping up and down.

"Darling, I love you, but calm down. That dress ain't made for jumping. We don't want any surprises."

"Oh, sorry." Eva smoothed her gown and took another sip.

"Surely, I can't be the only friend who came to support you. Where is Kate?"

"Oh, they couldn't make it. I haven't seen them in a long time actually. They've been helping Collin's mom renovate her house, so she can downsize."

"Eves, who is *that*?" Olivia asked her friend, pointing her champagne flute across the room.

"Huh? What." Eva composed herself and stood stiff.

"Over there. That tall drink of water staring at you from the hors d'oeuvres."

"Oh, great." Eva rolled her eyes and took another sip. "Probably just another idiot man that doesn't know how to keep his eyes to himself-"

Eva stopped talking almost as quickly as she'd turned to see the source of Olivia's question. A man her age, maybe just a few years older was leaning against the stairwell across the room in a black tuxedo. His chiseled face was as if he was searching for something. He had a confidence about him that went beyond his obvious physical strength. The minute her eyes fell on his deep hazel, the confusion in his face softened and relaxed. Eva felt locked into his calm gaze for a moment, then slowly turned back around to Liv.

"Who is that guy? Do you know him?"

"No," Eva whispered with her head down. Something stirred inside of her.

"Wait a minute. That's not that selfish son-of-a-b-"

"No, that's not him. I don't know who that is-"

"Hello, Eva," came a voice behind her, masculine, but gentle with the familiarity of a long-time friend.

Eva kept her head down, letting just her eyes plead up at her friend. "Help!" she whispered. But Olivia just smiled back, clearly amused by the situation.

"My name is Hunter King. I do business here in town," he continued.

Eva finally regained her composure and turned around to properly receive her guest. She wasn't about to let another man control her emotions, let alone a complete stranger, even if there was something oddly comforting about him. She also wasn't about to let him see her ease about him, though. "Oh, hello, thank you for coming," she said coolly.

There was a calmness about him that spilled into his hazel eyes. His combed-back, wavy hair was a reddish ruddy-blond and although Eva had gaged him at about five to ten years older than her, had not a strand of grey in it. He was tall, but not spindly. Strong, but not obscenely muscular. If ever there was a specimen for the perfect male build, Hunter could have easily been claimed.

Hunter gently took her hand and gave it a firm shake, to which Eva quickly drew back. "So, how did you find out about us?"

"Well, my aunt was so excited that you were here to care for the place, I pretty much got an earful the day you got here," Hunter replied with a deep, chuckle.

"Wait. Rose is your aunt? So, that's how you knew who I was."

"Yes, ma'am. Well, mother's brother's wife, but that's beside the point." There was confidence about him. He wasn't cocky or arrogant, although his looks could have earned him the right. He was simply matter of fact with an easy sense of humor. Eva guessed that most likely nothing rattled this man very easily. And the way he looked at her, there was nothing creepy about it. Hunter looked at Eva as though he already knew her, much like his aunt had when she'd first met her...but different.

"Speaking of, did she come with you? I thought maybe she would be here."

"Nah, it's not really her scene. She's more of a behind-the-scenes kind of gal. Well, it appears you've drawn quite the crowd and I don't want to keep you from other guests on your opening night. It was very nice to meet you, Eva." Hunter smiled a calming smile at Eva and nodded at Olivia before disappearing into the crowd.

Eva watched him for a moment trying to decipher the feeling in her gut. She turned back around to Olivia who was beaming ear to ear. Eva frowned and gave her friend 'the look.'

"Alright, now you just stop right there."

"What?" Olivia blinked innocently at her friend.

"I know what you're thinking, and you just knock it off."

"But darling, he's cute!"

"I know. And I don't care."

"Eva, honey, I love you, but what the hell is wrong with you??"

"You know what's wrong with me." Eva noticed Frank waving her over from across the room. "Anyway, hold that thought. And my champagne. It's time for the big speech." Eva went to hand her glass to Olivia but stopped halfway. "Actually, wait a minute," she said, taking one last sip. Olivia's eyebrow-raised smile evoked an excuse.

"You know, for posterity."

"Whatever, darling. Now, go get 'em!"

Eva gracefully made her way to the front of the room where an elegant middle-aged elderly lady was playing a classical piano. She smiled at the woman and took the microphone from her father. Frank gave his daughter a hug.

"Proud of you, kiddo."

Eva smiled sweetly at her father and turned to face her guests. "Well...isn't this a hoot? If you had told me two years ago that I would be moving back home and opening my own art center, I would have laughed...right after I got done crying because things were pretty bad back then." The crowd chuckled softly in response.

"In all seriousness, I want to thank each and every one here for being here to support this special night and what it means for the future. A year ago, I didn't think I had a future." Eva paused, looking down at her notes to hide the tears that were beginning to seep into her eyes. She fought quickly to hold them back in an effort to protect herself from having to explain their source. When she looked up, her eyes once again fell directly into his.

Hunter was standing in the crowd almost in front of her, a strong stance. His face held that calm familiarity, and in his eyes, pride. Not cocky, or boastful. Just proud, as if her speech was something for him to be proud of her for. He smiled softly at her. Eva ignored the invitation and turned away towards the rest of the group.

"And now, with the opening of The Artist's Reprieve, I'll be able to help others realize their futures. What this world needs is more support and less competition. More mentors who are friends. I want to provide a safe place for others to come and relax and create in whatever medium that speaks best to them, canvas, paper, clay, words, instrument. We'll have conversations and coffee (or tea) and snacks. But most importantly, we'll have community. Thank you for being here."

Soft applause peppered the air as Eva made her way through the crowd, warmly greeting her friends and guests. Eventually she found herself outside on the porch, which was glowing golden light from the lanterns.

"I got all gussied up to drive hundreds of miles to hicktown and all I got was this lousy balloon."

Eva snapped her head up to see a tuxedo-clad figure standing in the middle of the sheered banners. "Charlie?!" she yelled running across the yard, the gossamer of her dress flowing behind her, to where he was standing with a pink rose. Charlie caught her when she got to him, picked her up in a tight hug, and spun around with her in her arms.

"Stop! I'll puke, I just had champagne."

Charlie laughed and set her down. "Damn, you look beautiful."

"Yeah, you clean up pretty good yourself. What are you doing here?!"

"Eva, you invited me, remember?"

"Yeah, but I didn't think you'd actually come!"

"Wait a minute. You're actually *happy* to see me, right? And did you say the same thing to Olivia?" he asked pointing to her friend waving at him from the window.

"Always the jokester. Of *course*, I'm happy to see you! It's just surreal. I haven't seen either one of you in so long and now we're here celebrating this awesome thing."

"I know. I'm super proud of you, Eves."

"Yeah?" she said looking up at him.

"Yeah. And listen, it's not the only reason I came here."

"Uh, oh."

"I need to ask you something."

"Oh, no."

Charlie got down on one knee and reached into his tuxedo jacket.

"Charlie."

"Eva."

"Charlie, stop." Eva interrupted him before he could get out another word.

"Eva, I love you. You're my best friend. I know what you said the day before you left, but I've loved you since the first time we went and got ice cream together and you tripped, and a bowlful of chocolate peanut butter came flying at my shirt. The city's not the same without you. It's cold, boring. Eva, I want to marry you. You know I could have any girl I want, but it's *you* I want. My best friend." He pulled the box out of his jacket, opened it, and held it out to her.

"What the hell is that?"

Charlie blinked a surprised look at the box, then back at her. "Wha- what do you mean? It's a ring!" he exclaimed clumsily thrusting the ring back out, as if his explanation would make it more appealing to her.

"Yeah, I know what it is. I mean what's it doing here?"

Charlie shook his head and closed the box, slowly rising from his knee. He thought for a moment, then shook his head. "You know, Eva, I just don't understand you."

"I know, that's your problem."

"No. I don't understand how you could have a perfectly good man standing in front of you, one you laugh with and cry with and who gives you his shoulder to cry on, would give you everything he has and it's *still* not good enough for you."

"Charlie, it's not a matter of being good enough. I just don't love you like that. We've been over this before. And you just keep getting hurt. Seriously, how many more times are we going to have this conversation?"

"Eva...why are you so harsh to me? I mean, I know you and that's usually par for the course with you, but seriously. Why are you always so mean to me? Especially now? Haven't I always been there for you? Been a good friend? And now I came all the way here and I'm pouring my heart out to you. Can't you give a guy a break for once?"

"Charlie...you deserve to be with someone who loves you just as much as you love them. Not someone you have to convince to love you. And even if I said 'yes' because I knew I was safe with you, it still wouldn't be right. Because I'm not in love with you. You deserve more than that."

Charlie considered her words. "You've never put it to me like that before."

"Because I felt like you wouldn't listen. I just feel like you want this so bad you won't listen."

Charlie loosened his bowtie and stood up. "This is never going to happen is it." It was a statement more than it was a question.

"I'm sorry, Charlie."

Eva watched him sympathetically as he paced the soft green.

"I need to go."

"Okay...I understand."

"No...I mean I need to leave. New York's tired for me. I'm going out to L.A. I thought you'd come with me, but...it looks like that's not going to happen."

Eva tilted her head and sighed. Charlie walked over to her. "Look, Eva, if it's him you're waiting for, you've got to be insane." He took her elbows firmly and looked intensely into her eyes. "He will never love you the way I do."

"Charlie-"

"He's incapable. He's too selfish."

"No, Charlie. Stop." Eva broke free from his grip. "It's not going to change anything."

Charlie was quiet for a while.

"Promise me one thing. Don't give yourself away to just anyone. If it can't be me...at least let it be someone who loves you the way I do."

Eva slowly shook her head. "So... L.A., huh?"

"Yeah. I need a fresh start."

"It might be good to get some space."

He backed away from her, ready to leave, turning around, torn. "I love you, Eva. If you change your mind..." He turned to leave before he could finish his sentence. He wanted to hug her but couldn't bear the emotional weight of having something in his arms that he wanted so badly to keep and then having to let it go.

Eva walked back up the porch steps to return to the party but turned just as Charlie was turning at the end of the brick walkway. He stared at her as if it were the last time that he would ever lay eyes on her. "You really do look beautiful," he murmured.

Eva smiled in return and held up her hand to wave goodbye.

"Later." Charlie threw two fingers to the air, gave her one last smile, then straightened his jacket - very debonair - and strolled casually down the street, casually whistling as he went.

21 COMING CLEAN

"Need some help?"

Eva turned from the table she'd been tidying to find Hunter standing behind her, black tie loose, the same easy look in his deep green eyes. "You look like you could use a hand."

Eva looked down from her own hands full of paper mache and champagne flutes. "No, I'm good thanks." But Hunter was already reaching to clear her hands. Eva jumped back to avoid his touch sending a glass crashing to the ground.

"Oh, gosh I'm sorry. Let me help."

"I said I got it," came Eva's sharp reply walking over to get a broom.

"Of course, you do. I didn't mean to imply otherwise." Hunter looked hurt but held his composure. "I'll get the trash," he declared in his stoic, confidant voice.

Eva watched him for a minute before finally cutting. "Look, did you need something? The party ended an hour ago. What do you want?"

Hunter walked back over from where he'd set the trash by the door. His eyes searched hers with an unsettling familiarity. "I'm not sure you're ready for the answer to that question. Right now, what I want is to help you clean up and for you to let me."

Eva sighed under her breath, then gestured to the room. "Yeah, sure. Have at it."

Hunter made efficient work of picking up the rest of the room and then met Eva where she was finishing gathering up soft clouds of the gauze that had been moving in the warm breeze just hours before. Eva unconsciously stepped back at his approach. Hunter took note of it without comment.

Eva set down the shimmering fabric and locked eyes on Hunter. "Listen, I don't mean to be rude, but why are you still here?"

Hunter held her gaze for a moment with that soft, stoic expression. His hand reached slowly for something inside his tailored tux. Eva watched him with apprehension. "I wanted to thank you, Eva."

"Thank me? For what?"

Hunter slowly pulled a glossy card from his inside jacket pocket. "For taking this," he replied softly, placing the card face-down in her hand. Eva turned the card around in her hands and gasped.

"I was once told me I would find something very special through the eyes of the beholder. And then that day...when I saw you...Well, goodnight, Eva. I better go. Thank you for allowing me to help you tonight." And with that he gave a very gentlemanly nod with his reddish-blond waves and walked out the door into the night air.

Eva looked down at the thick glossy paper in her hands. It was the most widely, critically-favored picture she had ever taken...autumn twilight in Central Park so many years ago, the rich yellow and gold lace of foliage contrasted with sharp lines of city steel in the background - and in the near distance Hunter, staring straight into the camera, seated on a bench, with a look on his face that told her he must have just happened to look up at that exact moment to see the most beautiful sight in creation.

***

"You looked gorgeous last night, my love."

"How do you know what I looked like last night?" I am so tired of this!

"I saw your profile pic. You look absolutely stunning in that shade of blue."

"Alright, that's enough of this. I want to know who you are. You need to tell me now."

"Eva, I don't think you're ready for the truth?"

"You don't get to decide what I'm ready for."

193

"Oh, well, actually I do."

Eva knew exactly what he meant. He held all the power in his staged anonymity. She was free to go at any time, but not free to the pull he held over her. The pull of the hope of what could be. But something didn't sit right with her. Even though Alex had been cruel to her and said a few hurtful things; as this electronic relationship had progressed, Eva felt more and more that it didn't line up with Alex really was. She began to feel even more convince that this person she was talking to might not be who she thought after all.

"The guy who I think you are...Alex...you're not really him, are you."

"Eva, I've been trying to tell you for the past 5 years that I'm not him."

***

"In order to fully express a thought, you have to feel it. You've got to become it. No hindrances or obstacles. Nothing should stand in the way. Not your own fears or doubts. Not the idea of what other people might think or say. It has to be fully you. Fully free."

Eva encouraged her patrons as she walked slowly around the studio, weaving through the artists that had come to The Artist's Reprieve to create together; each manifesting a unique, personal work of art. They were separate in and of themselves, but somehow united; tied together by the common thread of a long-suppressed desire to create, now finally able to be released. Some painting, some sculpting, some writing, and one making music on a piano someone had donated to the studio anonymously.

Behind them, a cafe counter teamed with goodies, some of which Eva had prepared herself. A volunteer barista bustled about behind the counter, preparing his special pour-over brew should any of them require a caffeinated pick-me-up. The atmosphere was warm and lovely, and the energy of their connecting with one another brightened the room.

Just then, Eva turned to see Hunter walking through the door. The gold in his eyes sparkled as he gave her his calm, warm smile.

Eva, unsure of why he was there, felt herself blush as she looked away, returning her attention to her fellow artists. Hunter, sensing Eva's discomfort, directed his focus to the cafe counter and made his way towards a coffee. Eva snuck a glance after he'd walked past her. He was dressed more casually today, jeans, with a nice button-down dress shirt. No tie this time.

Why do I feel drawn to him? Eva shook her head at her own inability to make sense.

"Hey, thank you," Hunter accepted the outreached cup and saucer with a gentlemanly smile and nod to the barista before turning his gaze back to her.

Eva remembered her vow to make her studio a welcoming place open to all. *Well, I guess I better go see what he wants.*

"You're welcome to join the others, if you'd like," Eva greeted him with trepidation.

"Hi, Eva," Hunter spoke warmly. If he was ever embarrassed by his previous words, Eva never would have known it, though she was desperately trying to pretend that those cryptically meaningful words had never been spoken. "Actually, I'm here for a different reason."

Eva felt an instant peace wash over her through his fluid tone and golden warm smile. *No,* she told herself. "So, he makes a pretty good cup of jo', right?"

Hunter mused at her feeble attempts to distract him - and herself - and tried again. "Eva, I'd really like to talk to you if you have a minute."

"Well, if it's about what you said the other night, I'd rather not."

"Look, I know it must have come across as...odd."

Eva raised her eyebrows to emphasize his point.

"That's what I'd like to talk to you about. There is something I need to tell you."

"I think you've already said plenty."

"I don't blame you for being cautious after hearing what I said the last time we saw each other. What I'm asking you for is a chance to explain. Because there is more that you need to know."

I bet there is. Eva searched him with skeptical eyes. But his stance wasn't like that of most men. It was strong, but unintimidating, open. *What could he possibly have to say that I haven't already heard?* Remembering the picture he'd given her just a few days before, her curiosity got the best of her. *Well, if he made a point to come back, it must be somewhat legit.* "Alright. Let's hear it."

"Care to join me for a walk?"

***

"Eva, the day you took that picture in the park wasn't the first time I knew you.

"What do you mean?"

"I mean that I actually own *Highland Magazine*. I own quite a few things, under my namesake King Acquisitions. *Highland* happens to be one of them."

"Wait, what do you mean you 'own' *Highland*??" Eva mocked him with air quotes. "Mr. Solomon and his groupies own *Highland*. I should know, he fired me."

"Mr. Solomon and the other men are business partners, but I'm the true owner of the company. I'm a silent owner. When my reach began to grow, I couldn't focus solely on *Highland* without compromising my portfolio. I hired him to help me oversee it when I couldn't be there, which was often."

"Okay," came the only reply that Eva could think of to give. She had many questions, but figured it was best to let him speak.

"That's what I meant when I said I knew you. I knew of you from your work before I ever laid eyes on you. You were our most talented photographer. That's why I gave you all of our best, most important jobs. Because even though I didn't know Eva personally, I knew I could trust her...you. Then I heard about what happened and I had such a hard time with it. Mr. Solomon is supposed to discuss with me anything that he has a concern with *before* he does anything about it. He didn't have the authority to fire *anyone* without my say. He overreacted and I am so sorry, Eva. If I had been there, I wouldn't have allowed that to happen."

Eva stared at him in disbelief. "Wait a minute. If you didn't even know what was going on, how did you even find out what happened then?"

"They waited to tell me, they waited until they had a chance to move his nephew into your place, most likely because they knew I wouldn't have allowed it. I hardly think that the innocent dating of a coworker is grounds for letting our best employee go. Mr. Solomon was always looking for ways to grow his power."

Eva realized in that moment that it had all been a setup, that they never really cared about her relationship with Alex. Peter had been waiting with bated breath for his opportunity to move into her spot and that was the perfect opportunity. And he knew that his uncle would be onboard because it would have given him more stake in the company.

"But then how did you...? That day in the park, the picture. Did you follow me? How did you even know I was there?"

"No, Eva, I never knew what you looked like until that day. They didn't even *tell* me about it until that day! Oh, man, I was livid! I'd wondered why it had been so long since I'd seen your approval on any of the shoots and they kept dancing around it. 'You were out sick, you were on a personal shoot,' etc.

When they finally told me the truth, I was so angry that I went to the park to process everything. Before I left, I demanded your file, so I could find you and found out that Solomon had already shredded it. I told him this was not how I do business and would not do business with anyone who operated in such an underhanded way and then I fired him. As I was walking out, I happened to see your picture on the wall in the studio from one of Highland's parties. It was a picture of you and Ramona. I'd heard how close you two were, so when I saw that picture of the two of you, it just clicked. I knew it was you. Eva, I could not get your face out of my head knowing what they did to you.

I sat down on the bench. I thought about everything. When I looked up and saw you...I couldn't believe it. Eva, I was just sitting there and this voice inside my head spoke to me and said, 'That's her.' It was like God Himself said your name. When I looked up and saw you standing there with your camera...I was stunned. In my heart, I knew it in my heart. It felt so warm."

Eva shook her head, "No, I don't understand."

"I know it's hard to understand, Eva, and maybe a little bit scary, but I'm trying to explain. What stunned me was that earlier this year, I met a man with a sort of gift. He said to me what I said to you the other night...that I would find my wife through the eyes of the beholder. Eva, when I looked up and saw you that day at the park, I knew that it was you. Everything in my entire *being* told me that it was you."

Eva backed away from him in disbelief. "No. I don't understand."

"Eva, I wanted to go to you then, but I wanted to pray first, to ask for the words, to pray for you to have an open heart."

"No, it doesn't make any sense! Why didn't you say something then?"

"Eva, nothing makes sense when it comes to God. It didn't make sense to me that when I lifted my head from that prayer...after God had *just* whispered to me that you were the one...you were gone. You just disappeared. I couldn't find you after that. Then I saw an announcement in the paper that you were opening your own studio and I knew I had to come to you. I couldn't not *come* to you."

Eva's heart began to pull within her, "No, please don't."

"Eva, I didn't want to scare you. I don't ever want to upset you, but I can't just let you go. I can't just let you go when I know without a shadow of doubt that you and I are meant to be together. Please hear me. Please try to open your heart to see it. Please."

Eva looked into his deep green eyes and saw something she'd never seen in Alex's eyes, something she'd never expected to see from any man after what she'd been through. His eyes brimmed with security, safety, sincerity. Eva shook her head. *No, he'll just do to you what Alex did.*

Hunter took her hand and softly spoke her name. "Eva..." His eyes begged her to believe him. "Give me a chance. I don't know your whole story, but I know you've been hurt. I've seen glimpses in my mind of what you've been through and my heart aches for you. Please give me a chance to prove that I am not that man."

Eva fought viciously against her heart, which was pulling her closer and closer towards him second-by-second. He felt like home, which terrified her even more. She could not let her heart go to him when it was still bound to someone else. "No, you don't belong here. Someone else belongs here. He *promised* me." Eva let the words flow from her mouth. She told him everything. Everything she'd been through these past few years. She told him about the promises that were broken, the manipulation, the back and forth, and the mystery that she still could not solve.

"Eva...if he truly meant those things...if he truly wanted you...he would be here. He wouldn't be playing these games with you."

Eva snapped back at him. "What do you mean games? How do you know he's playing games? How do you know this is all a lie? You don't know him. You don't know anything about him!"

"Eva-"

"No! You don't know me! I don't know you! Leave me alone and don't bother me again!" Hunter opened his mouth to reply, but Eva was already turning to go back to her studio. She closed her eyes, but she could not close her mind to his words that were playing in her head.

Why is this happening again?

And that night, after she'd gotten home to her apartment and snuggled in for the night...that night was the night that the man who had eluded her from the day they parted ways...the man who had come and gone for so many years through text and through her heart...that night was the night he finally called.

She quickly moved her finger to press the touch-screen button that would end the call.

"Hi...."

It was him, but in a text message. Not a recognizable voice that she could finally put a name to.

"*Hi...Why aren't you saying anything?*" she replied, scared, but frustrated that although he'd finally gathered the courage to call, he was continuing with this charade of text.

"*I can't...please say something.*"

"*No... I can't...it has to be you. You have to speak. You called me. You speak first. Please.*"

"*I'm afraid.*"

"*Please...we're so close. Please, say something.*"

More breathing.

"*How is it that you're even able to text me while we're on the phone?*"

"*Same way you are. Eva, please believe me...I love you. I love you so much. Nothing will keep us apart once we're together. I won't ever let you go. You and I are one, we always have been. I love you. I love you so much!*"

Eva trembled as she paced her shadowed apartment. "*I know...I know you love me. Please say something...you're scaring me.*"

No response. Eva grew more and more uneasy. "*Okay...I'm hanging up now. You're really scaring me.*"

"*No! Eva, please don't!*"

"*Then say something! I'm not going to stay on the phone with you and text you at the same time! This is freaking ridiculous!*"

"I'm sorry, Eva." A low and dark whisper came across the phone that chilled Eva to the core. Now, even more confused than ever, she quickly ended the call.

Then it came again. *"You hung up on me!"*

Another text.

"You scared me!"

"Eva, please, I love you! I was just afraid!"

"No. You are really frightening me now. Please stop texting me. Please leave me alone!"

***

The next morning, Eva awoke to the sound of her phone.

"My love...why did you hang up on me?" It was a text from him.

Eva began to cry out of crushing frustration. *"Why are you doing this to me?? Please stop! Please just go away and leave me alone!"*

"Eva, you don't mean that. I was going to speak...but then you hung up on me. If you hadn't hung up, I would have spoken eventually."

"I was afraid! You were breathing into the phone and wouldn't say anything. It scared me. I didn't know what you were going to do."

"Eva, calm down. You know I would never ever do anything to hurt you. You're my love. If I ever hurt you, it would hurt me even more so. You're just not thinking rationally. Baby... it's me...remember? The one who holds your heart. Who knows you inside and out? I know the very essence of your being. Do you truly think I could ever even think about doing anything to hurt you... my one and only true love? That hurts me very badly, Eva."

Eva tears flowed, unstoppable, she was so torn. Could this man who had shared and spoke her hopes and dreams truly harm her? The one who had repeatedly confessed his undying love for her, over and over again for the past 5 years? Without even being able to see her face to face? Without ever touching her? No... a love like that, a love that could stand the tests of both time and distance was surely pure and meant to be. As the shadows faded into the morning sunlight, so did her fear. But still her heart ached. She could not bear the games any longer.

"Please...don't....I can't take this anymore. Please just admit who you are. I can't do this anymore." Tears streamed down her cheeks and onto her silk pillowcase.

"But you hung up on me! Now I'm REALLY afraid!"

"I'm sorry I hung up on you, but it was late, and I was so afraid. I promise I won't hang up this time. I will hear you out and listen to what you have to say, but if you choose not to, understand that I will block your number and never speak to you again. I can't continue like this. It's killing me. It's absolutely killing me! We've been at this for 5 years. If you can't come forward now, you never will." Eva was crying hard now, her tender heart overwhelmed with both love and fear.

Suddenly his number flashed across her screen. Eva was jolted out of her tears. She looked down as if it would bite her...terrified...and shaking, as if all of the strength she had found, having blocked him and starting over with her life, never existed. She sat up, letting it ring a few times before finally picking it up.

"Hello," she whispered into the phone, almost an expectant statement instead of a question.

More silence. She waited. 10 minutes went by. More silence.

Eva finally broke the knife-like silence and spoke very softly, "Come on, we can't do this again. Please...say something.... it's okay."

"I can't." More texting.

She spoke again, "What is God saying to you?"

"He is saying that this is the beginning of our lives together...but you will be upset and need time away...and then realize that you love me, and we will end up together."

"Oh."

"Will you please pray?" more whispering. Only this time it didn't frighten her.

Eva paused for a while, then relented.

"Okay."

"Thank you," came the whisper.

Eva prayed for strength and courage and when she was finished, the whisper on the end replied with a simple "thank you." Only the whisper was undecipherable.

"Please speak...I just prayed for you...please do this for me. If you truly love me...please...Don't take me through these games again. I can't bear it. Please just say something." Eva was desperate for an answer at this point.

"...Hi, Eva."

Eva suppressed a gasp and put her hand to her mouth. His voice...not a whisper this time...a full voice. And she recognized it immediately. *No... it can't be...*

"How are you?"

Her heart began to race as she tried once again to catch her breath, slowly realizing who he was. *No... I couldn't be... it can't be him...*

"It's so good to hear your voice again...I've missed it so much."

Eva couldn't speak as she recognized the man on the other end of the line. *Oh, my God....*It was Collin....Kate's now ex-husband... He'd left her suddenly without so much as an explanation and now everything made sense.

Suddenly, every memory came rushing in like a flood in which she fought to swim her way to the top, wave after wave pushing her back under to where she couldn't break for air. She remembered the day they met and how there was something off that she could not quite put her finger on, like he was hiding something, but had long since forgotten... How they had come to visit her... and the dream she'd had of someone watching her in shadows...only she began to realize it wasn't a dream...it was Collin who had watched her sleep...How she had unknowingly written him an email, as everyone in their circle had, reminding him of his faith and pushing him to go back to Kate when she first found out that he had left her without so much as a reason...

She remembered that he had been the first person to anoint her to her new faith when she first moved back home...how he had caressed her hand for a split second in prayer and how she had brushed it off thinking he had mistaken her hand for Kate's...He had told her years ago when she still thought he was Alex that he had been in love with her since they met... He had told her that he knew the moment they met that he was supposed to marry her. Eva closed her eyes. Eva had met him before he and Kate were even married. This could only mean one thing...That he had been in love with Eva the entire time he was married to her best friend...and that the entire marriage was a lie...a farce to keep him close to her knowing that if he had approached her while being engaged to Kate, Eva would have turned him down flat. And the story she had told him when she thought he was Alex...about her friends that had to wait to start their relationship until it was "right" and were now happily married...it was *his own story!* It was the story of how he and Kate had started their relationship and eventually gotten married. *No wonder he'd said it sounded like a great story! He knew it was a lie because it was his own!*

...No... *this can't be real...this can't be happening. Not like this.*

Eva felt light-headed as she realized the weight of the situation. The reality horrified her. And her friend...Eva would have never *ever* participated in this had she known the truth. Never would done anything to hurt Kate and now she realized that although she could have known it was Collin, she unwittingly was the cause of her friend's divorce years prior.

That's why he wouldn't tell me who he was...he wanted to keep me blameless, because he wanted this relationship to become real, and if it had, he wanted to keep it so that I could honestly say that I didn't know. He thinks he was trying to protect me.

Eva didn't know what to think. She dug hard to find excuses that would make this terrible wrong thing right. Surely, God could not have meant for a relationship to be that would have hurt her friend so badly and go against every moral compass. And yet he had admitted to believing Eva was the one before he had ever walked down the aisle. Could all of this have been because he had denied what his own still small voice was telling him from the start?

Either way, it didn't make it right. She wasn't even attracted to Collin, never had been. Never even had a glimmer of a thought of him that way. She had thought this was Alex the whole time, who had been the only one she had ever wanted to be with. And her already tender heart was now a battered, bloody mess of confusion.

This was the man that had seduced her soul...had known her inside and out, the very depths of her heart...had read her waking dreams to her...had gotten her to fall so deeply in love with him, she couldn't even see straight and now...*now* what? She could not see how deeply entangled in his snare she had become. She was so torn; she couldn't see reality. She'd felt love on the deepest level and was in complete denial of the fact, that the love she felt wasn't real. Compounded with the fact that she had attached it to Alex all of these years, never knowing it was really Collin who had tricked her into loving him. The thought of this love not being real was too much for her to let herself see and she looked everywhere she could for the excuses that would somehow justify this absolute and utter disaster of a truth revealing.

But if he knows me this well...if he loves me this deeply...if we have been through all of this...and my heart still says 'yes'...I think? ...God surely can redeem this...can't He?... if it truly was His will from the beginning?

"Eva?... Are you still there?"

Eva closed her eyes as she wrestled with her emotions on the inside. "Yes...I'm here."

"You're so quiet."

Eva was afraid to let him see her struggle. She wanted the time to figure out the mess before he might disappear again, leaving her with even more questions. So, she smoothed over her silence with an excuse. "It's just...I'm just tired...I didn't sleep well last night...in fact, I haven't been sleeping well lately."

"Well...that's about to change," he responded with a cool confidence.

Eva bit her lip.

"Eva, I know I've hurt you; I know you don't trust me, but I promise you I am going to come get you and make this right. I know your entire being...your very essence. You're mine. You belong to me. Every dream we've shared. Every story I've walked us through. It's all going to come true now."

Eva stayed silent, still processing what she'd been hearing, what was now the undeniable truth. She didn't know what to say.

"Eva, why are you so quiet? Don't you know that I love you?"

Eva squeezed her eyes shut, so torn inside to hear the words she longed for, but out of a man she didn't really know. "Yes...yes, I know that you love me."

"And I know you love me, too."

Eva squeezed her eyes and bit her lip. Although she had never been attracted to him before and although she wanted to deny them, she couldn't deny the *feelings* they had shared all of this time, regardless of her lack of attraction.

"Yes," she whispered, but her heart screamed uncertainty.

"You and I are meant to be, Eva. You are the most beautiful woman I have ever known. And not just outside. You have a heart of gold. I love your heart for God. I love your purity. And I have cried for you, I don't know how many times."

Eva sighed in despair. "Me, too."

"Eva, I'm so sorry." Now he was audibly beginning to cry. "I never meant for any of this to happen. All of the pain and torment I put you through. I love you so much!"

Eva's heart pulled towards him, still not ready to let go of the phantom she had been led believe was the source of her love.. "So... now what?" Collin was weeping on the other end of the line. "Why are you crying?"

"Because I'm afraid that God is going to punish me for what I've done to you. I'm afraid that God is going to punish me for ruining your life."

Eva felt a sting at that last statement. Was her life ruined? Did he know something that she didn't? If it wasn't him, did she miss what she was supposed to have? Was her life truly ruined? "So... now what?" she asked nervously.

"Now what? I'll tell you 'now what'...I'm going to come and get you and were going to get married and have the most amazing honeymoon you could ever imagine."

Eva's heart puddled again as she listened to him describe every imaginative detail of their future wedding, honeymoon, and life together. She looked at the clock and realized they had been talking for almost 4 hours.

"And I can't wait for the wedding night."

Eva didn't respond.

"Soo...hearing my voice...all this time talking...you know who I am now, right?"

Eva smirked a laugh, "After 4 hours, please tell me you're kidding."

"Seriously."

"Of course, I know who you are."

"Say my name...I haven't heard you say it yet."

"I didn't think I needed to."

"Please say it...I want to hear you say my name."

Eva sighed but relented. "Collin."

Silence.

"Okay, so are you happy now?"

"No."

"No?"

"No... that's not my name."

Eva knew he was lying. She felt the familiar pang of fear begin to rise up within her. "Please don't do this...I know it's you. Please don't play games with me again."

Silence...."I can't do this. Eva, don't rely on me anymore." The phone clicked on the other line.

"What?? Why?!"

But it was too late. He had already hung up.

Eva's heart came crashing to the ground and shattered into a million pieces. Once again, losing what she thought had been true. She called the number back, only it went to a strange answering service. She called him again, still no answer. Her heart twisted in her chest, and she began to sob. *No! Please don't do this to me again.*

"I'm sorry, Eva." A text message.

"What do you mean? Why did you hang up on me?"

"God's telling me to walk away."

"What?! But...you just told me He was telling you this was the beginning! You just spent an hour describing to me what our wedding will be like! You asked me to pray for you!"

"I know...and those are things that I want...but I don't know if they are things that I actually heard God say. I'm sorry, Eva, I have to go."

"Are you kidding me? You call me to suck me in deeper and demand my heart, demand that I believe you, go on and on about it, and after 4 hours you do this? Why?" Eva sense he was hiding more dark secrets and possibly another relationship. *Are you in another relationship?"*

"No."

"Then why? Please don't do this to me again. Please don't take my heart from me and then leave me again."

No response.

"Please don't do this." Eva was in complete denial. Because admitting it was fake, would mean she had wasted the last five year of her life. It would mean that she'd invested everything she had into something that was a complete mascarade.

"All of this...the past 5 years...everything. All leading up now to what? A

great big nothing?" No matter what she said, he wouldn't respond. All of her hurt, all of her love, her pain, her frustration at his lies...she let it pour like a waterfall into her messages. But without him in front of her to verbally express herself to, nothing could alleviate the searing, white-hot pain she felt deep in her heart. And she became even more frustrated at her inability to communicate with him outside of a screen.

"You're a liar! You sucked me into this. You deceived me! You made promises! You promised me knowing you'd never come through! Knowing this was a lie! You begged me and begged me for my heart until I gave it to you. How can you do this to me? After all of these years? I waited for you! I turned down any other man who showed interest in me. I trusted you because I believed that someday you would come through. And now you can conveniently slip away and leave me to clean up this mess by myself, while you leave me for dead?! It was all a lie! You couldn't have meant any of it! My dreams are shattered! I hate you! I hate you for doing this to me! You told me you had a BABY even! How could you lie like this??"

Eva was out of her mind with the grief of reality. She felt her heart continue to explode into tiny shards of glass as if each and every piece was a spontaneous combustion...her dreams shattering before her. She truly believed that this was the man she would spend the rest of her life with, that would take care of her, build a life with her, their dream life. It was so real to her that it never even occurred to her that it might not happen. It was not even in her realm of possibilities that it might not happen. And now what? Her future had been snatched away from her in the blink of an eye. It was over now. Her dreams were dead on the floor. She was beside herself with pain, sobbing and rocking back and forth on the floor. He had abandoned her. The man who had insisted for five years that no one could love her the way he loved her had abandoned her. If he could feel that way about her and still reject her, then no one would ever be able to love her to that depth and magnitude ever again...or even more. If she wasn't good enough for him, the one who kept her heart on demand, she would never be good enough for anybody else. Not even Hunter, who was flesh and blood standing before her just the night before.

No, it was too much. Eva couldn't take it. She remembered the gun in her nightstand drawer and slowly reached up from the floor to get it. Just as she was about to grab the cold steel barrel, a still-small voice stopped her...

"No, my love...this is not the way out of pain."

Eva closed the drawer, shaking as she sobbed, "Oh, God...I have nothing left. Absolutely nothing. This was nothing but a complete waste. And now my life is a waste."

Eva got up and grabbed her running shoes and sprinted out the door to the open highway. She ran and ran and ran into nothing. In the distance, she could hear the thunder roll against the dark gray sky. She ran further still...trying to get away from the searing pain inside...only it followed her...taunting her..."*See, Eva? No one wants you! You'll never be good enough for anyone! Your life is over!*" Eva ran harder, barely able to breathe.

The rain began to pour, and Eva fell to her knees...completely broken from the trauma. The rain dropped big and fat, falling fast running down her back, soaking her hair until the excess had nowhere to go, but to drip off of her. She wrapped her arms around herself but could not keep from shivering violently...from the cold and from the pain.

Night had fallen. And the rain continued, making her colder and colder by the minute. *If I just keep walking...if I just keep going...I can run away from all of this...and I won't have to feel this pain anymore.*

But that still-small voice would not let her. "Go home, My love. You cannot stay out here in the rain. Go home where it's warm and sleep. You need to rest."

"No... I can't take this pain." She lowered herself to the cold, wet asphalt as the thunder drummed around her in the rainstorm. "Please just let me die."

***

"Eva!"

"Eva!" came the voice again.

Eva jolted around; the rain slicing through her like an icy knife. "Wha..." She barely had the energy to speak. "Hunter?"

"Eva, what in God's name are you doing out here like this?" He didn't wait for her to answer, he had already removed his coat and was wrapping it around her. "Come on," he said, picking her up to carry her.

"No! I don't need you. I can get home myself." Eva pushed herself out of his arms and took a couple of steps back soaking wet, blue, and shivering. Her dark red hair plastered to her head from the rain.

"Damnit, Eva, we don't have time for this. Your father's worried sick about you."

"I don't need your help. I'm-"

He caught her just before she hit the ground. He wrapped her close in his arms and held her tight as he began to carry her limp, freezing body back home.

"It's okay," he whispered gently into her soaking wet hair. "You're safe now."

Eva was so cold all she could do was sink into him. It was a surprise to feel good in his arms. Peace washed over her like a flood, and a feeling crept through to her bones that she truly was safe with him, such a different feeling from the shame of a relationship she was lured into. Too weak from mental battle to resist, she let him carry her to the studio porch. He held her tight as he opened the door and carried her up to her apartment, and into her room.

"Alright, this is as far as I go for now. Please don't go to bed in those wet clothes on."

He grabbed a towel from the laundry that was folded on the chair near her bed. "Dry off and please," he spoke tenderly, concerned, "and try to get some sleep. I'll give you some privacy, but I will see you soon."

22 JAGGED EDGES

The next morning, that still-small voice stirred Eva out of her deep slumber, her hair still wet from the night before. *"My love, you must take care of yourself. You are going to get sick."*

She looked down at herself and realized that Hunter's hopes for her to clean herself up (for goodness sakes), were far from granted. She'd fallen asleep the minute her head hit the pillow. She sat up shivering and immediately put her hand to her throbbing head. A chill had set in as a result of sleeping in her wet clothes.

Eva padded sluggishly down the whitewashed, hardwood floored hall to the bathroom and turned on the shower to warm herself up, letting the hot water wash over her until she was no longer shivering. As the water ran down her face, she could not tell which was the water and which were her tears. Eva closed her eyes and pressed her pounding forehead against the tile to stop the pain...only it wouldn't stop. She turned off the water, reached for her big, fluffy white bathrobe, tied the sash, and dried her hair.

Now, finally dry and warm, she laid back on her plush, white sofa, put her hands to her heart, and closed her eyes. The heartache she felt was a new species all of its own...not the normal pit-in-the-stomach, foreboding kind of pain. Her heart literally felt sore...from her chest, through her heart, all the way to her back shoulder.

It was as if someone had shot an arrow straight through her heart with an intent to kill. Eva had never experienced this kind of emotional pain before in the physical. She pressed her hand to her heart and winced from the soreness. She ran her hand over her shoulder to her back directly behind her heart...more tender, soreness.

In that moment, that still, small voice spoke to her. *"...My love...evil has intent to destroy you. He has shot his fiery weapon through your heart in order to kill you. He knows how powerful you can be in this world, my love, and he is afraid. He has dipped his weapon into the poison of hopelessness, bitterness, and despair...to stop you...to keep you from your destiny, and to keep you from the one who will truly love you. This is the pain you are feeling in your heart, my love. You must fight it. You must overcome or your heart will die."*

Eva held onto her heart and sobbed, inconsolably. "I just don't know how!"

"You must let me heal you, my love. You must let me do a surgery on your tender heart. It will be painful, but if you do not let me, your heart will die and you will suffer the consequences of an unhealed heart."

"God, I don't care if I live or die. My heart is so completely broken. I'll never have joy again. Never. I'll never, ever love again!"

"My love, you cannot see My plans for you. You do not know what lays ahead. Pain endures for the night, but joy comes in the morning. I do not intend to leave you here. I intend to use this for what you cannot yet see. He is selfish, my love. He wanted you for himself knowing that he could never be with you. I told him many times to leave you alone, but he did not listen. He should have respected the marriage that he entered into. This is not the first time he's done this. I would not deliver you into the hands of a man who would destroy you."

"But, why, God? If we love each other, why can't all of that work out?"

"My love, do not be fooled by a fallacy. This is not love. And you know that deep in your heart. You're not grieving the loss of him. You're grieving the loss of what you thought this was. Do not worry about the answers right now...let Me heal you...restore you...and you will see the answers for yourself in due time. The love he has for you is a selfish love...it is not godly. He is not capable of holding your heart the way it needs to be held, My love. You are precious...special...you must guard your heart and not let it be overtaken by evil. This was never a true love. He deceived you from the beginning. Although, you do not see it, joy is coming. You must not give in to the enemy. You must not give up. You must fight this...or your heart will die."

Eva's heart sank further into despair as she began to realize the weight of the past 5 years. She thought of Kate who had been so heartbroken during the divorce. She remembered how angry she had been for her friend that Collin would do that to her; the seemingly "perfect" Christian man and devoted husband. And how the split had been a shock to everyone. She was taken into a first-person vision of their house...only it felt empty...one thing missing that should have been at the forefront...the foundation...love...love was missing. She felt her friend's emptiness and despair for the first time. She had no idea; they had always seemed like the perfect couple. She thought of how he was always around whenever the two friends hung out together. And how she had admired how strong their marriage was seeing that he and Kate were inseparable, now realizing it was all a facade. *No wonder he was always around...he wanted to be near me.* And that day in their house when she felt something was off...something very, very dark, but she could not put her finger on it at the time.

No wonder he was able to read her heart, know her so well. Kate was Eva's best friend. And she told her everything...And so Kate must have told him everything. He knew her so well...because Kate knew her so well.

Eva closed her eyes as the tears continued to fall. Once so strong and able to block out the world, she had no control over her tears now.

"So many tears, my love," came that still small voice again.

"God...I have nothing left. I have to know. I have to know why." Eva got up off of the couch and opened her laptop. Now that she knew his name, she could try to find more information. More insight into the situation. The not knowing was driving her crazy. His social media might tell her what she needed to know.

"My love, DON'T," came the voice again, loving, but stern. *"It will only wound you more deeply."*

"No! I've got to know!"

She typed his name into her social media page and waited. When his page came up, Eva's mouth dropped open in shock.

His profile picture.

It was him...

...with another girl.

The resemblance between her and Eva was uncanny save for the blonde hair. "She looks just like me," Eva whispered. "He let his fantasy play out by finding someone who looks just like me...? And how long has this been going? Since he was with Kate even?" She was sick to her stomach.

"I told you not to dig, my Love. Now you have caused yourself more undue heartache. Close your laptop and walk away from this. You forget, this was not real. He was married, he should have never spoken to you in the first place. The fact that he is with someone now is irrelevant to that first fact. I

know you want answers. I know you want to justify. Believe me, it is in your best interest. You MUST let this go."

But Eva kept scrolling, the twist in her bruised and battered heart getting the best of her. And then she saw it. Behind the happy looking couple with plastic-looking smiles was a banner, an engagement announcement. "Save the date!" Its white letters screamed from a loud mauve background. Eva narrowed her eyes at the screen...the date was one week from today. Her heart found a trap door beyond the depth to which it had already sunken. *He's engaged?* Suddenly, her mind exploded with rage. *How could he do this?? How could lead me on for years and lie to her??* But without a face across the room to receive her words, she had no verbal outlet. She couldn't yell, couldn't scream like she wanted to. Couldn't tell this man that she absolutely despised his actions.

And then a new revelation came...*It never was Alex. I believed all of this time that it was him, but it was never him?* It was an even crueler discovery. Because it meant that he never really cared about her as much as she believed he did. It meant that he really could so carelessly leave her waiting alone on a New York City sidewalk with no reason or response afterwards as to why. It meant that she had been giving life to something that had truly died five years prior. Everything Eva had known and believed to be true for the past five years never even existed. It was a *complete* falsehood.

***

The next morning, the charcoaled sky cleared. Warm rays of yellow beamed upon the sparkling, dewy green hills surrounding Frank's house. Buster, true to his name, just about busted through the door when he saw Eva coming up the walk.

"Hey," she greeted Frank as she came through the door.

"Well, there you are, finally."

"I know you were worried. I-"

"Damn right, I was, but...you're an adult. You make your own choices. And... Hunter came by and told me you were alright, so I figured I'd give you some time."

"He did?"

"Yeah, we had a good talk actually. You know...he seems like a good man, Eva Rose. Maybe that's something to consider."

"Oh, no, not you, too."

"Well, just hear me out. He's a nice guy, he's successful, and from what I can tell, absolutely smitten with you. What's holding you back?"

Eva hesitated. With her wounds still fresh from the day before, she wasn't sure if she was ready to go there with her father.

"You know, Eva, I can tell that something's hurting you. Something deep. I don't know what it is, but it's written across your face like white on rice. And frankly, no pun intended, it scares me. I worry about you. Did something happen to you when you were in New York?"

Eva looked into the mug of hot coffee he'd given her. If she couldn't confide in her own father, who could she confide in? "You're right, Dad. Something did happen and it didn't just happen there. It followed me here. I couldn't get away from it. I've gained a lot of solid ground since I've come back here, but it always resurfaces. I can't ever seem to get away from it."

"Uh huh," came Frank's lack of amusement for what he sensed was pain caused by an unworthy suitor. "And is that 'it' a guy, by any chance?" Frank replied, his heart softening for his daughter.

"Yes. Yes, 'it' was a 'he.' And now 'he' is gone."

"Wanna talk about it?"

Eva drew a long breath before responding. "No. Not really."

Frank nodded his head in understanding.

"It's not something I care to revisit. At least not right now anyway."

"It's alright, honey, you don't have to talk about anything you don't want to. I think I understand."

Eva gave a half-hearted smile at her dad, relieved that she wasn't being asked to dive deeper into the pain with which she was already ridiculously overwhelmed. It wasn't for lack of trust towards Frank. He'd always been at the front of the line as far as those she knew she could confide in. She knew someday, they would have that conversation. But today was not that day.

Frank poured more hot coffee into his daughter's cooling cup. "Listen kid, I know it's not of my business, but whatever you're going through now, Hunter seems like the kind of guy that could help patch you up. Make things a little brighter for ya. And I'm not just saying that because I like the guy."

Eva took a sip of coffee and held up her hand to signal her father to stop. She wasn't in the mood to hear it.

"Alright, alright," Frank held up his hands in surrender and stopped his musings out of respect for his daughter, never wanting to be a reason she lost trust.

Eva cocked her head and gave him a half-smirk and a firm headshake 'no.'

"10-4, kiddo."

***

Madge took a crooked orange carrot out of Eva's hand and blinked her thanks through shiny, long, black lashes.

"Good girl." Eva cooed and ran her hand along the shiny tan of her horse's flank. "We've got to do something about this hair, though," she said, now running her fingers through Madge's crazy black mane.

Madge whinnied in disapproval and gently nudged Eva's neck with her forehead. Eva laughed, "Alright, alright! I know you're not a fan of my horse-do's. Maybe I'll take you to my hairdresser instead!"

"Now that is a beautiful sound."

Eva turned around to see Hunter looking even better than she remembered. *Gosh, he really is handsome.* She was happy, even comforted to see him, but caught herself before allowing it to show on her face. Instead, she smiled and nodded her hello, pretending to be preoccupied with saddling up Madge.

"Look, I really appreciate your concern the other night and making sure my father knew that I was okay... but you need to know..." she paused.

"Know what?" Hunter gently encouraged.

Eva turned boldly to face him. "I'm fine on my own. I've been on this road for a long time. And I've been taking care of myself for a long time. I don't need you to help me."

Hunter walked to her. " Eva, I don't want you to need me," he responded softly taking her feminine hands in his. "I want to love you."

Eva looked away, unable to hear those words from another man, but then found the courage to look up into his face. In his glittering eyes, so full of love, she saw something that terrified her even more than that night on the phone with whom she thought to be a preying stranger - she saw her future.

"I can't," she whispered, squeezing his hands.

"Eva," he spoke sternly, but gently. "Don't you want to learn that love doesn't have to hurt? When are you going to even come close to letting yourself discover that?"

Eva's eyes turned cold, as if it was the most ridiculous question she'd ever heard. She sharply pulled her hands from his. "Are you kidding me? Love *always* hurts. I've never known it any other way! Haven't *you* learned *that* by now? When are *you* gonna learn that, huh?" She threw his question back in his face.

"Eva, I don't want to hurt you. I want to love you. You've got to stop this enough to let yourself see what's in front of you. I'm here. I'm not going anywhere."

"Please, do you know how many times I've heard that? You all say the same damn thing. What the hell is the difference here?"

"Well, if you'd drop that defiant, cornered animal act long enough for me to show you-"

"Look, you have no idea what I've been through! I won't go back there again. I refuse to go back there again. I'm absolutely fine on my own and I don't need *you*!" Eva grabbed her riding helmet and fastened the strap under her chin.

"Really, Eva? Are you? Are you fine? Because you certainly don't seem fine to me. Every move you make is in fear. You've lived with it for so long, it's engrained in you. I'm not asking you to go back to wherever it was that trampled your tender heart into the ground. I'm asking you to move forward with me into the *now*. Not the past, Eva. The *now*." His eyes pleaded with hers.

The past is over, and I know it tore a hole in you deeper than the Grand Canyon. A chasm so deep, no man can cross to even try to get to you. But I'm asking you to at least throw enough pillows in there to building up the valley enough at least let me try. Let me try to fill the pain with enough love to cross over to you. I'm not saying I will never hurt you. Love hurts sometimes, Eva. Even in its purest form. You know that. But the difference here is that I will never do anything to purposely hurt you. *Never*.

I'm not the men in your past who have hurt you. I'm the man in your *now* who loves you more than he's loved anything before in his life. Except for the big guy upstairs, of course. I'm a man who wants to give you something, instead of taking from you. A man who wants to love you for no other reason than the fact that I know that I am called to stand beside you, affect the world with you, take care of you...love you. I will go into the pit and find you when you can't find yourself."

She held up her hand to stop him. "Please stop. I've heard all of this before. And I don't want to hear it again," Eva shook her head. "I can't hear that again...ever." Eva turned to get up into the saddle.

"Not from me, you haven't!" He said, gently, but firmly taking her arms in his hands. "Eva, I am human. I will make mistakes."

216

Eva rolled her eyes, but he took her chin delicately, holding it in place before she could look away.

"And, Eva, *you* will make mistakes. But I promise you I will never do anything to purposely hurt you. You cannot expect to go through life without experiencing pain. It's a part of life, good or bad. But I promise you, I will never do anything intentionally to harm you."

Eva felt the familiar faint touch of fear rise in her heart. "No, let me go." She removed herself from his tender grip, got up onto her horse, and dug in her heels causing Madge to sprint away.

He called out after her. "Eva!"

She was gone.

"I'm not going anywhere," he called again. "I'm staying right here until you stop running."

Silence.

He looked out into the dark after her. "Forever if I have to."

23 CITY LIGHTS

Eva poured herself a hot cup of tea and sat down on her vintage couch, took a deep breath, and opened her laptop to pen him one last time. She pondered her New York life, her friends, the work she once loved so much… and Alex. She thought about the black cloud that had crept into her life, stealing every bit of joy until she was nothing but a shell of her former self. She wondered how she could have ever let that happen.

Then the realization came…she'd let it happen because she didn't know herself. She hadn't known the God that could have kept her from all of this. She hadn't met the version of herself that God had destined for her to step into; strong, resilient, unfettered. The never-ending unanswered "why's" would plague her mind until she could answer. She *had* to answer them. It was the only way she would rid herself of this poser forever and let go of her old life. Eva dug deep to find the words to end this for good, refusing to be a victim any longer.

"I hate what you did…and I hate how you tried to shove me aside like I meant nothing to you so that you could cover your tracks. I hate the lies. I hate the deceit. I hate that you caused me to hurt my best friend. You're married, it's true…but it's like a convenient excuse for you to hide now after this huge mess. You can't make it right, that is also true…but to say don't rely on you…when you were the one who wanted me, to take care of me, begged for my heart…is like a knife in my heart.

You don't realize how deeply the things you said to me affected me. It just makes me sick to my stomach. I never said I was relying on you…I needed to express how I felt…because you tore my heart apart…although, I realize now how fruitless that was. Because it doesn't change what is…it didn't make you who I needed you to be...who you promised. But that person never existed. You came to me... painted yourself into my future for years...lied and cheated...deceived and blamed me for things I had no control over and then wondered why I reacted the way I did. That's called reacting to abuse. You told me you were single, not in a relationship, etc. how could you say that?

I know you don't want to face that, but it's true...to promise me so many things and hide a marriage at the same time. To keep painting gorgeous pictures of the things you know that I would have wanted in life, and then give someone else the wedding you promised me, the honeymoon you promised me, the life you promised me, love someone else the way you said you would love me.

You told me that I was your dream. You said that you would never cheat. There is no way you could do those things with someone else if you truly loved me...your heart would never let you...unless you shoved it aside out of fear or the realization that you're a lying manipulator to anyone you're with. But to lead me on that way...how could you? Don't answer. It doesn't change what is and it doesn't make you what I needed you to be. You have completely damaged and defiled that love...was it ever even real? You said you were afraid I wouldn't want you, so you married her...when really you were afraid because you were married to my friend...why bother keeping me then? Why not just let me go? Why ruin my chances of being happy with someone real? Why did you lie to me so severely over and over again?? Because you're a selfish coward you would go so far as to disrupt my life to make no other man could have me.

You promised me that you would have fought to the death for me, regardless of the circumstances. I thought for so many years that you didn't because I wasn't good enough for you. I had no idea you were a completely different person than who I thought you were. But I will be more than enough to the man who truly loves me, and he will cherish me with his actions, not just his words.

You didn't have the guts to tell me the truth. And you made it seem like I knew everything you kept secret, like, this was just a normal choice when I knew nothing about what was going on behind the scenes. You KNEW that I would never agree to be with you if I knew that you were my friend's husband.

You promised me all of these things and then went the complete opposite. I'm glad you're happy...I wish you had cared enough to put first the happiness of everyone else involved in this before your own. But you kept the truth from me because you knew that if I had known the truth, that I would have nothing *to do with you. That I would never betray my best friend wittingly....and you were right.*

I am worth so much more than this. I deserve better than a 'you are my second pick, if this doesn't work out'...I have absolutely no words for that notion. I am special and I am rare. I am not a cheater, and I am not a shiny prize to be won by the highest bidder. I'm sorry you couldn't see that.

Your love is divided, and it is fake.

God bless your new life. Don't EVER contact me again."

*Ping! It was him.

"Oh, Eva can't you see? It's your fault I didn't choose you. You never trusted me.

Why did I do it in the first place? Well, I guess I just wanted to see if you would respond. And then you did."

In typical selfish fashion, Collin managed to point all of the blame back onto her, refusing to take responsibility for his part. She hadn't expected him to respond. She didn't want him to respond. It was more of a closing for peace of mind for her, than it was an invitation for him to debate. Even in the end, he couldn't respect her wishes not to contact her further.

She shook her head and snorted at his lack of accountability. She blocked his email address and turned off her laptop.

That night, as Eva laid her head down on her pillow and closed her eyes, she saw the arrows dislodge from her heart one-by-one. A bright light shone from the holes that the arrows had left until they were all closed up with gold, healed by love and made whole again.

"See, my love?", came the still small voice in her heart. *"This marks a new beginning. I am here. I will never leave you and I will never forsake you. My plans for you are true. No longer will the pain of the past hold you back. You are now free to step into the future that I have designed for you. Rest well, my love, for I watch over you as you sleep, and tomorrow is a new day."*

***

The air hung heavy with humidity the next morning. Eva took Buster and walked down to her favorite bluff overlooking the lush greenery of the hills that surrounded her. She sat down in the pillowy grass, closed her eyes and leaned her face back towards the sky and waited. "Okay, God. I'm here. And I'm listening."

"So much more in store that I have for you, my love. Do not think your time is over or that it is too late for you. It's never too late with Me."

"But God...I still make so many mistakes," she replied out loud.

"My love, you are learning. That will never end all the days of your life, you will always be learning as long as you are in Me. Now you are ready. Take the path that is before you."

Suddenly, the literal path before her turned to vision. She saw Hunter's eyes again, and the future she'd found inside them, and it was even more glorious than all of the broken promises of the past. She remembered how he had come for her almost unexpectedly in the night when she was at her lowest, as if like a thief, undeterred by the mess in her heart and the mess that she was, drenched in rain, snot dripping down her nose. What a picture!

Eva realized that the motivation was different. It did not match that of thrill or game. No. Hunter was motivated simply and purely by the love in his heart and a deep knowledge, a true understanding that she was the one that God had chosen for him.

And so, she went to find him. But when she got back to her house, she found a letter taped to her door. It was from Hunter.

Eva, I've gone back to New York to handle a business matter. Although I've left this place, I haven't left you. My offer still stands, as it always will. I will see you when I return unless you beat me to it.

I love you and remain faithfully waiting,

Hunter

***

The sparkling city was even more crowded than Eva had remembered as she made her way to the park. The setting sun colored a salmon and lavender sky behind the bright yellow and orange tree-lined park. She hurried down the familiar paths, her silk scarves flying behind her in the wake as made her way deeper into the park. *The Grand Promenade, that's where he'll be*, she thought to herself.

Eva looked around her as she made her way to the promenade, remembering that she once called this beautiful cityscape 'home.' A smile crept across her face as she realized how far she had come, not by a blocked-out barrier of protective memory-killing armor, but by the true inner work of digging deep into healing to find the treasure buried within. She laughed as she let the joy wash over her. This joy was a completely different animal than the false happiness she'd felt before.

"Eva!"

Eva slowed her pace at the sound of a familiar voice, stopped dead in her tracks, and stared in disbelief at the face in front of her.

"Alex…" she breathed.

"Gosh, you look even better than I remember you." He said almost apologetically.

"Thanks," she whispered, stunned to see him after so many years, and a little embarrassed at the details in-between. "Look, I really need to get going."

Alex moved in front of her to block her exit. "Look, Eva, I'm sorry. I am so sorry. I was such a jerk. I never meant to hurt you."

"Listen. Alex. I appreciate that, but I really don't think we need to go back there."

"No, we do. Because it's been bothering me since it happened. And then when I saw you at Columbus Circle and chickened out again…Eva, the night I was supposed to meet you downstairs in front of my apartment building… Listen, the reason I missed it… I got drunk and fell asleep. I didn't mean to leave you standing there like you meant nothing."

Eva just sighed shook her head. "Look, it's okay, it was a long time ago and-"

"No, it's not okay, it's totally horrible what I did to you. You were such a good gal, and you didn't deserve that. I wanted to reach out to you. I wanted to call you as soon as I woke up, but the phone was dead and anyway, I don't know, I guess I just figured it was too late at that point."

"Interesting. I never thought of apologies as something that had a time limit, but, I understand."

"Didn't you ever wonder what happened?"

Eva laughed to herself. *Did I ever wonder what happened…if only he knew! Actually…it's a good thing he doesn't know!* "Yes. I did wonder. And for a long time, I thought I knew. But… I was wrong. And that path didn't end well."

Alex looked as though this was a mistake that would haunt him the rest of his life. "I'm so sorry, Eva," he whispered. "I regret this deeply… and I hope you can forgive me."

"Alex, I forgive you. I mean, don't get me wrong. You absolutely broke my heart, but it wasn't the worst thing that's ever happened to me. Believe me."

Eva's eyes widened at that last point.

"I mean, maybe, if you're interested...maybe we can start over? I'd love the opportunity to treat you the way I should have in the first place. I mean...you were my friend even before all of that."

Eva felt bad for him, pouring out his heart. At one point in time, she would have given anything to hear those words. Now as they fell, she realized, though they were appreciated, they would never mean to her what they once meant before.

"Look, I think it's cool that we ran into each other after so long and I really appreciate the apology and finally being able to know what happened that night, but I'm okay now. And honestly, looking back, I don't think we were right for each other anyway. You and I are so different. We have different dreams, different goals. I'm happy to keep you as a friend, but I don't want anything more than that anymore. It's just over for me."

"I guess I really screwed things up, huh?"

Eva shook her head sympathetically. "It has nothing to do with you. No, I wouldn't say it that way."

"I guess I understand..." Alex let out a big sigh, "Well, it was great to see you, Eva. I guess I better get going now," he concluded, giving her a big nod and an embarrassed smile.

Eva watched as he turned sheepishly and walked off, shoulders slumped in defeat. But this time it didn't kill her. This time she was stronger. She knew her worth and would never let anyone take that from her again.

Alex turned back just as Eva was turning to leave.

"Hey!"

"Yeah?"

"Whatever it is that you're looking for... I hope you find it, Eva. You deserve to find it."

Eva smiled knowingly, "I already have!"

Alex gave her one last smile before turning back on his way.

"I already have," she reminded herself softly as she took the beautiful landscape in around her.

Leaves of rust, sunlight, and orange fell to the ground and scattered about like confetti. Not one to let a beautiful canvas go to waste even in the midst of an exceedingly important errand, Eva promptly pulled out her camera and began shooting. Eva clicked as she moved slowly towards her destination, the promenade.

And then, through the viewfinder, sitting on a black iron park bench, Eva saw him. It was Hunter smiling with the deepest adoration she had ever seen directed towards her. "Hi," he mouthed.

Eva pulled the camera down from her face, an expression mixed with pure joy and astonishment. "Hi!" she exclaimed as Hunter stood up from the bench and walked over towards her.

Eva laughed. She couldn't believe she'd actually found him in the park with thousands of other people bustling around. And even more so that he was there. Waiting. Just for her.

"I don't know what this means!" she spoke, unsure of what to fill the one foot-gap between them with aside from words.

"You don't have to know," Hunter gently replied, lovingly brushing a stray lock of auburn out of her eyes. "We'll figure it out together."

Eva looked at him in wonder and shook her head, "Hunter, I'm so sorry for what I said before and the way I acted, I-" Hunter took a hurried step to close the gap between them and to keep her from an unnecessary apology. He wrapped his strong arms around her and held her tight to his broad chest. "Shh," he whispered. "Don't. I know what you've been through."

Eva looked up at him with tears of happiness streaming down her face. "But I gave you such a hard time and I didn't mean to."

"Eva, I know," his soothing voice calming her racing heart. "I know. I knew what I was getting when I signed up to love you. I knew it was going to be a huge struggle for you to let me into your heart."

"Oh, Hunter, I just had to work through all of that before I could see you clearly. This thing was hanging over my life for so many years, I was beginning to believe it was a part of me. And then, I found out the truth. It was never what I thought it was! The whole thing was a game, a facade. And I just fell for it! And I had to see how horribly wrong I'd been about this whole thing.

And then, God started showing me who I was. And then *you* came. And you showed me what was real. I never thought it was possible for anyone to love me the way you love. So open and honest, with integrity."

Hunter cupped her porcelain face in his hands. Her face fit perfectly against the curves of his palm. "Eva....that's how I plan to love you for the rest of our lives." And with those words, he leaned in to kiss her lips. And Eva kissed him back. He felt like a long-awaited home-coming and she had never felt so safe in the arms of a man. She knew in that embrace that she was his and he was hers, not in the abusive, possessive way, but in the way that tells you, this is the person you're meant to be with because God is in it. He has put His mighty hand on it and His blessing is the orchestration, a life of two people living in their truest identity.

"Hunter," Eva breathed.

"Eva," he whispered back. "Come with me."

Eva followed him as he led her to the hot dog and pretzel stand. "Seems only fitting we do some planning on a full stomach. You up for it?"

"Oh, yeah," Eva replied, taking a pretzel from his hand. The two continued to walk as the sun set deeper and the sky began to fade.

"So, what are your thoughts? Do you want to keep your studio? Do you want to stay here? Go back home? Or try somewhere else?"

"You know, the studio was very healing, but I'm not sure I want to stay in my hometown. I don't want to just get rid of it, but I'm not necessarily wanting to stay there 24/7 either. I think it was what I needed for that chapter of my life. So many other artists enjoy it, though. I wouldn't want to outright close it. And I definitely want to keep the apartment for artists who might need a place to stay for a while."

"Okay. I think I might have a solution."

"You do?"

"Well, I had an inkling that you might want to move on after you'd had some time to rest and regroup and realize that I was the love of your life."

Eva laughed and squeezed his arm.

"So, I talked to my aunt, and she's been missing the place, especially after she saw what you did to fix it up and bring artists back in. She wants to buy it back but was afraid to talk to you about it in case you decided to give me the permanent boot."

"That's great! No, that's perfect! She brought it to life in the first place and it deserves to be loved by a gentle, creative-loving soul who will appreciate it. I'll talk to her about it and that will free us up to do we what want from here. So, I guess we get to create the life we want now, right? But what about your work?"

"Well, the good thing about that is, I can do that anywhere. Are you still interested in photography?"

"I do love it...but, I don't want it to be what it was before. When it's a hobby, I love it. When it's for work, it literally becomes a chore and then it's not so fun anymore."

"I get that."

"You know, I think I don't want to rush into a decision where that's concerned. This is all so fresh, and our lives are coming together. Why don't we take some time and really consider what to do next I've made the mistake of making my own plans and they all failed. I don't want to make that mistake anymore. I don't want to take another step unless I know it's the right one. Unless *we* know it's coming from up there." Eva pointed to the sky.

"I think that's a wonderful idea. You get to design your life. You don't have to follow the rules of what everybody else thinks they need to do. Do what is on your heart. I'll support you every step of the way. Just one more thing I want to ask you."

"Oh? And what's that?"

Hunter kneeled in front of her and reached into his pocket, pulled out a cream-colored box, and opened it. Inside the plush velvet-lined square, was a gorgeous sparkling black diamond surrounded by smaller white diamonds, set in platinum. Behind it, was a thick wedding band of diamond-patterned basket-woven platinum set with more precious stones of diamond and teal.

"Wow, killing two birds with one stone?" she teased.

"Well, you know I'm a veteran scout," he teased her, "I always like to be prepared."

Eva giggled softly and pretended to peer into the box pretending to critique the gift. "Eh, not bad."

"Aren't you at least going to jump up and down?"

"What you do you think?" Eva gave him a look that said, 'c'mon.'

"Darling, you're stealing my thunder here." Hunter chuckled and shook his head. "Eva, I love you. I promise to protect you. I'll protect your heart and I will fight for you no matter what life brings us. Will you start this journey with me and be my bride?"

Eva stalled for a moment.

"...Eva?"

"Well, I'm pretty darn sure I'm supposed to say yes, here. So, YES! Yes! A thousand times, yes!" Eva jumped into his already waiting arms.

Hunter pretended to wipe the sweat of anticipation from his brow. "Whew! I was worried there for a minute! You know, next step and all," he teased, winking at her. He gently set her down, took the black diamond ring from the box, and placed it on her finger. "See? Perfect fit."

Eva gazed at the exquisite perfection on her finger. "Perfect fit. But you'll have to keep an eye on me if we ever go swimming. I might sink straight to the bottom with this rock on my hand!"

"Don't you worry, honey, I'm an avid swimmer. Plus, I think that ring comes with its own life jacket. Didn't you see it in the box?"

"No, I think that's called 'insurance'!"

"*You're* my insurance!" Hunter teased, kissing her forehead and wrapping his arm around her shoulders as they walked.

"So, what now?"

"I've got some ideas. But why don't we start with coffee first?"

"As long as cheesecake is involved, coffee it is."

"Coffee. And then… you and me."

"You and me," Eva cooed back at him.

Hunter took her hand and led her to the 5th Avenue sidewalk that lined the park. They walked and talked along a tree-lined sidewalk with the lights of New York beginning to twinkle around them as they lit up the twilight sky, now a soft lavender with approaching night.

See, My love? Eva heard that still small voice speak to her as she walked down the glittering avenue with her future husband, *Darkness cannot stand against the light. Light will always win against even the darkest of days. And your future, my love, shines brighter than you can even imagine.*

ABOUT THE AUTHOR

Author, Sarah Lynn, is originally from Jackson Township, Ohio, where her dreams would eventually lead her to writing. She has lived in New York City, studied in Paris, and is currently acquiring her master's in mass communications from the University of Florida while working on ideas for future novels.

Made in the USA
Middletown, DE
06 January 2022

57930317R00135